D0839226

Her Name Is Rose

Her Name Is Rose

Christine Breen

St. Martin's Press   New York

This is a work of fiction. All of the characters, organizations, and events portrayed in this novel are either products of the author's imagination or are used fictitiously.

HER NAME IS ROSE. Copyright 2015 by Christine Breen. All rights reserved. Interior illustrations by Christine Breen.
For information, address St. Martin's Press,
175 Fifth Avenue, New York, N.Y. 10010.

www.stmartins.com

Designed by Molly Rose Murphy

The Library of Congress Cataloging-in-Publication Data
is available upon request.

ISBN 978-1-250-05421-0 (hardcover)
ISBN 978-1-4668-5723-0 (e-book)

St. Martin's Press books may be purchased for educational, business, or promotional use. For information on bulk purchases, please contact the Macmillan Corporate and Premium Sales Department at 1-800-221-7945, extension 5442, or write to specialmarkets@ macmillan.com.

First Edition: April 2015

P1

To Niall, Deirdre, and Joseph

Acknowledgments

I'm indebted to quite a few people—for without them this novel would not have become real. For her editorial insights I'm very grateful to Hope Dellon of St. Martin's Press. For believing in the story from the beginning, my agent Rowan Lawton at Furniss Lawton, and to Rachel Mills and Caroline Michel at Peters Fraser and Dunlop, who carried it further. Thanks to the members of the inaugural National Academy of Writing in London and its administrator, Rena Brannan, and especially to its director, Richard Beard.

To the members of the Kiltumper Book Club, I am grateful for their continual reminder that storytelling counts first and foremost. And I thank them for putting up with me as their facilitator these seven-plus years. Thanks to Marie O'Leary, Siobhan Phelan, and Isobel O'Dea, and especially my sister Deirdre Breen, who read the story in its first draft.

But most of all, I owe more gratitude than can be expressed

Acknowledgments

in words to Niall Williams, the man who has believed in me
since that first day we met in a university café in Dublin many,
many years ago. Without him—and our children—I would never
have had this story to tell.

Plants are always from some sort of family.
　　　　—from *Swimming Home* by Deborah Levy

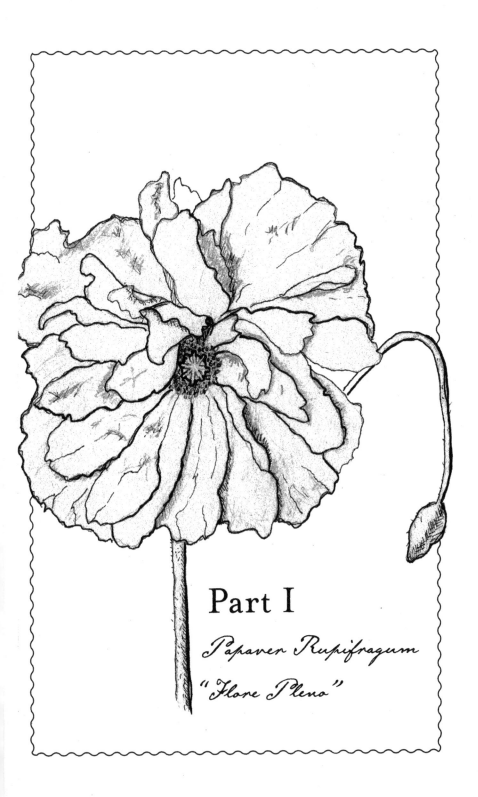

Part I

Papaver Rupifragum

"Flore Pleno"

One

The nurse who performed the X-ray had a magenta streak in her short dark hair. She had a Dublin city accent and her name began with "L." Maybe it was Letitia? Loretta? Latara, maybe? Iris had been too apprehensive to listen. In the center of the windowless room stood an old diagnostic thing, a white metal machine. By the door was a black plastic chair with chrome legs and in the corner, a half-wall-half-glassed-in partition, inside of which L stood. Half-hidden.

It had been one of those days for Iris. That morning her editor had asked her to call in to the offices of *The Banner County News* and she'd arrived thinking he was going to offer her a permanent spot. He'd sat her down. What he offered was coffee. He'd never done that before. Then he propped his short legs in their beige cords against the desk (a somewhat Scandinavian-looking piece, very minimalist) and explained the newspaper was taking a new direction. They didn't see gardening articles as appealing to the newspaper's current market.

"Of course, *I* love your pieces. Even read them. But, that's progress isn't it?" He looked at his watch. "I'm sorry. I have to tell all the freelancers today. Not just you. There's crosswords. He has to go, too. And the books guy."

Iris had looked out through his wooden blinds onto the street.

"I know, Iris. Rotten luck. But it's coming down from the board. Things are tight and we have to cut. Cut, cut. You know how it is these days." Arthur Simmons was the son of the owner of the paper and ten years her junior, and for a moment she had thought how stupid his hair looked, sticking up like a modern mohawk. He hadn't even got it right. And he was too old for it. And *he* certainly didn't know how it was these days.

She felt he was expecting her to say something but as she hadn't, he straightened away from the desk and looked down on her. She was looking at the fine wool floor covering.

"Are you all right?"

She had forced herself to turn her upset face to him.

"If not coffee, tea maybe?"

"No." She ran her hands through her hair, then smoothed it. "I've got to be somewhere." She stood up. "As of when?"

"Sorry?"

"When do I finish?"

"Well. Actually . . ." His hands were in his pockets and he rocked back on his heels. He had an apologetic look on his face. "As of today . . . so sorry."

She had looked at him for one long moment. His face had reddened. *Was* he sorry?

"I just thought . . . it was going well," she said. "I've been getting questions from readers, you know. 'What's the best time to prune an apple tree?' "

"Iris, please."

" 'When can I move my peonies?' 'When's the best time to transplant carrots?' "

He tightened his lips together, raised his eyebrows, and slowly he shook his head. Apparently, there was nothing more to say.

She walked toward the door, had her hand on the handle and was about to open it.

"Listen. Wait," he said. "Wait . . . I'll tell you what. We're starting an online version of the paper. A blog might be perfect for you." He paused. "I mean, if you don't mind doing it for free . . ."

A pair of secateurs had just sliced through her little moment of hope.

". . . just until we see what traffic it generates." She turned back to the door. "Iris?"

"I'll think about it." She was about to step out into the corridor when she swung around, looked directly at him, and in a voice solid and unwavering she said, "You never transplant carrots." And then she was gone. Out through the maze of other Scandinavian desks and past *The Banner County News* staff with their averted eyes. Did they all know she had been let go? Keeping pace with a thrumming in her chest, she had gone down the stairs and out into the street.

"Are you still having periods?"

She was jerked back by L's question.

"Yes."

"When was your last?"

"Two weeks ago."

Stripped to her waist, Iris was directed to the machine and positioned, or rather her breast positioned, in place. First the right.

"Turn this way. Put your arm here. Like you're hugging it."

"*Hugging* it?"

"I know. It's only for a bit. And I'm sorry, it's cold."

With Iris's cheek turned sideways and one arm stretched around the contraption in the opposing direction, L lowered the plate. The radiographer was so close that Iris saw the butterfly tattooed behind her right ear. And she breathed in the scent of the sea off her hair.

Then the left.

It had hurt, the squeezing, but not as badly as Iris expected.

L said, "It'll just take a few minutes to scan these." Iris went back and waited, half-naked, on a small bench, in a blue cape of crepe paper in an airless cubicle with the door closed. Her hair clashed with washed-out blue she was sure. She reached into the rattan basket she used as a handbag and found an old lipstick and steadied her hand to put it on. "There," she said to the back of the door.

People used to say Iris Bowen was beautiful, what with the wild weave of her red hair, the high cheekbones, and the way she carried herself like a barefoot dancer through the streets of Ranelagh on the outskirts of Dublin city. But that was a lifetime ago. That woman, the woman Luke had said was the most beautiful he'd known, was now wearing a blue paper cape and her best summer shoes, a pair of thinly strapped black sandals. How vulnerable she felt, half-dressed.

The old linoleum was so polished that with every move, as she crossed and uncrossed her legs, it squeaked. The chill in the air made her shiver. She clutched her breasts. Nobody had touched them since Luke. She held her breath and counted. Exhaled long. Breathed again. One, two, three—

"Mrs. Bowen?" L knocked on the door and opened it a crack. "We need to retake one. Left side. The X-ray hasn't turned out good enough to my eye. Sorry, but it has to be clear for the radiologist." L was used to anxiety, but her chosen professional manner came in short sentences. "Don't worry. Happens all the time. Doesn't mean anything. These old machines." She guided Iris back to the mammography unit. "We're due for a digital machine next month. They get much better results." L laid bare Iris's left breast on the cold, black square. She sandwiched it with her clean hands and lowered the machine. As she squeezed down Iris thought of the word "mamma." And with that came sudden fear. Nothing but cold white fear.

She waited again for L to view the result. Panic rising, she forced herself to picture her garden—her poppies, the ones she'd grown from seed that were looking gorgeous. Yes. Gorgeous. They absolutely were. And she thought, *It takes many people to make a garden: those who dream it and those who create it. Without gardeners, flowers are like orphans* . . .

"Mrs. Bowen, it's all right now. You can get dressed."

Iris let out a slow exhale and in her shiny black sandals and paper cape went down the corridor to get dressed.

When she reappeared in the X-ray room, L said, "The results will go to Dr. O'Reilly as soon as the radiologist has read them. Probably early next week. Sometimes . . . just sometimes . . . the radiologist will send them on to the consultant in the Breast Clinic in Limerick. But only if there is the slightest doubt."

L looked up from her clipboard long enough to break into her version of a reassuring smile.

In the long corridor with its tea-colored walls and hand-sanitizer dispensers, Iris passed a woman she recognized from the village where she lived but she cast her eyes down. She sensed the woman pause and lift a hand but Iris kept walking.

The day was warming up, with patches of blue appearing here and there, clearing from the west. Iris decided not to stop in town and instead head for home but first she texted Arthur: *Ok. I'll do it.* She left out: *And BTW fix your hair. You look ridiculous.*

Because Iris was the kind of person who sometimes lacked patience, the minute she got home, without stopping to make herself a cup of tea, or check her post, or listen to phone messages, or feed her cat, she started on her first blog post.

A red-orange poppy, bright as an African sora, opens above a sea of green in the flower bed, shocking everything else in sight like some electrifying force. It clashes with the pink French rose.

A minor collision of color. Cerise digitalis towers beside delphiniums and red phormiums.

Butterflies hop from dying tulips to the fired-up flowers.

A lonesome dragonfly whirrs.

Iris stopped. It was awful. She needed to find a better voice. This one was pink, sickly pink, pink like a marshmallow sweet. She needed bloodred.

Poppies—they explode and crack open like popped champagne corks and spill out those red silky yolks, taking the gardener's breath away. Watch, and within the hour they will unfurl into big fat cups and hold the twilight until morning. They can be sloppy though, those capricious ladies of the garden. After their garden appearance, they get, well . . . blowsy. Like women who have stayed out too late, they need to be escorted home.

Okay, better, she thought.

From the table where she sat she looked up and out across her garden—the wild garden she'd been cultivating under the inconstant sun of the west of Ireland for twenty-five years in Ashwood, the middle of the Clare countryside.

Cultivating wilderness, that's what she'd been doing. And she'd given part of her soul to it. Beyond the high fuchsia hedges bordering the garden, the land was boggy and rush-laden—rushes tall as hazel rods and the earth full of clay, but inside, the sticky soil had become a rich loam. Seaweed, gathered off the rocks at Doughmore, and leaf mold, gathered from the ash and sycamore trees, and her own kitchen waste and garden clippings had turned the blue gley soil a healthy black, and yielded exotics like the rare lady slipper orchid. Three perennial borders sloped southward toward the unseen River Shannon.

A rose bed lined the eastern edge.

It was Luke who'd insisted on the rose bed because roses had meanings in his family. The Bowens, from Dublin, had their customs. You gave a rose when a child was born. You gave one on a significant anniversary: a fortieth birthday—a Just Joey, a fiftieth—a Gertrude Jekyll. You planted a rose in the name of someone who had died. Luke had taught her that.

Between the living and the dead, a rose, he'd said.

From that April day in 1987 when she and Luke first arrived— when initially it seemed only the brambles thrived—the wilderness had been tamed, season after season, into a garden that shone at night when the moon was out. The white anemones in late summer were like fallen stars.

Now in the last week of May, when the garden would have been at its peak in earlier years, the wilderness, always at the perimeter, was inching forward like some monster mollusk. Even the slugs brazenly slithered on the path in the middle of the day, not waiting for the cover of nightfall. A battle that Iris was losing.

She moved from her writing table in the sitting room to the kitchen and switched on the kettle. Waiting for it to boil, she inspected her hands and their unpainted nails half-lined with black earth. Her hands felt like claws, stiff and fixed. On the granite worktop she pushed them down hard, as if she could press them into a different shape, perhaps the hands of a long-fingered musician.

Her claw hands planted on the counter, she flattened them as best she could, bearing down upon them, pressing the hollow of her palms, and stretching and spreading her fingers. Supporting herself like this on the cold counter, she looked out through the near window. The blue clematis, Alice Fisk, flaunted herself across the wooden door of the stone cabin, her tangle of twisting vine holding it in place. (If Iris had clipped Alice back like she was supposed to, the door would have fallen into the drive.) How she loved that clematis. Gutsy, tenacious. A real beauty.

A breeze blew the starlike petals and scattered them across the drive. And behind the vine, through the now blistered black paint, the cabin door revealed sploshes of crimson. Ten years earlier Luke had painted it. It was spring. Their daughter was about eight or nine at the time and she'd pleaded with him to make it look just like the one in a photograph from one of her mother's gardening magazines. She'd said, "Can't we paint it red? Dadda? Look. Look, Dadda, how pretty it will look." And she'd shown the photograph.

Luke agreed, as he always did, and together they'd painted it. He'd been pleased such a small thing could make her happy.

The phone rang. She let it, for a moment. Then, she released her hands from the counter and answered.

"How are you?"

"Tess . . ." Iris let out a sigh. "It's you."

"Yes, pet. It's me. Are you okay?"

"I'm okay."

"How did it go?"

"Not *toooo* bad."

Neither of them spoke for a second. Then Tess continued, "Will I ring you back? You're in the middle of something?"

"Sort of. Do you mind? It's been a full-on day and—"

"Not at all." Tess paused. "Iris?"

"What?"

"Don't worry. It'll be all right."

Tess was Iris's best friend. They'd known each other ever since they'd struck up a conversation in a queue at the supermarket. That was ten years ago. In Tess's shopping cart that day were several liters of low-fat organic milk and potatoes and cabbage and organic apples and flour and butter. "Dinner," she'd said and smiled at Iris, who was holding three bars of baking chocolate and butter.

"Me too," Iris said and smiled back.

Tess was a social worker in town and worked with disadvantaged teenagers, and although into things like organics and yoga, she wasn't one of those New Age yogi types and didn't plague Iris with alternative-health aphorisms. She'd tried more than once to cajole Iris into joining her at a yoga class but Iris said it hurt her back. "Exactly the reason you should be going! You're only ever using the same old muscle groups. You'll end up like an upside-down U if you don't watch it. Too much of anything isn't good for you." Iris was about to say something but Tess had already read her and cut her short. "Not even gardening." She smiled. "Gardening is *not* the new yoga."

Her friend understood why Iris now shied away from doctors, medicine, and hospitals and one day a few weeks after Luke's death, she'd arrived with a basket full of vitamins and herbal teas. There was St. John's wort and omega 3s and magnesium and melatonin. Something called gamma-aminobutyric acid, tablets of which she still had in the cabinet above the sink. And chamomile and passionflower and valerian tisanes. Iris took the bath salts and a lavender herb bundle and the plastic bottles of supplements and lined them in a row on the counter under the cabinet where she kept tea and coffee.

"Thanks, Dr. Tess, Medicine Woman." At the bottom of the basket was a bottle of wine. The Malbec Iris liked.

"That's if none of the others work." They'd laughed then and it had felt okay to laugh and Tess took Iris's hands and folded her own over them. "It's over now and you're going to be able to move on. And if you don't, don't worry, I'll be here to push you! And while we're on the subject—"

"What subject?"

"Taking care of yourself."

"Ri-ight."

"You need a mammogram."

"Do I now?"

"You do. You're in the high-risk category for breast cancer. Come on, Iris, you know that." It was a touchy subject but Tess was not put off by touchy subjects, she'd continued. "For starters, you didn't breast-feed."

"No medals for stating the obvious. And?"

"I hate to remind you—"

"Then don't."

Tess smiled. It seemed there was almost nothing Iris could say that would offend her friend. She was permanently in good form even though there was plenty she could complain about. She lived her life half-full, not half-empty.

"Iris?"

"I know."

"In America they start you at forty, and you're—"

"Thank you." Iris had glanced at her friend with a look that said, *Please don't say any more.*

"Go for one, will you? So I can stop pestering. And don't get worked up about it . . . until you have to. Nothing to worry about. Just arrange it, okay?"

It had taken her almost two years to make that appointment.

The thing about poppies, which one is inclined to forget when one is standing in the garden admiring their pomposity, is that they make frightful cut flowers. Most unsatisfying if not downright depressing.

If you are to have any success with bringing your poppies indoors, you must take a flame to their bottoms.

Until blackened.

With fire.

A well-known British gardener suggests dipping them for thirty seconds in boiling hot water after collecting the flowers in the morning when the stems are fully turgid.

Long live those turgid stems.

Two days after the mammography, on the first of June, Iris had passed L at the entrance of the supermarket in Ennis. The nurse-out-of-uniform was wearing combats and a black T-shirt and if it hadn't been for the purple-streaked hair, Iris mightn't have recognized her. The combats must be some sort of defense strategy for nurses who perform breast scans, she thought. As the two women passed, the nurse averted her eyes and declined an invitation to be recognized. Iris was sure of it. She quickened her step and by the time she returned to her car, breathless, she felt exposed, like a dug-up plant whose knobby roots were shriveling in the cold.

Iris spent the next few agonizing days waiting for Dr. O'Reilly to ring. She busied herself in the garden: mowing the lawn, pruning the spirea that had finished flowering, and spraying the rose bed with a Bordeaux mixture recommended by her friend at the Ennis farmers' market. (She left the fixing of the cabin door for another day.) When she'd finished all her jobs she retrieved her sketchbook from her bedside table where she'd locked it away in a drawer after Luke had died. Making *pretty* pictures then hadn't felt right. But now the Icelandic poppies in the front border inspired her to try, to just *try*. She was attempting to sketch one when the doctor's office finally telephoned at the end of the week.

"Mrs. Bowen? Will you hold for Dr. O'Reilly?"

Iris paced with the phone from room to room. Her cat was asleep in a square of sun on the sitting room floor, just under the pine table. She left him sleeping and made her way to her daughter's room where light slanted through the open curtains.

"Iris, how are you?"

"Fine. I'm fine. Well . . . not really, but—"

"I know. I know. I have the results of the X-ray now. And I want to tell you first of all that I don't think there is anything for you to be concerned about."

"O . . . kaaay . . . ?"

"One of the X-rays was sent down from the Ennis Hospital to the Breast Clinic at the Limerick Regional. Just for confirmation. It appears there's a disturbance, what the radiologist calls an 'architectural distortion.' "

Iris took a sudden in-breath, and held it.

"This is *really* important to hear . . ." The doctor softened her voice like she was sitting beside Iris holding her hand. "The radiologist phoned me this morning to say it's *nothing* for you to worry about, but they *do* want to see you next week."

There was silence from Iris's end. *Architectural distortion?*

"Iris?"

"Yes." Iris replied finally. "Sounds iffy all the same, but you say I shouldn't be worried?"

"I can guess what you must be thinking, after Luke and everything, but it's not bad news, Iris. Really. The radiologist just wants to make sure. Nine of out ten callbacks are what we call false-positives. The Breast Clinic has already sent you an appointment by post. You should get the letter on Monday."

"All right."

"Do you have someone to go with you?"

Iris hesitated. "I do."

"Okay, then. Cheer up, *please*, and *try* to have a good day." She paused. "I'll be in touch after you've seen the consultant. And Iris?"

"Yes?"

"Call me if you need to."

Iris didn't know what she was feeling. It was like nothing. Just a void. Or an empty air pocket. Or that moment when you've been asked a question and you don't know the answer but you know you should. And you panic and suddenly you feel paralyzed. Why hadn't she asked more questions. Architectural distortion? What the hell? Iris replaced the telephone and hauled herself outside with a crippling sort of feeling, as if her legs had lost their power.

The sun was shining and she noted how odd that felt. The lawn was dappled in patches of different hues of green. If she could have drunk it in, like some green elixir, it might have calmed her. But as it was she stood a few moments, a frenzy building, then she grabbed her secateurs from the wooden table under the porch and scanned the freshly opened poppies. Crimson goblets with beads of light shining through them.

She ordered herself to get a grip. It was a thing of nothing, the doctor implied.

Iris sliced one stem, two stems, then three stems, clear down to the base of the plant.

The cuts were swift and clean. The poppy stems a foot long.

She brought the flowers inside and laid the stems on the counter, balancing them without bruising their petals, their faces clear. She would put these poppies to the test to see if they'd *really* hold their shape until morning. She'd photograph the sequence of singeing their cut-off ends and arranging them in a vase, and she'd photograph them again in the morning and upload them to her blog.

The flower heads floated above the sink. Striking a match with her right hand, she took up the first long hairy stem and held the flame under the cut end—just like the blonde on *Gardener's World* demonstrated. ("Until blackened," she'd said.) It sizzled and oozed a greeny liquid. She laid each down and photographed their burnt ends. Then, with three poppies scorched, she placed them in a tall glass vase and centered them on the counter. She stepped back and for a few moments stood staring at them, half expecting the petals to separate and fall. She challenged them. Go on! I dare you. But in a kind of numbed stillness their open faces and dark centers held their pose and stared back.

She took a few deep breaths. Tess had taught her: In with positive energy, out with the negative. In with white light, out with gray.

In the empty house in Ashwood, the phrases "architectural distortion," and "nine out of ten callbacks," and "false-positives" boomeranged about her.

White in, gray out.

Water up, fire down.

Two

Sunshine pouring through the window of her Camden Lock flat in North West London reminds Rose of the song about a Chelsea morning. The one with the milk and toast and the oranges and butterscotch. It reminds her of her mother singing when the spring sunlight returns to the kitchen in Ashwood—sometime in the middle of March—before the cuckoo comes, before the swallows return, and the tulips fade. For six months of the year no sun shines in the north-facing kitchen until that first ray of spring light squeezes in from the east. Her mad, loveable mother would start singing, nearly as good as Joni Mitchell.

Rose sings it now to herself as she stretches in the bed. She kicks off the duvet and slides to the edge, looking out her window on the canal below. Early-morning kayakers paddle. Seagulls squawk above the lock, noisy and loud. She loves the noise here compared to the utter quiet of the west of Ireland. She observes her room a moment before standing to dress, and counts, "One, two, three!" Three tea mugs. Not a record. She smiles, remembering the sort of Mexican stand-off she would sometimes have with her mother.

"So here's where all the mugs have got to, Rosie!" her mother would say, stepping into Rose's bedroom to retrieve them, sidestepping music sheets and books and clothes. "How you manage to emerge from this . . ." she would say, somewhat exasperated, looking about and holding out her hands as if to receive piles of dirty laundry in her arms, ". . . is beyond me."

"Don't know, Mum . . . just do."

"You're like a butterfly coming from a cocoon."

"Yup."

"Mother find mugs?" Her father would ask when she hopped into the car later, not a minute too soon. He'd be sitting, waiting patiently to drive them: she to school and him to work.

"Three."

"Not a record so. You could make her happy, if you wanted," he said, looking at Rose seriously for a moment, "by giving your room a little tidy."

"I know, Dadda. I'm sorry."

"Was she cross?"

"No. Not really."

Back then, Rose was at secondary school, and Luke's law office was in the town near the old limestone courthouse. It was a daily ritual. Rose was always only just on time. Her father was the kind of man who felt being exactly on time was already being late. So in order to avoid the kind of confrontations Rose and Iris sometimes had—it being only natural with two females in the house—he allowed her to think he needed to be at work twenty minutes before he did. It was easy for him to make allowances for his daughter.

19

A breeze stirs, the curtains move a wind chime. She plans to phone her mother later to say her room was flooded with light when she awoke. That's what she will tell her—there was a song outside my window, Mum.

Grabbing a pair of jeans, Rose lifts a gray cotton string top from among small piles scattered across the floor. She grabs a black cardigan and turns to her image in the mirror. She decides not to braid her long hair but tucks loose ends behind her ears. "Rosie dear, *please* tidy your room, soon. Now, there's a good girl." She carefully folds a black jersey dress and slips it into her rucksack.

The sitting room is strewn with her roommate's tissue-paper patterns and toiles. In the corner a tailor's dummy is half-dressed with a print chiffon. "Hello, Dummy." She writes a note and pins it to the dummy's breast.

Isobel, gone to master class. Wish me luck! Talk later. x Ro

The Pirate Castle at Oval Road on the edge of the canal is below her flat. The stairs alongside it are iron-rusted and gum-stained. A paper cup sails on the gathered green algae. Rose now walks along the narrow sidewalk, dodges cyclists coming toward her, and hurries under the dark part of the railway bridge. She passes the floating Chinese restaurant at the canal's turn at Regent's Park, where she joins the stream of morning commuters and dog walkers.

This morning, Tuesday, the grass verges of the Broad Walk in Regent's Park are flaked with pink droppings from the horse chestnut trees. Blossoms pirouette in the wind. It's snowing petals. For a moment she stands, closing her eyes, waiting for one to hit her face. She's a girl standing still in the green heart of the moving city. She opens her mouth and sticks out her tongue to catch a petal and taste its pinkness, but without luck.

The petals toss about in whirlwinds while she continues along at the edge, where the grass meets the pavement. Two petals land on the back of her head, wed themselves to her dark hair. There's a man in a smart suit walking beside her, and he looks as if he wants to say something. She's seen him before, on the daily commute through the park, one of those familiar strangers in our lives. But he doesn't speak. Rose hoists the weight of her case on her back from one shoulder to other. The businessman follows a few paces behind.

Rose is humming as they cross Chester Road, and she turns slightly right to walk along the western side of the Avenue Gardens, passing the colorful parrot tulips. At Park Square she turns right again in the direction of Baker Street and the Royal Academy of Music on Marylebone. The man pauses. He stops to watch her. She is like a picture of a girl in painting. The petals adorn her hair like gemstones as she heads up the steps of the academy.

On the top step she turns, pauses momentarily. The young businessman crosses the road and walks east toward Portland Street. Another time, she thinks. Today is not the day. No. Today's agenda is already full. No room for flirtations. She's having a master class with Roger—Mr. Kiwi Dude, as some of the other students call him—in the afternoon but has one last practice with him this morning. She passes the porter. His crooked lips ignite into a smile.

"Miss, you forgot to sign in."

She spins around and returns to his desk. "Sorry, George." She signs. She senses his glance at the birthmark on her cheek. He can't help himself. Rose knows; she's used to it. She'd decided at the end of her teens not to keep trying to cover up the small, darkened stain and so, as she signs her name she smiles, hands the pen back to George.

"There you go."

When George returns his eyes to the desk a pink fragment has appeared, like a thumb-size piece of silk, on his record book. As Rose moves off down the hallway the old porter shifts the petal to beside the girl's name.

Mr. Kiwi Dude is a handsome New Zealander and a virtuoso violinist. In addition to giving master classes, Roger Ballantyne is Rose's tutor at the academy. She's lucky. He used to play with the Sydney Symphony Orchestra before moving to London to take up the professorship in strings for second-year students. He isn't one of the stuffy types they have there. He's cool, the type of not-quite-fifty-year-old who looks not-quite-forty because his skin is permanently tanned and his curly hair is hardly gray. It has sun-bleached highlights. Does he dye it? Now that *would* be cool. Rose heard a segment on BBC radio about men wearing makeup. And why not? That would have made her father laugh. Too bad Dadda would never know things like that, like how she feels about men wearing makeup, or how she loves to take the tube around London, finding her way to places like Columbia Road Flower Market in Shoreditch, or discovering random hidden gems like the Fan Museum in Greenwich. Sometimes she visits the British Library just to see what's on in case it'd be something her father would have liked. She knocks on Roger's door.

He opens and holds it. He's wearing flip-flops and jeans and a brown T-shirt with the logo of a white wineglass. "Hey, Rose. Come in." He steps aside. "Excited?"

"Hi. Yeh . . . I am. Nervous, though."

"No worries . . . you'll be fine."

Rose senses something about him is off but she continues, "I'm scared, actually, and feeling kinda hyper."

"Your final master class can do that, but it's the end of a great year, Rose. You've done well so far. Don't be worried." He looks at his cell phone. "Anyone in your family coming to hear you today?"

"No. There's only my mother and she's in Ireland. I told her it was next week. She gets too anxious for me. I'd be more worried for her being worried for me than I'd be nervous to play."

As if he really wasn't listening, he says, "Maybe next year."

On the wall of his small office there is a poster of a surfer on a wave. Rose lays her case on a chair below it, unzips the cover, and undoes the clasps. Her violin lies open with a mottled layer of white just under the bridge. Crap. Light from the window overlooking Marylebone shines on the varnish as she takes her instrument up by the neck. Tiny specks of rosin run off the surface. As she bends slightly to position herself, the second pink petal falls from her hair onto the floor. Rose only notices the shower of rosin.

"That dust I'm seeing, Rose . . ." He pauses. His fingers are tented under his chin. He taps them lightly. He looks at her like she's a child. And the look makes her feel like one. "Rosin won't make you play better, you know. Here, give it to me." He takes her instrument and wipes the excess with the cloth he keeps on his music stand.

Rose gets her sheet music and sets it up. The excitement of the morning is gone. Her head is a jumble. The sheet music trembles as she adjusts it on the stand.

"I was practicing last night. It was late." She feels chastened, embarrassed. Her fingers have a clammy mind of their own as she takes up her bow and tightens it.

When Roger hands back her instrument he is not pleased. "Begin with a G-minor scale, please. Three octaves."

Roger "the master" is preparing Rose for her first solo performance of Bach's *Sonata in G Minor*. Serious stuff, she gets it, but this coolness increases her anxiety. What the hell? The student recital and master class is scheduled for the afternoon. Roger's other students will be there. Some performing. Some not. Maybe he's anxious, too. She lifts her violin with her left hand and brings it to her shoulder. Is he angry with her? It wasn't that much rosin. Her chin senses for the familiar place on the rest and nestles into position like a cat finding a place in the sun. She bends her fingers and squares them, placing them in position for the scale. With her bow raised she takes a moment, counts to three, scans the room: the poster, the warm light that angles in from the window, Roger standing beside the door, his arms crossed over his chest. She begins. G A B flat, C D E flat, F G . . .

"Good," he says. "Again."

Again Rose plays. She relaxes and thinks, Okay, I'm feeling more confident now. Her old teacher, Andreas, appears for a moment in her mind.

"Ready?"

"Yes."

"Begin."

With the top of the bow hovering just a whisper above the strings, she nods imperceptibly to the surfer and begins the adagio, the first movement of the sonata, with a sweeping run into an arpeggio starting with a slow bow.

Everything is good, Rose believes. She's relaxed. She's playing really well. Somewhere near the end of the second movement, the fugue, Roger's cell phone rings.

It rings once.

She plays on. He'll silence it in a second. She's into the challenging ascent, and is careful not to lose the singing line, the melody line, but the damn phone is still ringing.

A fifth ring. A sixth. And then he answers it.

He opens the door and he goes out into the hall. He actually walks out. Worse, he gives a slight wave of his hand in her direction indicating she should continue playing. The door doesn't quite shut. It hangs ajar and she can hear him in the hall.

"Ah. No. Don't do that. We can meet later. I know. I know. Hey, why don't you come, it'll be fun. What? No? We can go for a . . . no. Please . . . Victoria?"

Silence.

Then, "Fuck!"

A sharp thud thunks against the door.

Rose plays on, by now just beginning the third movement, the *Siciliana*. She plays it slow, emphasizing the dotted rhythms like Roger has shown her. After a few minutes he opens the door and walks behind her to the window without a beat of acknowledgment. She keeps playing. This movement is melodic and Rose is swaying. But suddenly he stops her, puts up his hand, and says, "You're not moving slowly enough into the strings. Approach it from underneath. And . . . *re-lax* . . . the tension in your left hand." He checks his watch. "I've told you that before."

Rose lowers her violin and bow. Her head is turned slightly, her small birthmark fully visible. She's uncomfortable with him, with the way he's looking at her. She's suddenly very self-conscious. They stand facing each other but saying nothing. He turns back to the window. Sounds of buses rise into the stillness of the room.

"I can't do this now," he says, and walks past her. Out. It happens in a second. She hears his footsteps flipping and disappearing down the hall and down the stairs.

Rose stands, holding her violin and bow at her sides, closing in on herself like she's a deflated party balloon. She stops breathing and listens. She expects he'll be turning around, turning around any minute and coming back. Coming back to apologize, or something—to hear her finish the *Siciliana* at least.

She waits, waiting to be revived, but he doesn't return. She stands at the window, bow in one hand, violin in the other. Roger has left the building. She sees him crossing the street and heading down Thayer.

"Feck!" she says. "Crap!" A wave of bewilderment quickly turns to something else. Part of her feels frozen, part of her feels fuming; her movement is jerky as she starts to pack up her bow and violin. She's shaking between anger and humiliation.

Before closing her case she eyes the slip of paper taped to the inside velvet covering, the one Roger had given her the first day she started practicing the sonata with him.

Rose,

Practicing Bach for me is like a meditation, even a daily prayer. It connects me with a higher power. May it be the same for you.

As ever,
Roger

She pulls it off the velvet, crumples the note, and throws it down.

Still shaking, she stands in the corridor outside his office.

With a little over an hour to pass before the master class, she hopes she'll run into someone, anyone she can vent to, but the hallway is empty. She thinks about finding the two friends she's made at the RAM. Leonard and Freya. They're studying musical theater, but they have their final projects this week, too. There are only the muted notes of string-playing instrumentalists she can hear behind the closed doors of the small practice rooms. Ysaÿe. Kreisler. More Bach. Rose slumps down against the wall. She feels like vomiting. Do they all play better than she does? Today was meant to be a celebration. She was looking forward to performing, to staking out her territory, to claiming her place alongside the other brilliant students in her class, and to ringing her mother with triumphant news. Now she feels cast out, inadequate. An amateur. A craftsperson at best. Not an artist. She makes no sound in the hallway although tears shine in her eyes.

A door opens and closes somewhere down the hall. What is she going to do now? Hang out here until Roger returns?

What the hell?

And who is Victoria?

In the ladies', she sees her red face in the mirror. She stares while trying to control her breathing. She's gulping for air.

Finally, she takes out her makeup bag. The birthmark is flushed with feeling. She looks closely at it, as if in seeing it, it somehow pulls her back into herself and she begins to calm down.

"It's shaped like a rose," her father said.

"A tiny tea rose," her mother said.

When she was old enough to understand such things, they had told her: "That's why you were named Rose."

She'd thought about that for a moment and then asked: "What if it looked like an elephant? What would I have been called then?"

"Ellie, of course!"

They went on like this, making a game of it. The story of the rose always preceded the story of how she arrived in Ashwood on August 23, 1990, when she was eight weeks old. She wasn't an orphan, but "placed" for adoption following her birth in the month of June. Both stories always worked to make Rose claim her identity. Her father was right, the edges of the birthmark on her right cheek do look like the curved petals of a rose tattoo. But that's not why they named her Rose. She knows that. But the story always comforts her. She's grown used to it, just as she'd grown up with the idea of being adopted. Just another way of being in the world. Most of the time she doesn't even notice. It doesn't really matter, most of the time.

When she was sixteen her parents decided to give her the letter from her birth mother. She had cried when she read it. Rose keeps the letter tucked inside a music book that is on the shelf in her bedroom back in Ashwood. Her birth mother hadn't written much. It was a short, handwritten letter. She wanted Rose to know she was very much loved and it was because of that love she'd been "placed" with a wonderful couple who would give her all the things she couldn't—a house and home and, most important, two parents who really loved each other. *Always remember you are doubly loved. By me, forever, and by your parents.*

She touches her cheek and thinks of her father. What would he do now? She knows her mother would be raging mad at Roger. In fact, now that she thinks about it, she's sorry she didn't tell her mother the master class was *this* week, because if she had, her mother would be on her way to the academy, bursting in without stopping for George, marching right up the stairs to the office of Mr. Roger Ballantyne and waiting for him to come back, to ask him what the hell was he doing walking out on her daughter at a critical moment when she was trying so hard to be perfect. She would be a storm coming at him. And for a moment Rose lightens up just thinking about her impassioned mother.

But her father, now what would he do?

Leaving the makeup bag on the edge of the sink, Rose takes out her ensemble for the concert, strips off, and steps quickly into her sleeveless black dress and ballet flats. She returns to her makeup and underlines and overlines her eyes in black. Sultry.

Feck 'em. Get your Irish up! her father would have said.

Yes. Feck them.

She picks up where she left off with the *Siciliana*. The acoustics in the ladies' room are amplifying. Her *Siciliana* is a long, anguished sigh. She leans into the phrases like Roger taught her, goddamn him, giving them room to breathe without letting them fade like petals withering on a stem. The heartbeat in her chest is a metronome, silent to the outside world, but keeping time with the music.

An hour later, she gets her Irish up and goes to the recital hall. Roger returns five minutes before the master class and just nods to her as if nothing has happened. He doesn't offer any explanation or apology. She opens her case and gets ready. She's up first. Bowen before Ferguson and Kowowski. She steps to the stage in a sort of half dream. Dust motes swirl in the glare of the stage lights. She doesn't look out at the audience of fifty or so. She doesn't want to see the gathered students and their parents and the other professors come to assess the best of the academy's talent. She settles her chin and begins. She plays her heart out. She keeps the melodic contours without losing the balance. Her phrasing is intense but elegant. She is playing it beautifully.

But she is wrong.

"Wrong. Wrong. Wrong," Roger Ballantyne says, taking center stage. "Stop moving, Rose. You look like you're trying to draw pictures with your scroll." He looks to the audience, as if he's said something clever. "You are playing too fast between the sections. Wait . . . until . . . the sound . . . comes out and we can *hear* the change of colors."

She continues. Louder. But over her playing, he is calling, "Don't be so polite. It's Gypsy music! Play it like it was written."

She plays. He is strutting on the stage. "Your vibrato is exaggerated."

She tries to exaggerate less.

"It sounds like you are ironing the strings. Rose!" There's an actual murmur from the audience. Stifled laughter? "Make them sing like a song. Let them breaaaaathe."

Roger crosses the stage and picks up his violin. "How you manage to make Bach sound sterile, I don't know." Rose stops as Roger starts into the fugue, to demonstrate. He's superb, of course, and when his attention is focused on the audience, lost in his own magnificence, Rose grabs her case, violin, and bow and walks out. She doesn't look back and she squeezes her tears. She hopes for one moment Roger will call after her, she hopes he will stop performing and call her back, that he will feel her humiliation. But he doesn't. Murmuring from the audience doesn't stop him. It's all about him. He has his audience, and plays on.

The next moment Rose is into the cool corridor. She kneels down and puts her violin in the case, then gets up and keeps walking, pushing out the front doors until she is out onto the rainy, steamy street. Too wet to walk back to Camden.

Five o'clock and the mood of the crowds on the busy night on Baker Street is a clash-and-bang cacophony. Rose jostles her way to the tube platform, barely conscious of where she is. She stands, hollow and waiting. When her train comes she steps inside just as the doors close. They catch her violin case. She tugs it free and loses her balance. A man beside steadies her. Collapsing into a seat, she hoists the case onto her lap and stares at the black mirror of reflected faces and lights as the train whirs through the tunnel. At King's Cross she gets out to change to the Northern Line. Up the escalator, a hundred bodies judder as one, except for Rose Bowen, who stands immobilized, apart, void of thought or emotion. *Euston. Mornington Crescent.* Rose gets out at Camden. As the train pulls away, she stands on the platform and looks back into the carriage. The doors close and when the train shudders into motion, she watches her violin topple from where she has left it leaning against the window. It slides down onto the seat. Then off it heads. *Chalk Farm, Belsize Park, Hampstead, Golders Green, Brent Cross, Hendon, Colindale, Burnt Oak, Edgware.*

Gone.

Three

It had been Luke who'd decided what they should name their baby. When Iris suggested Poppy he'd turned his eyes upward.

"No, Iris, be serious! Poppy? Come on. Her name should be Rose."

After four years of waiting, Iris would be a mother and Luke a father and two would become three. For seventeen years the Bowens were a trio—two flowers and a "fLuke," Luke had said.

"Fluke?" Rose asked when she was old enough to wonder what it meant.

"That's right," Luke would say and wink at Iris. "I'm the odd one out. Did you ever hear of a flower named Luke?" He looked at Rose with his eyebrows raised to their highest and she shook her head. "No, then. As I said, we're two flowers and a fLuke." And that's how it was—until the beginning of that wet summer two years ago when three became two again.

A pain in Luke's back had become pancreatic cancer.

They'd sat in the peach office of the oncologist Dr. Conway. The office was on the second floor of the Limerick Regional Hospital and Iris remembers looking out at the traffic, the buses and cars and taxis, and thinking, This is just a bad dream. A bus stopped and two older women helped each other off. One was wearing a red hat and a black-and-white-checked jacket. Everything was so *normal*. Middle of a Wednesday afternoon in early March. Blue sky. Spring. A few clouds. But at a tidy desk with a brown folder a voice was saying, "I'm afraid it's not good news."

When they came out to the car park that day Iris couldn't find the parking ticket and she pulled everything out of her bag, pulled it all out and let it fall on the ground. Check book, old shopping receipts, wallet, a packet of tissues, lipstick, her hairbrush, sunglasses. Loose coins. Everything. A man came up quickly behind them and said, "Here, take mine," as though he knew all the people coming and going from that particular car park might have just heard, *I'm afraid it's not good news.* Maybe by giving her his ticket his news would be better.

Next came the treatments and the short spells of hope, the urgings of good cheer, visits from neighbors and friends all wanting her to hope for the best. *There's always room for hope,* they'd said. Iris had a mania for feeding Luke green leafy vegetables and juicing arugula with lemon and olive oil—good for the liver and pancreas, Tess said. But that passed when he couldn't eat anymore, when he lost his appetite and became the thin figure with no strength left. Then she tried to feed him applesauce. They nursed him at home and Sheila, a hospice volunteer, came every afternoon. Every day Iris brought something fresh in from the garden. Petals of forget-me-nots, like blue confetti, lay sprinkled on top of his bedside table. The CD player was playing Bach concertos, and then sometimes Luke would ask

Rose to put Israel Kamakawiwo'ole's "Somewhere Over the Rainbow" on repeat.

Luke's health declined quickly. (He hadn't been feeling well since early December, but hadn't let on.) Then, one afternoon in the week before he died, he reached for her hand across the cream candlewick bedspread. Iris had looked at him with fear in her eyes that this was the end. But she was surprised by his sudden strength, and briefly, like a sun ray breaking through a storm cloud, a glimmer of hope eased her face.

"Luke?"

He angled himself up in the bed. He took a moment to moisten his throat, as if the words were hard and dry, and yet he had to say them. The green of his eyes had deepened. "Luke? What is it?"

"Iris . . . after me. If anything happens to you—"

"Stop. Nothing is going to happen to me. Lie back."

"Iris. Listen . . . I—"

"No."

The pressure of his fingers on her hand tightened.

"Listen to me. Please. I don't want Rose to be alone."

Iris turned to look away out the window, tilted back the tears, and held her mouth tightly.

"You . . . need to make sure that doesn't happen. Iris, you . . . have to explore all possibilities. Without you . . . there will be no one."

"Nothing is going to happen to me," she said. "Lie back."

"*Say* you understand."

She hesitated. "Do you know what you're asking me?"

"I do."

But did he? Did he really? It pained her to think about what he was asking. This man she'd loved for nearly three decades was dying but he was talking about life. Not his life. He was talking about life *after* him.

"I'm going now," she said. He loosened his grip. "Rose has her French practice exam tomorrow." Then, to make him laugh (because they all knew she was hopeless at languages), she added, "I promised I'd quiz her on grammar." But he didn't laugh.

"I just wanted to make you smile."

There were tears in his eyes; there were always tears in his eyes now, just on the edge of spilling.

"Iris. Please . . . she'll have no one. Do it for me."

Iris held her breath.

Then he spoke the words she didn't want to hear. "Try to find her . . . find Hilary."

He didn't know what he was saying. Find Hilary? It was an impossibility. They'd had one meeting with her. The three of them and a social worker. Years ago. It was crazy. Iris rose from the bed and went to the window. Pulling the curtain aside, she saw the poppies needed staking.

Iris tidied the bed tray, smoothed the blanket, poured water into a plastic cup, and straightened the pile of magazines—*The Economist, Wine Spectator*—and the novel Luke was still hoping to read, *The Third Policeman*. She couldn't think straight but she pretended calmness. He knew. He knew her inside out. When she came to kiss his forehead, he caught her arm. His voice was hoarse.

"Iris, we have to keep showing up for each other, for Rose." He closed his eyes and fell back.

She kissed him on his forehead and let her cheek linger on the side of his face. The softness of his skin at that moment was extraordinary. As though he was already becoming transparent, already leaving the world.

She whispered, "I'm sorry. I'm so sorry this is happening." She clenched her teeth. She didn't want to cry. They'd been all through this. The unfairness of it. The sadness. The end.

"Say you'll promise." He held his grip on her arm.

"I'll make a phone call this week," she'd said. Then she held his face between her hands. "I promise."

Luke died a few days later on a sunny day at the end of May, two weeks before Rose's Leaving Cert exams, a month before her seventeenth birthday.

Iris had rallied as best she could. She'd coached their daughter through the exams because there was no other way. She had to take them, but she only had to pass. And somehow they'd got on. Somehow they did. Iris and Rose, with a lot of help from Tess. Then, four months later, Rose entered London's Royal Academy of Music.

The surviving pieces, after the center had been blown out their lives, fell into place, as if ordained from on high, as if in compensation. The life insurance benefits were held in trust for Rose, and after paying her rent and school fees she had a monthly stipend for living expenses.

Iris stayed in Ashwood. And in the unyokedness of being a widow she was adrift in the world, like a dandelion when its yellow florets have died and turned to seed, parachuting into the air, like a ruptured cloud burst. She was all over the place. No center to hold on to.

She'd never imagined a life without Luke. She hadn't prepared. And yet now here she was, a damp morning in the beginning of June standing in her kitchen with the radio playing requests, wearing her nightdress with its watering-cans-and-Wellingtons pattern Luke had given her one Christmas, and her long, wavy red hair that Luke never wanted her to cut, having to imagine the possibility of a cancer growing in her, too. What were the odds? *Nine out of ten callbacks. False-positive.* It was simply unimaginable, and yet.

Instinctively she moved her hand to her left breast, and then took it away.

"You're fine," she said to no one listening. "You're perfectly fine. Don't go getting all dramatic. You're fine."

She stood at the counter, looking at the poppies she'd singed and propped in the vase. When she'd come into the kitchen the next morning, the day after Dr. O'Reilly telephoned, she'd expected to see their turgid stems bare with petals fallen on the counter. But the flowers were perpendicular, just as she'd left them. Alive, erect, and vibrant still. The BBC gardener was right. The purple stamens nodded as she turned the vase around and a fine black dust whispered down the inside of the petals.

She opened her laptop and brought up the blog page on *The Banner County News* Web site. The country had gone from boom to bust and there were neither new houses nor new gardens, but there were still gardeners. Gardening doesn't stop when the economy tanks. She took a moment and then tapped the keys in a flurry.

Bird jam. Listen to the dawn chorus. To calls, whistles, trills, cackles, coos, chattering, and twittering.

Omens are everywhere. Birds are everywhere. Love is somewhere.

Anxious to lift a corner on the veil of the future, we are attracted to omens and birds. In the days of the Romans, a bird appearing at a person's right indicated fortune. A bird to the left . . . well, you guessed it . . . avoid it.

The blog seemed a lesser thing to Iris. Did anyone care? And who the hell out there was ever going to read it? Yet the blinking cursor was alive on the white template. It could *link* anywhere. Connect to perfect strangers, even. By such a thin thread she could connect with the world beyond Clare, she thought. She'd set up a Wordpress site and she owned the domain IrisBowen@wordpress.com. She could hyperlink between the two blogs now and felt a little pleased with herself. When she missed Rose and Luke the most, she could blog. The blog could be her dialogue . . . with somebody. Anybody. She looked out down the slope of the garden toward the trees. She watched the sudden flight of a blue tit heading for the cherry blossoms. Then she typed:

A bird flying to you is a benediction. Grab it before it flies away.

After uploading the poppy photos (the sketch she'd attempted was laying, half-finished, beside the telephone), and writing step-by-step instructions and posting, Iris went outside. Suddenly she wanted to hear the cuckoo. She walked eastward along the front of the house, along the border that was stippled with wild columbine, and turned right to face the valley. Nothing.

"Where are you?" she asked toward the treetops.

Listening for the first call of the cuckoo was a thing she and Luke used to do. In the brightening of spring they'd keep track, year on year, who would hear him first. (Luke, fourteen. Iris, eleven.) *The cuckoo comes in April.* She walked backward in case her left ear should catch him. Then she stopped and faced east. No sound. *He sings his song in May.* Sing, cuckoo.

She called: *Goo-ko, goo-ko,* willed him to fly up from the valley and sing across the top of the spruce forest.

Goo-ko, goo-ko . . .

Nothing.

All she could hear was Tommy Ryan's van from half a kilometer away as it stopped and started to deliver post into neighbors' boxes along the road. Still wearing her nightdress and one of Luke's shirts, her hair undone, Iris hid behind the hedge. Tommy was a kind man but she was in no humor to speak with him. He played cards most nights in Nolan's pub since his own wife had died suddenly of a heart attack at fifty-two. Now when he saw Iris he seemed to look at her like she was wearing some dark mantilla of sadness that he felt somehow obliged to take away. She wanted to say, "I'm fine. Thanks, Tommy. Really. Don't worry. And stop looking at me that way."

As he stepped from his van, leaving the door open, she could hear the noon Angelus ringing on the radio. He opened the box and dropped in her post. Out of nowhere, Cicero, her black cat, appeared at her bare feet and started mewing. She mimed to him to shush, but Cicero paid no attention to mimes and mewed louder and Tommy called "Sibby, Sibby" outside the hedge. (Why all cats in the west of Ireland were called Sibby, she never understood.) He might have come to the gate to see then, but Iris plucked the cat up into her arms and held him tight.

"Sibby, Sibby?"

When Tommy's van passed away back down the road, Iris slipped through the gap in the hedge. Between the electricity bill and a copy of *Gardens Illustrated* was a letter from the Breast Clinic. She opened it and read:

A client's path through the symptomatic breast clinic is tailored to the individual and may not require anything more than a clinical review (especially in younger women). The medical history will be discussed and the client will be given the opportunity to ask questions regarding their symptoms and future management. A small number of clients require a biopsy. This is a minor procedure where tissue is removed from the breast using a needle under local anaesthetic. Most women experience little or no discomfort with this procedure. The center is equipped to perform a biopsy during the client's initial assessment, although occasionally biopsies are performed at a later date to facilitate accurate guidance with the mammogram. The tissue is then examined under the microscope. Most clients who have a biopsy do not have breast cancer.

It is very important that you confirm your appointment: Friday, 12 June, 10:30. Dr. Denise Browne.

She folded the letter into its envelope and put it in her back pocket and walked up the path, unable to deny it was real. This distortion thing. Swallows reveled in and out of the barn, ignoring her, and Cicero made little cackling noises. The tip of his tail shivered. The appointment was at the end of the week.

"What? Don't look at me like that," she said. But he did. Expectant. She turned to face again the trees. The female cuckoo would be encamped high up, somewhere out there, biding her time, awaiting her moment. This was the time of year she'd drop her egg into the nest with the meadow pipit and, in the way of nature, the meadow pip mother would raise the baby cuckoo as her own. But where was the cuckoo's mate? Iris wanted to hear him. It was absurd, but she did. No sound came from the sky except a wind noising in the spruce. She made it across to the stone steps at the top of the garden and sat down, clutched her knees. She rocked back and forth. Tears streamed down her face.

———

Iris had decided not to disturb Tess's weekend. But on Monday when she rang, Tess hadn't answered, so Iris had left a voice mail: "Guess what? I have a distortion. Ring me."

Now Iris sat in a iron garden chair with a bottle of red wine and a tumbler at the round table under the porch. She sat out in the falling night air with the garden perched on the edge of explosion of more poppies, lupines, and geraniums. A swelling greenness turned the new growth of the boxwood hedge neon, even in the darkness. The swagged layers of Mt. Fuji, the Japanese cherry, had reminded Luke, she remembered, of the bustle gowns in *Femmes au Jardin* by Monet, with its branches billowing in the wind. Cicero composed himself in a clef shape across the table and played with the pieces of cheese Iris fed him.

"One for you and one for me."

Evening began to fall. She finished the wine and went inside and lay down on the couch.

A few hours later Tess woke her.

"Good evening, pet," she said, raising her eyebrows and looking at the blue Wellies still on Iris's feet. "A little self-medicating?"

"Never hurt anyone," Iris said somewhat sheepishly, sitting up and feeling at once a sharp ache at the base of her neck, under her left shoulder, and yes, there, dead center of her spine. "What are you doing here?"

"Got a missed call from you earlier. You sounded funny, so I thought I'd pop over."

"Oh, right. Sorry. I must have fallen asleep. What time is it?"

"Ten." Tess picked up the bottle on the floor. "Californian. Yum." She smiled. "But mind yourself. Okay?"

"Yes, Dr. Tess, Medicine Woman."

"Iris?"

"Okay. Yes. I hear you." Iris kicked off her boots and rose crookedly from the couch. Her head was sore. The blue of the summer night sky was finally yielding to darkness.

"Tea, I think, before you tell me exactly what the doctor said."

In the kitchen, Tess switched on the light and Iris put the kettle on. "Poppies are fab," Tess said, looking at them and, without lifting her eyes: "So the doctor said they found—"

"A distortion." Iris looked at her for a long moment. "What is . . . an 'architectural distortion'?"

Tess came around the counter toward her. "I know it sounds very clinical and not very encouraging but—"

"No, it really doesn't."

"—I looked it up." Tess smiled, hesitantly at first, then laid her arm around Iris's shoulders in a robust kind of way. "It's just common medicalese, pet. An abnormal area of density. It shows up as shadows or white spots on the mammogram." She'd brought her PC with her and now had it opened on the counter.

"Shadows or white spots?"

"Apparently. Fatty breast tissue can look similar to a lump."

"Fatty!"

"Iris, seriously, that's it. An architectural distortion—"

"Can we stop calling it that!" Iris opened the cupboard and took out aspirin.

"Did you drink the whole bottle?"

Iris didn't replied. She *had* drunk more than she'd meant to. Her back was to Tess for a few moments. "Look, I got this." She reached into the back pocket of her jeans and showed Tess the letter from the Breast Clinic. "It came today."

Tess took the letter. "They don't waste any time." She read it. "That's good, Iris."

"Yeah?"

Tess nodded. "Really. The sooner, the better. Right? Doesn't mean bad news. Just . . . let's get on top of this." She paused a moment before continuing, "So . . . Iris . . . the distortion . . . it says here . . . just requires a bit of further exploration by ultrasound. It's not unusual"—Tess lowered her voice and narrowed her wide eyes—"in older women."

Iris suddenly burst out laughing, startling her friend. "Oh, thank you! Now I'm fat *and* old. I wish Luke could hear this."

She brought the teapot and cups to the table and Tess read more: "An architectural distortion is an abnormal arrangement of tissue strands of the breast, often a radial or random pattern." Tess looked up. "*But* . . . without any associated mass as the apparent cause." She continued reading as Iris poured the tea. "There is no visible mass." Tess read silently for a few moments.

"And?"

Tess held up her hand. "Here. Listen. The number of women in which the architectural distortion would actually represent invasive breast cancer is very low, perhaps five to seven percent. Clearly, most architectural distortions found on mammography are due to benign causes. There!" Tess sat back. "See?"

For a few moments both women sipped their tea, feeling somewhat relieved that perhaps the "distortion" was a thing of nothing, just as the doctor had said. Iris then showed Tess the sketch she was working on.

"Not bad, pet. Not bad at all. You're a constant surprise, Iris. Really. I'm in awe of you."

"Yeah?"

"Really. No, it's good." Tess reached across the table and squeezed Iris's hand. "You know, I'm really proud of you. What with the uncertainty of your job at the paper and now this. You're handling it so well."

Iris got up and faced her friend and, as if rising to the occasion that all would be just fine, she stretched the back of her neck straight up and stood firm. "Anyway, it's not like I *have* cancer. Sure it's not? I'm just going back for a second mammogram and ultrasound. To be sure. End of story . . . maybe a biopsy."

"Absolutely." Tess knit her brows.

"But I can tell you for nothing, I am a *little* nervous." She relaxed her stretch and started to clear the table.

"Don't be. Let me be nervous for you."

Iris nodded, feeling the genuine warmth from her friend.

"And I promised Luke I'd look after you. And a promise is a promise is a promise," Tess said.

Suddenly, Iris was looking at Tess as if she'd just seen a ghost walk past, as if it wasn't Tess who was speaking.

"Iris? What is it?"

Iris turned away. "Nothing." She went to the sink and put the teacups in and washed them. Until that moment Iris had kept the words "promise" and "Luke" well apart from each other. Ever since that horrible afternoon toward the end when Luke had asked her to promise, she'd closeted that word, locking it away in the farthest cupboard of her mind. There had been too much to do just to get on with living. Anytime she'd revisited the moment when he'd reached across and grasped her arm and said he didn't want Rose to be alone, she thought, *She isn't alone. I'm here!*

But now, hearing the word "promise" and thinking of her appointment, she felt suddenly cold, like an iceberg had melted and pulled her down in its freezing chill. Had Luke glimpsed some dark future? Had he *known* something?

A year had come and gone. And another. *He who was living is now dead*, the poet wrote. With each passing month she'd let herself forget what he'd asked and began to believe he'd only "wished" it to himself, and she'd merely overheard it. In the weeks and months after his death she hadn't thought of anything but getting through. She'd had to take care of things, figure out things, learn how to do the dozens of things Luke had always done. And she did do everything she was expected to do. Tidied up his papers. Wrote thank-you notes. Sent memorial cards with his picture. Settled with the solicitor and executor. Squared away the insurance for Rose and got her through and off to London.

And now, *what if?*

What if you were in that most delicate and tender part of your life as a gifted young musician just lifting your bow to add to the beauty of the world and suddenly not only was your father dead but your mother, too? What music would be left to you then? Luke and Iris were "only" children. Iris's parents had died within a few years of each other when she was thirty. Luke's parents, too, were both dead. His mother had a stroke and died shortly after and his father lived out the rest of his life in a nursing home in Monkstown, overlooking the sea. Luke had visited him as often as he could, even after his father no longer recognized him.

Rose was too young, too talented, too vulnerable to be parentless.

She had no one else.

"Are you all right? Pet?"

Iris determined right then and there, in the middle of the

kitchen with her head pounding, her left breast with a phantom-like pain, her blue Wellies tossed on the floor in the sitting room, the poppies with their still-turgid stems, that she was going to make the promised phone call. She believed this was the right thing and *only* thing to do, she believed this more than anything. That yes, she must find out if Hilary, her daughter's birth mother, was somewhere out there.

All this and more Iris thought about as she stood frozen by the sink with Tess watching her. It had been many years ago, in the summer of '90, but Iris remembered: It'd been raining the day they met her at the Adoption Board offices. Steady gray rain falling all over Dublin. Streets gleaming. Hilary had kept her khaki raincoat on over a print skirt and white T-shirt. Her legs were bare and her loafers wet from walking. She was twenty-one or twenty-two. Iris remembers feeling sorry for her yet strangely elated that Hilary was choosing them. (That's how it happened in those days.) Hilary had her pick of five couples. She didn't say very much. She didn't mention the birth father, or why she'd decided to place her baby up for adoption in Dublin. All they knew was she was an American student doing her master's degree in Irish literature and the baby she'd given birth to just a few weeks earlier was already in the care of a foster mother. She was tall, Iris remembered. Tall and thin with dark shoulder-length hair that had a bit of curl to it. But that's all she could remember. The encounter had been too brief to remember anything else. As their meeting was coming to a close, Luke asked, "Is there anything you'd like us to do?"

"Just one thing," she'd said. Iris looked at her. What color were her eyes? They were light. Were they blue or gray?

"Yes?" Luke said, reaching for Iris's hand.

"Her name—"

Luke and Iris looked to each other. They'd already picked out a name.

"Would you keep it?'

"Well . . ." Luke started, "we actually picked—"

"Her name is Rose."

"You all right, pet?" Tess asked again and reached across the table.

Iris came back from the memory. "Yes. Yes. I'm fine."

Your life can change in a moment. In a moment you're living or you're dying. *I'm afraid it's not good news.* Immediately after Tess left, Iris rang the Adoption Board in Dublin intending to explain her situation—all of it: Luke's death; her upcoming callback to the Breast Clinic; Rosie alone in London and that she was coming to up to Dublin the following morning, but a recorded voice apologized. The office was closed. What was she thinking? It was nearly midnight.

That night she tossed and turned in the too-big bed. When she came down to make herself hot milk in the small hours she saw that one poppy, but only one, had dropped its petals on the granite counter.

Four

The next morning was Tuesday. Feeling the particular kind of heaviness that comes with no sleep (and a little too much wine), Iris boarded the train for Dublin at Limerick Station armed only with a gardening magazine and a bottle of sparkling water and the notion that what she was doing was the only option. Dressed in what Rose called her "uniform"—smart olive green trousers with a camel-colored cardigan twin set—she'd even put on eyeliner and brought her lipstick. Where she was going she wanted to make a good impression.

After twenty minutes the train left the outskirts of Limerick city and began its passage into the deep, green middle of the country, past the silver mines, into northern Tipperary, and into rich, horse-breeding farmland. Hedgerows of whitethorn blooming squared off green fields. She thumbed through *Gardens Illustrated* and read about treatments for a new strand of boxwood blight. She learned how applying cow dung to the base of plants would give the fungus plenty to think about. It was worth a try. She jotted that down on a scrap of paper. In another article she read about an organic gardener's experiments with a homeopathic remedy called *Helix tosta,* made from crushed baked snail shells, to keep slugs at bay. Her blog readers, when she gets any, might like that.

When she arrived into Heuston Station she'd been feeling absurdly positive. The possibility of rescuing her boxwood and protecting her plants from slugs (and the birds from poison) lifted her heart. In a small thing there can be hope. She focused on the thought of saving the box hedge and for a time raked aside all the rest of it. She'd ask Tommy Ryan next time he was passing for a load of manure. Standing in the taxi queue, she imagined how much she would need for a ten-square meters. But the moment she entered the taxi and as it took her along the bus lane beside the quays heading toward O'Connell Bridge, and cars honked, she lost her sense of hope. As the taxi approached Trinity College her heart raced. The crowds along Dawson Street seemed to be racing, too, all on urgent missions of their own. Camera-laden tourists stood before the great oak doors to the college, snapping photos. Students jostled, rushing to end-of-term exams.

Iris asked the driver to let her out at the front gates. She paid, then walked slowly under the arch and out along the cobblestone path of the courtyard toward the bell tower straight ahead. She skirted its perimeter, remembering the myth that it was bad luck to walk beneath its dome. This she knew from her days as a student there. She'd planned to walk through the campus and exit right out onto Kildare Street but in choosing this path, she'd tempted fate. She knew it. Luke was everywhere, everywhere around her. His presence, like the ringing of the Trinity bell, was loud and clear and reverberated through her whole being.

She nearly lost her footing on the cobbles when the clock rang noon. On a bench not far away she sat, laid her basket at her feet, and closed her eyes, feeling the vibrations of the chimes.

Iris had met Luke on a rainy afternoon when she was waiting for the 46A bus. Her first glimpse of him was walking, a long, grounded stride and sheltering under a black umbrella. He'd been heading down Pearse Street, toward the seafront to his home, he later told her. As she waited, herself umbrellaless, protecting her books from the heavy rain, a notebook slipped from her bundle onto the edge of the pavement, just as he was passing. In that instant while Iris considered how to retrieve her book without tumbling more books, Luke had stopped and snatched it up. Rainwater gathered quickly in the gutter. Years later when they told the story to Rose, Iris said Luke had bumped her accidentally on purpose, but Luke said Iris had dropped the book just as she saw him coming. "I think your mother imagined she was dropping a handkerchief." And Rose laughed.

"Here you are," Luke had said, shaking the book free, and, satisfied it wasn't too wet, he'd landed it gingerly onto the pile she was holding. His smile intoxicated her.

"Thank you."

"Waiting for a bus?"

"I am. Forty-six A. Going to Ranelagh." Iris squared her books together. "You?"

"No," he said without moving and holding the umbrella high enough to include her. "Trinity?"

"Ah-huh." She nodded. "First year."

"Me, too . . . but not first year." He moved closer. It looked as if he was going to wait with her. Submerged under a sudden wave of warmth Iris was caught for words. Even though she was eighteen she was not very experienced with the currency of flirting.

"A rucksack might be a wise investment," he continued, "if you're going to be leaving home without an umbrella, that is. This is Dublin. You know the saying. We have four seasons: rain, rain, rain, rain."

She considered his green eyes, gauging whether he had said this in good humor or good old Irish sarcasm. It was both. It was a trait she'd come to love—his self-effaced delivery of facts.

"I know. But I was rushing this morning. Lecture at nine. I overslept."

His square face creased as he smiled. "I had company law this morning and I *should* have slept in." The skin around his eyes was pale, thin, and freckled.

"Was it worth it?"

"What?"

"The lecture?"

"Oh. Yes . . ." she blurted. " 'The Wasteland.' "

He paused. Thought a moment. *"Memory and desire* . . . right?"

"Yes. *Stirring dull roots with spring rain.*"

"Impressive." He smiled.

She blushed. "Not really. It's the next line. Ask me to recite any more and you'll see I belong at the back of the class."

Luke was from the south side of the city near Sandymount Strand, where he lived with his elderly parents on Gilford Road, one block from the Irish Sea and half a mile from the Martello Tower of Joyce's Stephen Dedalus. His parents, Agnes and Eugene Bowen, married late in life. They maintained a dental practice together. Like two bookends they supported his life, he'd always said. He later told Iris he never once took for granted the serenity of their life, nor their devotion to him. The sea air around Sandymount was like a tonic, he said, infusing tranquility into the Bowen house. It'd had been a charmed life, he knew.

51

When they got to know each other better, Luke showed Iris the old leather sofa in the front room where he studied every evening. His mother would bring him a cup of tea and a ham sandwich and slip quietly away. It was so much a part of the fabric of the workings of their life—mother and son—that neither needed to acknowledge her care nor his gratitude. "It just happened like clockwork," he'd said, "like it was somehow always meant to be that way. Like it was ordained. That's what I want one day, Iris." On Saturdays when the dental practice was busy with fathers and teenagers, Luke would bring his mother tea and biscuits at just the hour when he knew she'd be beginning to fade.

From that chance meeting on a wet November day Iris and Luke's beginnings had been set in motion. He was three years ahead of her in college. When he trained at Blackhall Place to become a solicitor, Iris was completing her final year at university. Then they moved in together to a one-bedroom flat on the Beach Road in Ringsend. After Luke passed exams and Iris had graduated with a degree in literature, they married in the late summer and had a small reception in Iris's parents' back garden in Ranelagh. By autumn they'd moved to the west of Ireland, where Luke accepted a job as a junior solicitor.

It ran just like clockwork.

They rented a house near the village of Seafield thirty miles from Ennis so Luke could be near the ocean. (It's where he'd always felt safest, he'd said.) A few years following their marriage, Iris's parents both passed away, first her father from heart failure and then her mother, who died in her sleep. With the money left to Iris they were able to put a down payment on an old cottage, ten miles in from the Atlantic, beside a grove of ash trees with a garden overgrown with wild blackberries and grass and nettles and rushes. They called their new home Ashwood and, when Luke went off to Ennis every morning, day by day Iris began the slow process of resurrecting the garden. It was then she really fell in love with gardening.

Three years after they'd moved to Ashwood, their GP, Dr. O'Reilly, advised them that if they wanted children they would have to adopt. She asked if they wanted to know who was—

"Deficient?" Luke had said. "Found lacking?" He looked at Iris who said, "Barren, you mean?"

"No. We don't need to know," they'd said. The next week they rang Social Services to inquire about adoption.

"Please take a seat, Mrs. Bowen. One of the social workers is on her way down." Iris was sitting inside the large foyer of a Georgian house on Merrion Square, in the offices of the Irish Adoption Board. Moments after settling, self-consciously, into an old wingback chair, she heard footsteps and stood quickly. A tall, slim woman, carrying a brown folder, came down the wooden stairs, then paused at the bottom. The unsmiling receptionist nodded toward Iris. The woman with the folder introduced herself as Sonia McGowan and led Iris into a nearby room with a corner window. She motioned to a chair to the left of a center table and sat opposite.

"Thank you so much for seeing me," Iris said. She was breathless with rising excitement.

"It seemed we had no choice." Ms. McGowan said.

"I'm sorry it was—"

"Yes. Well." Ms. McGowan smiled thinly. "Hearing that you've come all this way, Mrs. Bowen, we thought it best to agree. We do appreciate your circumstances. But you should have made an appointment. We're very busy. With cutbacks and—"

"I know. I'm sorry. But considering what's happening, or might happen, I mean, I thought you might . . ." Iris felt her face flush. "I just need some information."

Sonia said nothing and for a second Iris thought she would be asked to leave. Sonia went on, "It's really up to your daughter—"

"Yes. I know that. But . . . as I *hoped* I'd explained clearly to the receptionist, I just need to know one thing. Just in case. Because obviously I don't want to tell Rose unless the news is not good. About me, I mean. About the cancer scare. I have an appointment on Friday!" Iris's voice rose. "Do you see? I mean, what if?" With her eyes tearing up, Iris fumbled in her bag for tissues she knew were not there. She felt Sonia's eyes keenly on her.

"I do understand. First let me say, Mrs. Bowen—"

"Please. Call me Iris."

"All right. Iris." She handed Iris a tissue from a small box decorated with yellow ovals on a white background. Iris dried the corners of her eyes, then held the tissue between her hands. She folded her fingertips into her palms, hiding her chipped nails. After an awkward pause, Sonia finally spoke, but this time with a kind of chirpy drone.

"And how *is* your daughter getting on?" She laid down the folder she'd been holding, placing it beside the tissues on the side table between them. "Your daughter has gone to college in London to study music. You must be so proud of her. I understand it's not often an Irish student gets into the Royal Academy of Music." Sonia's breathing was measured, as if she was doing yoga in her mind. Everything about her was now measured and straight, as if she was schooling Iris in the ways of conducting oneself in stressful situations. Her fingers were soft-skinned and her nails were lightly polished. Her flat shoes were unscuffed. She might have walked in from a photo shoot advertising women's office clothes with her gray cardigan and smart pencil skirt.

Sonia McGowan was a woman in her early forties. And once upon a time she might have been eager and full of the energy young social workers initially possess, but on this day what Iris saw was great weariness. It was around her eyes. A few strands of gray peppered her otherwise shiny black hair.

"Rose . . . her name is Rose. She's doing well. Considering. She's very gifted. Her father would have been so proud of her. And she loves London. And I'm happy for her, but . . . I miss her terribly. What I really want—"

"Sounds very exciting, although I can also imagine your anxiety for her . . . and for yourself." Sonia was definitely pacing the meeting, injecting it with a balance of feigned interest and composure.

"Yes. And now, this . . ." Iris's voice stalled. Her hands went to her chest.

"I'm sorry. It hasn't been easy, I can imagine—"

"No, it hasn't been easy. It damn well hasn't. That's why I'm here," Iris cried. "I have to. I have to find. I have to find Rose's birth mother. I have to find Hilary."

Sonia's eyes knitted together, but if she was stunned at hearing the name she hid it well. She looked down and reached for the brown folder.

"Mrs. Bowen, Iris, I'm afraid it's not good news then," Sonia said finally. She turned her head toward the door in a way that suggested to Iris that she was suddenly uncomfortable. It was as if she was willing it to open, so she could escape. "We won't be able to help you. That information is private, available only to

the birth family circle and its adoptees. I'm afraid you don't meet
the criteria. The rules are very strict. Yours was not an open
adoption." She allowed just a few moments to let those words to
sink in, avoiding Iris's eyes, looking at the folder. But she didn't
wait long before she continued, "Your daughter can request this
information." She looked at Iris squarely. "And I promise whatever we have we will give her." Then she placed the folder back
down. "I hope you understand."

Iris's mind was in overdrive. She thought of Luke reminding
her that in situations like these, when her back was up against
the wall, she needed to lighten up. But he wasn't there. She had
to do this on her own. "This isn't good enough. *I'm* her mother!
I have a right to know."

Sonia McGowan may have had a storage of responses tucked
away behind her perfect hair and might have been able to deliver whichever of them was needed to calm clients down in situations like these, but this time she chose the wrong one.
"Actually, no. You don't."

Iris was on her feet in a flash.

"Please sit down, Mrs. Bowen. It's all right. I do understand."

Sonia moved to the edge of her chair and waited for Iris to
sit. Then she leaned forward, her voice quiet.

"I've looked through the file and what I can tell you is that we've
lost contact. So, really, even we would find it difficult to trace
her today." She continued, "We try to follow the birth mothers
for the first few years—as you probably know. And—"

"Her name was Hilary. Right? We met her, you know." Iris
had softened her voice, too.

"Yes, I see that. But the thing is, according to our records,
your daughter's birth mother"—Sonia was talking with that
scripted calmness again but she dropped her voice—"Hilary . . .

stopped responding." Sonia inched forward as if to reach out and touch Iris.

Iris's heart beat double time. She thought she might choke. The room was cold, and the armchairs were older than Iris, and the floor was so polished that her shoes squeaked when she shifted position in an effort to ease her panic. "When was that?"

"About sixteen or seventeen years ago," Sonia said, her voice low, nearly a whisper.

Iris wished it all was easier. The whole thing. Just as she was working her way through the grief of having lost Luke, now this. She'd anticipated she wouldn't be given *all* the information she needed, but she had not prepared herself for this. A dead end. Full stop. She sat back, covering her eyes, then looked up and spoke quickly, her voice now straining.

"Where does that leave me? I mean, is that all there is?"

"What more do you want?" Sonia asked, somewhat puzzled. "I don't understand, what more could there possibly be?"

"I'd expect more . . . more information," Iris said now, edging forward on her chair. Wasn't she entitled to something more definitive? *What* was Sonia not getting? "This can't be the end of the line. It just can't."

"I'm so sorry . . ." Sonia said reaching out to touch Iris's arm.

"No, no, no." Iris pulled away. "I *have* to have more information. What about the parents . . . I mean *Hilary's* parents. Can't I, or you, or the agency, contact them and find out where their daughter is?"

"Okay, Iris, calm down . . ."

"Addresses. Birth certificates. *Something*. Don't you know anything? Is that legal? Birth mother just drops off the face of the earth and that's all right with you? Well, it's not all right with me! I'm sure Luke . . . you know, my husband was a solicitor . . . I'm sure he wouldn't agree with this. What if something happens to me? What don't you understand? I could die! Who's going to look after Rose? You?"

Sonia froze. And for a long moment fingered the cuff of her cardigan. Iris stared at her. "And what about the birth father?"

"We don't request details about birth grandparents," Sonia replied, then shifted her gaze out the window and went on. "There's no mention of a birth father in the file, I'm sorry. Nor does his name appear on the original birth certificate. I'm afraid he's not in the picture."

"You can't do *anything* to help me? Is that what you're saying!" Iris heaved herself back against the armchair.

"I'm sorry, Iris. I really am." She reached forward and laid a hand on Iris's knee.

Iris didn't move. She was free-falling into a black empty space and it hurt. Was this it? The end. *What about my promise,* she wanted to shout.

After a few moments, when the only sound came from a bird across the road, Iris looked up because she heard Sonia lift the box of tissues from the side table and rise. With a hand on Iris's shoulder she said, "I'm going to make us a cup of tea. Okay? I'll be right back. A few minutes. I'll only be a few minutes." She placed the tissues on Iris's lap and closed the door behind her.

Breathe, Iris, just breathe. Slowly in, and slowly out. White in, gray out. Count to ten and breathe again. She couldn't do it. Her heart raced away on its own, beating hard. She gathered her hair in one hand and twisted it around with the other, making a rope that tightened with each twist until the nape of her neck hurt. She stood up and as she did the tissue box fell with a soft thump. Crossing her arms against her breasts she looked out at the gray wall outside the window. Where was that bird? She could still hear him. Her shoulders stiffened. She held her breath, then paced the room. When she came back around, it was then that she noticed the file.

How long does it take to make a cup of tea?

Iris quickly crossed to the table and picked up the folder that Sonia had left on her chair.

I'll be right back. A few minutes.

She stood with her back to the door and leaned against it, her shoes anchored on the floor. *I'll only be a few minutes.*

She opened the folder.

Inside, was the consent form to adopt, application order, and the notice of legal order from the Adoption Board. Nothing there she didn't already know. Stapled to the inside-front cover was a photocopy of the legal birth certificate for adoptive children naming Iris and Luke as Rose's parents. But there was also a copy of the original birth certificate, stapled underneath. She held her breath. Here it was. It named a Hilary Barrett as the mother. *Barrett!* Was there more? She flipped from the front of the file to the end. Paper-clipped to the back-inside cover of the folder, as if in afterthought, was a handwritten-addressed envelope. It said: *Adoption Board, Merrion Square, Dublin, Ireland.*

"Iris?"

Iris froze.

"Would you get the door, please?"

Iris quickly returned the folder. The paper clip fell to the ground and she brushed it away with her foot and went to get the door.

Sonia carried in a small tray with two mugs and settled the

tray on the side table. She looked at Iris, her eyes pausing on the chair a moment before picking up the folder and sitting down with it securely in her lap.

"I hope you've had a few minutes to recognize, Mrs. Bowen that the Adoption Board can do nothing more for you as the adoptive mother." She passed Iris a tea mug. "I am so sorry. It's just the way it is. And has been for many years. And until the laws change—"

"I understand." Iris paused a few moments and, still standing, took a single sip of the tea and then said, "Actually, I have to go. I have to catch the five-twenty train back to Limerick." She put her mug down. "I have a long way to go from here." She waited for Sonia to say something but Sonia only looked at her own mug. Then she, too, stood and the two women faced each other.

An instant of silent understanding passed. Nothing was explained nor questioned. But there was a moment—definitely, and a powerful connection—and for that fleeting moment Iris and Sonia were co-conspirators against the chaotic universe.

A moment that could possibly change a life forever.

"Thank you for your help," Iris said.

Sonia smiled weakly and weariness showed in the circles under her eyes, as if each day she prepared to face the world but it was wearing her out. She walked Iris down the wide Georgian hallway to the front door. A partial ellipse of light shone from the fanlight above the door onto the marble floor.

"Good-bye then, Iris," Sonia said, and she held Iris's hand very firmly. "Good luck . . . with everything."

Stepping across the street and onto the footpath, Iris reached out to hold on to the black railing enclosing the small park. She turned back to see the blue door of the Adoption Board close, the city street now a blur of noise and traffic passing. She took from her pocket the envelope she had torn from the folder. She had folded it small, but now gently opened and pressed it flat. She'd got what she'd come for. In the top, left-hand corner, inked in faded blue writing, was an address.

"Luke," Iris whispered. "Hilary . . . Hilary Barrett. 99 St. Botolph Street. Boston, Massachusetts."

Five

There is no difference between the fiddle and the violin—Rose had learned that by heart and said it in response to neighbors and friends in Clare who often asked why she played the violin instead of the fiddle. The fiddle was traditional, it was what a child was expected to learn in the west. "Sure it's who we are," Tommy Ryan had said one day hearing her play. But Rose was a girl who wanted to form her own identity. They're not really different, she would say, just played differently. When she played a jig she'd say she was playing the fiddle, but when she played a sonata or a concerto she was playing the violin. "Same instrument. Just played differently. Traditional and classical. I'm both."

When, as an eight-year-old, she'd showed an interest in learning an instrument Luke and Iris took her to a music school in Ennis, where she sat in on several classes, including fiddle. It was Andreas the violin teacher, an Austrian from Salzburg who'd moved to Ireland, who'd captured her imagination. A stocky man with a head of thick, gray hair. On her first lesson, he'd said, "Mein Roslein, the music's in you and you're in the music. Keep practicing and one day you'll find each other, and then you'll be famous. I know this." And with his help, year by year, she'd come though the exams and then won a gold medal for her performance of Beethoven's *Spring* sonata. She was accepted to the Royal Academy of Music in London in the summer of '08.

When she was sixteen Andreas had advised it was time for her to get a really good violin. He'd suggested an Irish violin maker called Conor Flynn who'd studied to be a luthier in Cremona, Italy. Andreas explained that Conor's mother was Italian and a musician herself and now played with the Irish Chamber Orchestra. Conor had learned to play the fiddle when he was young, Andreas said, but when he visited his grandparents' home in Verona at a young age he got it into his head that he wanted to make his own violin. Andreas laughs when he tells the story. "Imagine, mein Roslein, a five-year-old boy wanting to make a violin instead of an airplane or a tractor of some other wooden toy! And now he is one of the best young violin makers in Ireland."

Incense burned and two ginger cats were asleep in an open violin case on the window seat of Conor Flynn's workshop inside an old Irish farmhouse in North Clare on the day Rose and her parents walked in. It was early January. Wood shavings were scattered across the floor. Hanging on the walls were silver molds and templates, and on a blue nylon line hanging, like strange washing, were several unfinished violins. Against the wall was a long, thick table with several ceramic jars holding tools and a docking station with an iPod playing. Rose recognized the end of a Haydn concerto, but the next piece was a surprise. It was

"The Lonesome Touch" by Martin Hayes, the Irish fiddler from East Clare.

"It is all about the wood. Baltic spruce and Bosnian maple. The great Cremonese violin makers got their maple from the *Acer pseudoplatanus*," the blue-eyed luthier said. He was young, not even thirty. He was wearing a wooly cap with ear flaps, and from him came the scent of the sea and his sandy-colored hair was long and tied back. Rose watched wood dust drift from his fingers when he lifted his hand to point to the samples on the plastered wall. She looked to her mother, expecting a response, her mother knowing about plants and trees and such things, but Iris only nodded, eyes down, smiling faintly.

"The higher up the trees grow, the better; generally, the air is purer," Conor continued, a little nervous, Rose thought. "Wood is highly absorbent."

"Is it?" Rose said. She knew it was, but she'd felt Conor's eyes on her cheek and she needed to say something to break his stare. She turned to look around the studio and then out toward the sea. A dozen white heads of snowdrops bowed in their terra-cotta pots on the windowsill outside.

"Yeah, it is. Things penetrate the wood. Acid rain, things, you know. . . . Like when it dries out, toxins may remain"—Rose turned back to him—"in the wood, I mean. But it gives it . . . *character*." His eyes held hers. "You know?"

"Yes," she said.

For a moment it had seemed as if there was only Rose and Conor and the violins in the room until Luke smiled and said, "Character is important."

Iris straightened the stencils on the worktable.

"Used to be that natural materials used in violin making were unpolluted," Conor said. "They did stuff like cutting the trees down with the waning moon to make the best tonewood. So"—he waved his hand toward the display—"if you pick the cuts here, then I'll adjust them (and here he looked at Luke) to the *character* of whatever wood you choose." He bowed theatrically to Rose. She couldn't stop herself smiling. Something inside her stirred.

Iris, who'd watched the exchange unfurling between them, turned to Luke. "Maybe . . . we should just buy a really good *used* violin?" Her thoughts might have well been audible: waning moons, blue eyes, blond hair in a ponytail, *and* he makes violins?

"Up to you." The violin maker turned back to his worktable. The tune had finished on the player. "It makes a difference, of course, if the wood was grown in sunshine or in shadow."

Two months later the violin with a bright, rich sound was hand delivered by Conor on a radiant early March morning when Rose was studying. She wasn't expecting him. He hadn't let the Bowens know he was finished.

"I read about you in *The Banner County News*. Congratulations," he'd said when she'd opened the glass door and he breezed in. "Not many Irish get accepted at the RAM, I mean. That's really cool. RAM. Good for you." He was wearing the same yellow wooly cap with the ear flaps.

"I guess." Rose didn't know what to say because his arrival as well as his enthusiasm had caught her unawares. "I have to pass my Leaving Cert, though." She motioned to the French grammar book and practice tests open on the table.

"Sure, of course. But no bother. It's a couple months away, right?" He opened the violin case as if presenting an offering. "Will you play it, *ma chérie*?"

She shot him a look. Funny guy. "I don't know . . ." She didn't pick it up, and after a bit he put the open case down on the table beside her books.

He gazed at her one long moment, gauging the possibilities, working out the chances, and when at last it looked like he'd made up his mind, he blurted, "You're really beautiful."

Rose glanced away and fingered the open face of the violin, tracing the inside of the *f* holes ending in a swirl. Then she looked to him and said, "No, I'm not," and turned away.

Iris and Luke weren't home, they'd told Rose they had business in Limerick that afternoon. Rose didn't know if she wanted Conor Flynn to stay around. He was intense, or something. She wasn't sure what was happening. Her face reddened. He kept looking at her but she'd decided not to play for him. She walked toward the door.

"So, maybe you'd let me know how my violin stands up to the rigors of that academy, once you get there, I mean. Tell them there's an Irish fiddler by the name of Flynn you can recommend. That is, if you like the sound." He laughed at himself but continued speaking and followed Rose to the door and stood close beside her. "You'll be my first true professional customer. I slipped a few of my cards in with a gift for you—some rosin. It's a secret recipe a guy in Belgium makes." From him came the scent of the sea and wood dust. He said he hoped maybe she'd invite him around during the summer just so he might hear how the violin sounded, in case it needed any tweaking, but he'd been playing it for a month and was happy.

"All right, so, I'm off. Taking Gerty to Doughmore Beach." Rose cast her eyes downward.

"Gerty's my van," he said quickly.

"Oh." She smiled and laughed. "I thought you had—"

"A dog in the van? No, the cats wouldn't like that." He paused. "I'm a surfer." He put his hands in his pockets and waited in case Rose had changed her mind and wanted him to stay, but she only looked away out the window down across the garden.

They'd exchanged numbers and he'd wished her luck on her exams and in doing so placed his hand gently on her back. He moved closer so that his body was against hers. It was just a moment. And as quick as the flick of a downward bow he bent and kissed her.

"For good luck!" he said. Then he was out the door, through the gap in the hedge in her mother's garden.

Rose followed after a moment but it was a moment too late. She saw the back of an old red van heading toward the sea.

When he'd gone, she looked at his cards: *Conor Flynn, Master Violin Maker, Kinvara, Co. Galway.* She tucked them back into the small velvet box under the scroll. He'd explained her violin's sound would deepen, that it would travel through the layers of varnish like air through puff pastry. Rose would eventually think back on this as the thing that had opened the door and left an imprint on her heart. That he'd *thought* this and *said* it. It wasn't what she expected and she liked that. That night after dinner Rose played "O Mio Babbino Caro" on the new violin and her mother cried. (Her parents hadn't yet told her that Luke had been at the doctor's office that day.)

Until now the music had never let Rose down. Sometimes she'd had doubts and wondered if she was *chasing* the feeling instead of *flowing with it.* But at her best, at the very height of her rising skill, she could disappear into the sound like a surfer riding through the tunnel of a long wave. And for that she had lived.

Now, as Rose Bowen exits Camden Town tube station after the crushing master class and turns at Camden High Street, wandering along Parkway, that all seems a long time ago in another world. In that world she might have answered Conor Flynn's texts that first summer. Returned his kiss even. In that world her father would still be living and they would be laughing and he'd be telling her this very minute that the Kiwi dude was a "proper bollocks." And all would be okay. And he would say something philosophical, like even though the teaching is external the learning comes from inside, and not to doubt herself. But it's not that world, and it's not all right. Conor's texts had stopped and her father was not living.

Now she is just a girl moving through the night of the dark city, alone.

She passes the Jazz Cafe where a late-night crowd is queuing for Imelda May, the Irish rockabilly star. She keeps walking. It's getting darker. The tables on the sidewalk outside of Dublin Castle are crowded with young people drinking beer and smoking. The girls wear short summer skirts and string tops and briefly fill the air with their tangled perfume. The guys are skinny with hair that hides their faces.

A lightness on Rose's back where her violin should be makes her shoulders feel bare. It's as though she'd had wings, but hadn't realized it until now—now there's a vacancy. Her feet slap the pavement as she crosses Gloucester Road. In the falling coolness she walks through the iron gates of Primrose Hill Park where the lights along the path make white patches in the grass that look like snow. Rose climbs the hill. Wind through the fingered leaves of horse chestnut trees makes a noise like rain, and hanging in the sky just above the tree line to her left is a half moon. A runner jogs with a golden retriever. A couple pushes a baby stroller.

At the top of the hill, Rose sits down on a wooden bench and lowers her head to her knees, dark hair sliding along her legs touching the pavement, where it curls across the top of her shoes. A text beeps on her phone.

Rose, please ring me. Need to talk to you. ASAP. x Roger.

Red and purple lights of the BT Tower pulse in the distance. The light on the screen of her phone fades and leaves her face in darkness. As the late night folds around her she vows to sit still there above the city until she knows what to do. She ignores Roger's text. She wants to call Iris but she can't do it. She can't confess to her mother just yet the madness that has happened. She wouldn't be able to explain what she has just done or why she has done it until she can explain it to herself. It seemed that in the moment it was what she had to do. It was as though something prompted her to abandon the violin, as though she had no option but to bring the whole business of London and the academy and Roger to completion. Was she *really* any good? *Who* was she? She sat and stared down at the lights of the city.

Iris *would* understand, wouldn't she? Yes. But. But she'd be heartbroken for her. So how could Rose tell her?

If Rose could have asked God for a mother, she would have asked for Iris. Good old Iris. Strong, yet able to bend like a flower in the wind. She'd have asked for a proud mother, a brave one, an understanding one, a fierce one who could be pigheaded, impulsive, determined, yet delicate, too, who wanted the best for her daughter in everything and would move whatever she had to just to make that happen, a mother who always had just the right amount of humor.

Stars pixelate in the night sky and remind Rose of the day

before she left Ashwood for London at the end of August the previous year. She and her mother had lain out on beach chairs in the garden past midnight. They'd watched a meteor shower and counted twenty-four shooting stars. They'd held hands and agreed they'd come through an entire year and second summer without Luke. Somehow they had managed it. It was a miracle in a way and Rose had pressed her head against Iris's apple-scented hair.

There are times she wonders about her birth parents (she'd be lying if she said she hadn't thought about them, ever), but only in a matter-of-fact kind of way because Rose knows she's lucky to have been adopted. She knows how much she was wanted and that in a way, she was *chosen*. That has always made her feel special. Life as Rose knows it—has only *ever* known it—has been as the treasured child of Iris and Luke Bowen, the mother and father who raised her, nurtured her, encouraged her, took care of her—like that time with the chicken pox when all she wanted to do was scratch her face to pieces and her mother kept bathing her in calendula oil. Or, when she fell from her bike, broke her collarbone and her mother had to do everything for her. Everything. Or the time she failed French in her Junior Certificate exam and was gutted. Then, her mother's cups of tea and homemade scones were like some magic recipe to which only Iris knew the secret.

That's what she needs right now, as she sits on the park bench in the fettered dark—magic. But there is nothing and no one. She's on her own. A boisterous group arrives at the top of the hill and looks at the lights of the city. They don't speak English. They are laughing and pushing and hanging off each other. Rose doesn't understand them. But one of them has an iPod playing through headphones and something about the thin music escaping jolts her like a bolt of electricity.

Oh my God.

Oh my God, what have I done?

She jumps up, pushes past the group, and races down the hill and out through the gates. She tears down the High Street, past the pet shop, the greengrocers, the Primrose Hill Bookshop, past the now-closed pubs and chic restaurants and cafes, the street empty except for black plastic bags of rubbish and stacks of folded cardboard. Across the railway bridge she races down into Chalk Farm tube station. On the platform the tunnel wind blows her hair. The lights glare into her eyes and she feels disgusting, she feels like some insect wanting to run for cover. She walks quickly toward the red light so she can step into the first car as soon as the train comes and when it does, she pushes in through disembarking passengers when the doors open.

Next stop is Belsize. Did she get on the right line? Feck. Her anxiety is such that she gets out at Belsize to check. She jumps back in just as the doors are about to close. Hampstead, Golders Green. How long will it be to the end of the line? Brent Cross, Hendon, Colindale. Places she's never been, never even heard of, doesn't want to know. *Burnt Oak.* That's what she feels like, she thinks. Burnt Oak. *What have I done? What have I done?*

Dadda?

Finally, Edgware. The tube doors open and Rose is first out. She's frantic. Takes the stairs two at a time. Her heart is hammering.

I was stupid. I was stupid. I was stupid.

At the top step she looks quickly around like a frightened mother looking for a lost child. At the turnstiles other passengers

71

come and go. She is wild with alarm, yet with hope, too, that somehow the violin will be here.

She flings her Oyster Card onto the Reader. Her eyes sweep across the ticket windows. Will someone recognize the look on her face and know that she's not running from heartbreak but toward something? Will someone help her? Know this must be the girl looking for the violin that was brought in an hour earlier by some decent passenger? This girl with the flushed face and tossed hair must be her. It's crazy ridiculous but it flashes through her mind just the same— *It'll be there. It'll be there. It'll be there.*

But the ticket windows are shut.

No porter stands by any turnstile.

And there is no sign of a violin case as she peers in through the black windows of the office.

Exiting passengers flow past her. She keeps staring in. It's not there, but she doesn't stop looking, she doesn't stop hoping. Then, at last, like a slow breath exhaling, Rose slides down the cold tiled wall to the dirty floor. People pass but they do not look. She's just another drunken nightclubbing girl of London at one o'clock in the morning.

It is the second-hardest thing Rose Bowen has had to do, to get herself back to Camden, but somehow she does. It takes a long time. A long time to reconcile what she has done with what she had hoped this day would bring—achievement, recognition, a sense of belonging. Her so-called *sterile* Bach wasn't part of her plan or her tender hope to shine as a rising star for whom the academy might sit up and take notice, of whom her father would be proud. Rejection is all she feels. She can't escape it. Yet, somehow, she finally gathers herself, presses her Oyster Card again on the Reader, and makes her way down, down into the Northern Line.

She rides back in the spotlight of the nighttime Tube in a trance, not sitting but standing, swaying in a slow oscillation through the dark and light of Colindale, Brent Cross, Hampstead, Belsize, Chalk Farm, Camden . . . until she makes it back to her flat. There is a note from Isobel.

Hey Rosie, Hope the master class was brill! Hope you nailed it. Sorry I missed you. Aaron and I are off to Dublin. Back in a week. xxxoo Izzy

She sits on her small balcony with the bottle of champagne she'd brought the day before and drinks quickly. The bubbles spill down her chin. She has not eaten. Too late to ring her mother and confess all. Below, across the canal under a streetlight, a guy with a guitar sings reggae. The music swells every memory of the day into one tidal wave of emotion. She finally breaks. The guy with the guitar pauses his playing and looks for the sound of a woman crying. When he cannot locate it he plays Bob Marley's song "No Woman No Cry."

Rose will find out if it is the end of the world when she contacts the Underground's lost property office in the morning. But now, dizzy from drinking too fast, she steps back into her room, closes the curtains, and falls to her bed and sleeps.

In her early-morning dreams there are people in a crowd. They are waiting for someone. A man comes toward her but she can't make out whom it is. First it seems like it's the man she sometimes sees on her way to college. Then it's the violin maker. Then it's Roger. Then Bob Marley. There's guitar music and violins tuning. The man whom everybody is waiting for becomes solid. He approaches through a blue haze and when she recognizes who he is, she runs. She runs straight at him and flings her arms around him. The man hugs her tiny child frame. Her head turns in against his chest and she cries. "Dadda, come back to me. Come back to me. Please. *Please*."

Part II

Cosmos Bipinatus

"Sensation"

Six

Iris had never been across the Atlantic. When she arrived into Boston's Logan Airport at four on Thursday afternoon after an eight-hour flight from Shannon, she was travel weary, in a bit of a daze. So she followed the crowd through to the arrivals area where people in summer clothes looked like they knew where they were going. They seemed happy to be there. Happy to be on holiday. Happy to be home. Happy to have arrived safely. With a little trip of her heart, Iris believed that happiness belonged only to these people. Not to her. She slumped and let go of her suitcase. Gone was the confidence she'd felt walking away from the Adoption Board—a woman with a mission, doing nothing but charging forward until she would arrive in Boston and find Hilary Barrett. No distractions in between. She'd let no one know. Not Tess. Not the postman. Not the Breast Clinic. Not Rose. Especially not Rose. She expected to be back in four or five days. (She'd left enough food for Cicero in one of those plastic funnel

self-feeders but, she was suddenly remembering, had ne-
glected to reschedule her appointment with the Breast Clinic.)

In the center of the concourse the crowd she'd been following dispersed in a dozen directions. Iris stood by her suitcase and
looked around. She hadn't thought this through. Now what? Now
what the hell? What the bloody hell! There, under the bold bright
information kiosk, stood a young redhead. As Iris approached
the counter she saw the girl was wearing a green HI! I'M KERRY
nametag. She had the kind of face you see on old postcards of
Ireland, the ones with donkeys in Technicolor and freckled,
curly-haired children. Iris angled her suitcase against the kiosk.

The girl looked up from her work.

"Can you find me some place to stay?" Iris blurted. "I mean,
please, can you help me?" She was hot and gathered up her hair
to let the air-conditioned air cool the back of her neck. "I'm afraid
I haven't booked a place. It was last-minute."

"First time to Boston?"

"Yes."

"I'll be happy to help." Kerry smiled. Iris noticed her teeth
were straight and perfect and white. Her red hair was more au-
burn than Iris's. "In the city?"

"I'd like to stay near St. Botolph Street. Is that in the city?"
Iris didn't know what size city Boston was or, foolishly, she was
now realizing, how expensive. She'd already spent a fortune on
the last-minute flight.

"Sure thing. St. Botolph Street? Ummm." Kerry's eyes
squinted into the distance. After a moment she said, "Oh, right!
I know where that is. I pass it all the time." She said it with such
obvious satisfaction that it made Iris smile. "I can look for a hotel around Copley Square. The Copley Plaza maybe?" Kerry
leaned slightly forward and asked, "Single?"

"Single," Iris said quietly and made her best silly middle-aged-lady face. "I don't know what I was thinking, not booking accommodation. It really was a last-minute decision."

The girl smiled and looked down. Her fingers padded a keyboard behind the counter while she scanned the PC's screen. "Um . . . sorry. Copley's booked. It's the weekend." She paused. "Like, how nice a place do you want? There are lots of great places. But, some of them are—"

"A small hotel, I think." Iris placed her hands on the counter.

"No problem."

"Like a B-and-B, maybe? But near St. Botolph Street," Iris quickly added.

"A B-and-B? We don't really have B . . ." Kerry thought a moment, looked at her watch, then back to Iris. "Just a sec." She picked up the phone.

Iris's eyes rose from her hands to Kerry's young face. She wanted to say more. She wanted to confide in her the way one does sometimes with strangers. In fact, right then she wanted to confide to anybody who might listen. And for a few seconds she imagined walking right out into the middle of the concourse, walking into the flux of the arriving and departing, the helloing and good-byeing, and saying: "Hey. Listen. I need your help. I have to find my daughter's mother." But of course she didn't, and the flow of people continued, each face carrying its own story, like worlds within worlds.

She'd kept to herself the whole flight from Shannon, flicking through her gardening magazines, and back and forth between films she didn't really care to watch, eating and not eating, drinking a gin and tonic after takeoff and then two small bottles of pinot grigio somewhere over the mid-Atlantic when she realized she wasn't going to be able to nap. She'd been eight hours in a silent cocoon with the name "Hilary Barrett" and the words "architectural distortion" flying around in her head. Everything was up in the air, literally—her appointment at the Breast Clinic; her promise to Luke; and just what she was going to say to Hilary Barrett when she found her. It had all been colliding silently in seat 16D for eight hours. And now, now she was desperate to talk to someone. Just that. Talk. She turned from the counter to watch the crowds negotiating the concourse, a non-stop rush of families, friends, and other strangers moving purposefully across the polished floor, and then she looked through its wide windows beyond where cottonball clouds floated above the city on the horizon.

Kerry returned and scribbled something down on a little "Welcome to Boston" pad. Her short nails were painted purple. She produced a map from below the counter and as she leaned forward, she tossed her hair back over her shoulder. "Here. Here's a nice place," she said quietly, looking around her and ringing the location with a pen. "She has a vacancy. A Mrs. Hale."

"Thank you."

"But I have to tell you . . ." She lowered her voice even more. "She's not *registered*, exactly. Not like, officially. But I know her. She's a bit, um . . . she's *really* nice. I think you'll like her." She looked at Iris, quizzically, as if to see that she understood.

But Iris's eyes were scrambling over the map to see how close this was to St. Botolph Street.

"Okay. That sounds okay."

"Good." Kerry smiled. "See here? This is the T stop, just a few blocks away." She outlined with her pen. "You can walk from the T to here, and then, here."

"The T?" Iris flagged her hair against the back of her neck and wondered for a second if jet lag made you hotter.

"Public transport. It's called the T." She laughed. "You can take it straight there. I've done it many times. Or you can take a taxi. But it's Friday. Rush hour, you know."

"Is it far?"

"On the T? No. And it's a lot cheaper. Don't worry. I know Mrs. Hale. She's my mother's friend. They play tennis together over near Berklee."

"What's Berklee?"

"Berklee College. It's near the South End. Near St. Botolph Street. Where you're going. Look. You take the Silver Line" —Kerry indicated with a wave of her arm across the concourse in the direction of the T—"to Newton Street Station. Then walk here. Where St. Botolph Street is." She circled it, too. "Very close." She handed over the map but Iris didn't want to move away from the information booth.

"Thank you. Kerry."

As if sensing the lady in front of her wanted something more, Kerry said, "Are you Irish?"

"Yes." Iris's face brightened.

"Me, too! My grandmother's from County Kerry." She pointed to the name tag. "That's how I got my name." Her Boston accent was now, Iris noted, heavily pronounced with its missing Rs. "One day I hope to get *over there.*"

This brief recognition was just what Iris needed, one tiny connection to inch her along. She nodded. "I hope you do. And thank you so much for your help." She smiled as genuinely as she could and grabbed the handle of her bag and headed toward the Silver Line, leaving the girl at the counter dreaming, probably, about the day she would return to the birthplace of her grandmother in the Kingdom of Kerry. Midway across the concourse, Iris turned to wave back but the crowd was already whirring between them.

Mrs. Hale's was only a few blocks from the station stop but with each step—pulling a resistant brown suitcase whose wheels seemed to have swollen in the heat—Iris withered. She stopped on a corner and looked up. Tremont and West Newton. My God, it was hot. Heat rose from the sidewalk and channeled through her feet up to the top of her head.

It was commuter time. People passed around her. Well-dressed women in running shoes and men with suit jackets off, their ties loose around their necks. She fanned herself with the map and walked toward the shade under what looked like maple trees. She rested a few moments. Through the canopy of green she looked up at the blue sky. In the middle of a puzzle, the pieces will fit somewhere. Trust. White in, gray out. Water up, fire down. She steadied, went another block, and arrived at the steps of a red-brick building with a fancy wooden sign: HALE 116.

She rang the bell, and after a few moments a middle-aged woman with a shock of cropped golden-white hair and the reddest-painted lips opened the door. She was a good few years older than Iris.

"Oh, hello!" the woman beamed. "Come in. Come in. Hot out there, huh? Yes. The heat is just gruesome today. We're having a heat wave. Right?" It was like she was giddy with it. Iris stepped in. Air like a cool breeze rushed toward her.

"Mrs. Bowen, yes? Have I got it right?"

"Yes, that's right."

"Grace Hale." She offered her hand. "Not up for this heat, are we? Not even we Bostonians are. And golly, look what you're wearing. You must be ready for a tall glass of lemonade. Or something."

Iris took Grace's hand, which was cold, and said, "That would be lovely. Thank you."

"Here, let me take that," the woman said, beginning to reach for Iris's bag, then shouting, "Billy?" She seemed as if she was either just coming in or just going out. Pink seahorses rode in the white of her knee-length shorts and the pink socks she wore peeked above her white tennis shoes. Mrs. Hale called down the cool hallway, "Billy? *Billy!?*" and turned back to Iris, who was still holding her bag. "Oh, leave your bag. Billy, my helper, will bring it up. Eventually." She led farther along the hallway, past framed prints of landscapes and city scenes that hung on green-painted walls.

Mrs. Hale explained that she'd had a phone call from Kerry and was happy to let out the room. "It's a little arrangement Kerry and I have." Iris followed her up two flights of old wooden stairs and into a small room with wallpaper patterned with bird boxes. "Kerry only sends me special people." The bed was tidily made up with linen pillowcases and a dresser held a small pile of books and brochures. "I'm not exactly registered with the tourist board, you know." Everything in the room was wooden except for a soft leather armchair. "Maybe next year I'll apply for my license."

"I'm very grateful," Iris said, feeling she should say something, but now wondering if she should have declined Kerry's booking and found a Best Western or something.

At the window Grace Hale moved the voile curtain aside and said, "It's not much to look at, but you'll be glad because this corner is nice and quiet in the morning."

"I'm not here for the view."

Grace Hale didn't follow up; she just smiled. "You'll find everything you want." Grace's round eyes opened wider and she scanned the room, nodding to herself as if ticking off a mental checklist: fresh towels, a bar of soap, bottled water, and a drinking glass. It was all there. "And now, what about a bite to eat? You must be starved. Right? I mean, what time is it? I can bring you up a light supper and something to drink."

"Really? If it isn't too much trouble," Iris said, thinking how she'd love a glass of that lemonade she'd been offered at the door. "Thank you."

"Gosh. Not at all. I couldn't send you out into this heat." Grace Hale leaned slightly out the door. "Billy?" she called down the stairs, then turned back to Iris. "Lemonade? Or . . . something stronger?"

Iris paused. She was unable to match this woman's energy and before she could reply, Grace laughed. "I'm famous for my chicken sandwiches. Wouldn't that be nice? Yes? Toasted?" She spoke quickly, as if used to one-sided dialogues. "I'll get that and I'll leave you now, unless there's something else—"

Of course there was something else. "No. That would be wonderful. Thank you, Mrs. Hale."

Grace stood a moment longer. "It *used* to be Mrs. Hale," she said "but my husband, Bob, died a while ago." There was a tiny puckering around the corners of her eyes then, a little resigned upturn on her lips, as if it was a story she was finally able to tell without crying. "Please, call me Grace."

A young man with black hair and a black T-shirt and khakis finally appeared with Iris's suitcase. "Hi, I'm Billy. Welcome to

Boston. If you need anything I'm usually downstairs. I'm helping Grace out—" He was about to say more when they both heard Grace calling "Billy!" from below, and he shrugged and said "That's me," and headed off down to her at a saunter. "Coming, Mrs. Hale."

Iris closed the wooden door, stood a few moments feeling at a loss, then unpacked. And as if she needed evidence that she had made her decision to come too rashly, here it was: no nightgown and too many cardigans. Three. "Well done, Iris. If they get a sudden freeze, you'll be fine." She pulled aside the curtain and looked down into an alleyway, listening to the sounds, inside and out, of the early evening. A soft whir of traffic hummed. Someone walked by her door outside. The floors creaked. A vent above the door to the bathroom made a hissing noise, but Iris didn't mind. She was glad of the cool air. She checked the bathroom and was grateful to see a tub. A white cotton bathrobe hung on a hanger on the back door. It was belted at the empty waist. She could sleep in that.

At the airport there was no phone service. Here, too, her old phone said "no service," but yet her battery was half-full. She walked around the room with it held out as if to catch signals. Then suddenly, like a pulsing in her heart, she thought of Rose in London. Was it wrong she hadn't told her? Of course it was. But I'll be back in a couple of days. But I still should have told her something. And ruin her practicing for her master class? No. No. This was right. This is what a mother does. Get it done. And get back. Carry on. Make no fuss. You don't want to ruin everything. Rose would be in her own world practicing like mad anyway. She had an important master class next week. She wouldn't be in touch. She was like that. She needed her own space and she'd be coming home soon for a short holiday anyway. Best to say nothing. Just get it done. I'll buy a phone card, she thought, and phone Tess *and* the clinic.

There was a knock at the door and Iris opened it to see Grace—now in a cream muumuu with a thick leather belt girdling her waist. On her wrist was a square, gold bangle. "Toasted chicken sandwich with lettuce. Potato chips. A pot of tea. And a half bottle of red. How's that? Nice, right?" She laid the tray down on the desk.

"Very nice." There was no sign of lemonade.

"And just what the doctor ordered," Grace said, stepping backward to the door and lingering there. She straightened her belt and looked at Iris a moment. Iris wasn't sure if she was expected to taste the famous chicken sandwich right then and there. Grace didn't stir.

"Will you join me in a glass?" Iris said at last. She didn't really know why she'd said it; she was tired and hungry and needed to gather herself for the morning's mission of tracking down Hilary. But then it seemed inviting Grace in was the right thing to do, and Iris liked to do things that were right. Because here was a woman like herself, although a decade older. Widows in arms. A sort of ally, Iris thought.

"Well, yes, that might be fun!" Grace's eyes broadened. "Yes! I'll be right back," she said and scooted down the stairs. Moments later, with a second glass and a full bottle in her hands, Grace reappeared. "Here we go." She unscrewed the top and poured the glasses. "You save this one for later." She placed the unopened half bottle on the bureau, then pulled the chair around from the desk and settled, somewhat ungracefully, down onto it. She sat only a moment. "Grace Hale, where are your manners?" She popped up. "You sit here. You have your supper at the desk . . . and . . ." She hesitated. "I'll sit there." She indicated the leather armchair and thumped down again, dislodging a cushion embroidered with a tennis ball and racket.

Iris angled the chair at the desk and sat facing Grace. She began to eat the sandwich, but thinking now—what unusual accommodation Kerry the redhead from the information kiosk had booked her.

"This was Bob's chair." Grace said quietly, and she picked up the cushion that had fallen, hugged it for a moment, then tucked it back behind her. "Five years and I'm still getting used to his not being here." She looked at Iris. "Do you know what I mean?" But before Iris could answer that yes, she did know, she did understand, that her Luke was gone, too, Grace went on. "Bob was in investments. What I don't know about derivatives and hedge funds, and options and futures!" She laughed and patted her knee with her free hand in a manly way as if Bob's gestures came with inhabiting his chair. In between quick swallows of wine she told Iris how Bob would come home in the evenings and spill out all the office politics and whatnot and how she listened to him like it was the most important thing in the world. How on weekends they played tennis together in the park and, having no children themselves, they had traveled to see their nieces and nephews. Before he died they'd taken a cruise to Alaska and seen the bear and the salmon.

"Bob *was* my world," she said, and turned toward the open door, and Iris got the feeling Grace expected Bob would somehow appear. When Iris had finished her sandwich and emptied her glass, Grace sprung up and refilled it.

"I'll take this away," she said and removed the tray to the hallway. "The tea's cold, I'm afraid. Would you like another?"

"No. That's fine. Wine's good." Iris felt a slight lift, as if she were delicately floating.

"I'm afraid I've drunk more than my share," Grace said, sitting down. "Ever since Bob died I've had trouble sleeping, although I don't know why. He was such a snorer! Now I find a few small glasses help me sleep." She paused, sinking further into Bob's chair. "Sometimes he slept in this room, when he had to get up early. So as not to wake me."

The memory of it took her away into a quietness that Iris welcomed. She calculated what time it must be in Ireland. After midnight. She looked over the travel brochures on the desk and fingered Kerry's map of the South End. She glanced at Grace, who seemed like she might fall asleep at any moment. Then Billy appeared, and seeing that Grace looked about to doze, knocked sharply on the open door.

"You're wanted downstairs, Mrs. Hale." He looked at Iris with a knowing smile.

"What? What?" Grace stirred.

"Downstairs. Hector."

"Right," she said, rising quickly. "I'll be there in a minute." She straightened up, looked in the mirror, then turned to Iris and said, "Well, that was perfectly lovely." At the door she paused. "How lovely to meet you."

The sun through the thin curtains woke Iris at nine. It was later than she'd intended, but she'd slept poorly in the early part of the morning and dozed off and on all night. Her eyes opened on the map of the South End that lay on the desk beside the bed. St. Botolph Street was marked in blue ink. She was dying for a cup of tea. She looked around the room again. Not like Ireland, she thought. No kettle in sight. She might ask Billy for one. She showered quickly and dressed in the only "nice" outfit she'd packed, a periwinkle blue linen sleeveless that Tess had bought with her one day.

"Get something Rose would be surprised to see you in," Tess had said. "Instead of those ratty blue jeans and Luke's old shirt." They'd chosen the linen dress because it was the kind of thing she could dress up or down, with heels or sandals. She chose the black sandals. She hadn't worn a dress in so long, she felt uncomfortable in it. She'd folded it carefully between tissue paper but that hadn't prevented it wrinkling. Oh, hell. She tugged at it as best she could. Looking at herself in the mirror now as she was ready to go downstairs, she felt acutely like an imposter. (What does one wear when meeting the woman who birthed your child?) She sat down on the edge of the bed and took off the sandals and put on the heels. She wanted to look *smart* meeting Hilary Barrett. She wanted to look like she'd measured up to the mother Hilary had probably hoped for when she gave her baby over to the adoption agency all those years ago. She tried to think about what she was wearing that day, but she couldn't remember.

Would Hilary remember her?

In the breakfast room another guest was already sitting, a tanned man in a Hawaiian-like shirt, who sat in the corner by himself. He looked to be in his mid-forties. Iris sat down near the window at the only other table for two. She'd prepared a friendly smile to offer as she passed, but he didn't look up. His straight back was leaned forward, his head fixed over the table. His unfinished plate had been pushed aside. He was writing something. He mustn't have heard her, she thought. Then a sound, like a low humming, haphazard in rhythm, reached her and she looked over. It was coming from him. A low music somewhere inside him was humming and he was moving his head to its rhythm.

"Good morning, Mrs. Bowen." Billy had startled her and she looked up. He'd come in without her noticing. "Mrs. Hale says she hopes you slept well."

"You can tell her, thank you, yes," she said in a quiet voice. She kept her eyes on the man in the blue and green and white shirt.

The humming continued.

"Coffee. Or . . . would you like tea?" Billy asked, taking no notice of the guest in the corner. "Mrs. Hale says you might prefer tea."

"Tea would be lovely. Yes," she almost whispered.

"Coming right up." He turned. "Morning, Hector," Billy breezed past him, but the man made no acknowledgment except a slight nod of his head.

Letting the fall of her hair curtain her face, Iris glanced at the humming man, who was now making small circles in the air with his long-fingered hands, like butterfly wings fluttering. His lips were moving *bap bap bap bap*. He looked up and stared at her blankly, then returned his attention to his writing.

"Where are you off to today?" Billy was back with the tea and toast.

"I haven't quite decided," she replied quickly.

"If I may suggest?"

"Yes?"

"If you haven't seen the Mapparium, then you should go. Just around the corner, across Huntington."

"Mapparium?" She pretended to be interested.

"Yeah, it's awesome. It's like . . . it's hard to explain actually. It's a giant walk-through globe with a map of the world painted on glass. Inside out, like. Like you're in the middle of the earth looking out. Really cool. The acoustics are unreal, and—"

From butterfly hands came a groan. "Hey, Billy, pipe down, can you? I need to finish this." The man hadn't looked up.

"Yeah, sure, Hector. Sorry, man." Billy moved so he was masking the tall man from Iris's view. He raised his eyebrows and shrugged and lowered his voice a notch. "Anyway. It's three stories high and there's over six hundred glass panels held together and they're individually lit from behind. And there's a glass bridge, midway though the earth, that takes you across from one side to the other and—"

"It's the world as it was in 1934," said Hector. He stood up then and strode from the room in a kind of whoosh, but not before first looking directly at Iris, then back to Billy. "And don't forget to say it's a *whispering* gallery." *Whoosh.* He was out the front room. *Bang.* He was passing in the street below the window, striding away, his fair hair like wings beating behind his ears.

"Was it something we said?" Iris said, trying to make light of what was feeling to her like an awkward situation.

"Don't worry about it. Sometimes he's like that, Professor Sherr. He's a real good friend of Mrs. Hale's. He's Californian. He stays here a few times a year. He *can* be really nice, when he's not composing."

"A musician?"

"Yeah. He's playing tonight at the park." Billy pointed through the room and out the window. "Jazz."

Iris felt her face blush for no reason at all. Billy kept chatting and he told her he was helping Grace out while she took in a few guests over the summer. He told her he was a sophomore at Boston University, hoping to major in computers. "I'm a bit of a computer geek," he said.

"So, you're about my daughter's age, then?"

"Twenty in September. Twenty-ninth."

"My daughter's going to be nineteen at the end of the month."

Iris didn't wait for Billy to return with the brochure on the Mapparium that he'd proposed to get. Instead she went up to her room to change her shoes again and brush her hair. She looked at herself one long moment. *Will she remember me?* A few minutes later, map in hand, she left the guesthouse and walked in the direction of St. Botolph Street. The day was already hot. Iris passed alongside a long expanse of iron railings that enclosed a park. Children's voices rang in the near distance. Redbrick townhouses, like Mrs. Hale's, with double wooden doors and bowed windows with lead glass lined the other side of the street.

Would Rose have come from a house like this?

Would she have played in this park?

Would she have loved growing up here?

Anxiety, which had been briefly diverted by the Hawaiian-shirted man, returned. Her breath quickened and her chest hurt. *What* was she was going to say to Hilary Barrett when she found her? She'd been operating on gut instinct and her usual impulsiveness, but had she really thought it through? No. Of course not. Of course you didn't, Iris. For a moment she wished she could beam herself home and wake up, relieved, as if from a bad dream. But there was too much at stake; she'd come too far to turn back now. At the end of the park, an almost paralytic terror gripped her.

I am keeping my promise, Luke.

At the intersection of West Newton and St. Botolph, a three-story building spanned the corner, curving with it. It was unlike the other buildings on the street. This one was a bit more elegant, with a kind of turret at its corner capped with lead. Iris walked across the street, closer to it and looked up at its doors, which stood at the top of a set of brick steps.

99 St. Botolph Street.

These numbers were etched in a glass panel above its black frame. If this is the place, nothing about it said it could be the home of Rose's birth mother. It might have—once upon a time—housed apartments, maybe, but what Iris now saw as she stood fixed to the sidewalk was not someone's "home."

Iris climbed the steps to the door and knocked.

Nothing.

She knocked again.

Nothing again. No one came to answer the door.

She turned around and half slumped her back against the door. A surge of heat rushed to her chest and face. She tugged on the neckline of her dress and felt perspiration gathering in the folds of her skin. How could 99 St. Botolph Street be the home of Hilary Barrett?

It was a restaurant.

After a few moments she went down the steps and crossed the street. She walked dazed, an ache in her heart, a kind of numbness buffering the pain of her thoughts. She turned abruptly and came back. There was a fruit and vegetable stand outside a small shop called Megaira's Market. Botolph's was across the way. She stepped into the market and, feeling conspicuous, took up a *Boston Globe* from the stack of newspapers just inside the front door. She looked back toward the restaurant, peering through stacked shelves of cans of tomatoes and lentils and jars of stuffed cabbage leaves and boxes of rice. A stoic-looking lady with small dark eyes and gray hair, standing inside behind the counter, snapped at her.

"You want that paper?"

"Sorry?"

"*Globe*'s two dollars. You want it?"

Iris crossed to the counter and stood for a moment in the whir of a fan.

"They're not open," the woman said, opening the till.

Iris looked at her questioningly.

"Botolph's, not open until lunchtime."

Iris smiled weakly. "Oh."

"Where you from?"

"Ireland. I'm Irish."

"Ireland? Never been. I always wanted to visit places where *foreign* languages were spoken."

Iris didn't know what to say to that, although she could have said, *The world feels like it's speaking a foreign language today and I don't understand.*

From her post at the checkout the woman eyed Iris but as Iris met her gaze directly, something in the old woman lightened.

"You looking maybe for a place to eat?"

"No, thanks." Iris put her things down and opened her purse.

"Looking for a job? Maybe you got an interview or something. You meeting someone?"

"No."

"None of my business, then," the woman said, this time sounding cross.

Iris was about to pay when she spotted some postcards of an urban garden. "I'll take these, too, please."

"Titus Sparrow Park."

"How much are they?"

"Six for five."

"Unusual name," Iris said.

"It's Greek," the woman said and shuffled along behind the counter and made a noise that sounded like spitting.

"No, sorry. I meant . . . I meant Titus Sparrow."

A noise behind Iris got her attention. And then a voice. "Don't pay any attention to Mrs. Kostas . . . often cranky midweek." An elderly man in a red baseball cap had come just inside the door, half inside, half out. "Isn't that right, Megaira?"

"Ah, *áfisé her ísihi!*" She took a ten-dollar bill from Iris and placed the postcards on top of the newspaper.

"You got that right, though, ma'am." The man smiled. "It's an unusual name, but a nice name." He glanced at Megaira. "And TSP's got a nice long history, too. Titus wasn't a bird, a sparrow, you know. He was a great man. And once upon a time, before the park was named after him—in honor of his teaching tennis to poor kids—Salvation Army had a home for unwed mothers and—"

"Hey, Amos, old man . . . *you* want something?" Megaira interrupted.

"Just the *Globe* today, Megaira. Read about my Sox beating Baltimore."

"Two dollars, then. And go away." Despite herself, Megaira Kostas had softened in response to the Red Sox fan, and her downturned mouth evened out. Iris was reminded of home, of standing in the post office listening to Tommy Ryan when he'd be collecting the post from Josephine and she'd be giving out to him because he was five minutes late. And Tommy would laugh and say something that made Josephine bark even louder. The world is small, Iris thought. And, maybe, not always, so foreign.

Amos smiled and did a neat pirouette. "As I was just saying," he said, lowering his cap and looking sideways from beneath it at Megaira, "we've got community gardens and of course tennis courts and—"

"And as I was just saying, Amos, you want something? *Else?*"

"No. You know, I guess I don't." He winked at Iris. As he began to saunter away he turned, "And if you're interested, it being a summer Friday, there'll be jazz tonight in Titus's park."

"Amos! Scat!"

Amos tilted his head and was gone. From outside, Iris heard him sing, *"Nothing but bluebirds . . . be dee and doo da bah . . ."*

"Someday that man might buy more than the *Globe*," Megaira said.

Movement from the dark windows across the street caught Iris's attention. She hurried out.

"Hey, lady? Your *Globe!*" Iris heard the woman yell after her, but she didn't turn back.

She crossed the street, climbed the steps, and this time she absolutely hammered the door knocker. The door was opened sharply by a man of about sixty, nearly bald, in a white shirt. His trousers, shoes, and belt were black. "We're closed, lady," he said point-blank and more than a little annoyed. But Iris was fired up now. Something about the baseball fan had sparked her courage. She walked past the bald man into the restaurant and didn't look back until she was well inside.

"When do you open, then?"

"Didn't you read the sign? We're open for lunch on Saturdays and for Sunday brunch," he said. "Today is? Friday. You can come back for dinner. Open at six." He turned his eyes to the door.

She'd missed the sign. Iris reached for the top of the nearest chair. Suddenly she thought she was going to faint. Her courage hadn't lasted but a minute. She tried to steady herself but her eyes were dizzy, taking in the tables covered in white linen, each with a tall vase of single flowers, cosmos maybe or daisies. Suddenly she couldn't remember what they were called even though she knew well their name. The tables were swimming and Iris's legs were feeling limp. "I think I . . . could I sit down?"

The man moved toward her. "Hey. Hey! Okay, Look, here," he said. He pulled a chair away from the table and Iris slid into it. When Iris was seated he rushed through a swinging door. A pulse thumped along the side of her neck. Her head felt light. A mixture of humiliation and panic seized her. If Hilary Barrett *was* here, was Iris going to collapse at her feet?

The man reappeared with a glass of water. "Now. Here, drink this. Slowly."

Iris sipped. "I'm sorry, I'll be all right in a minute." She steadied her hands on the table. He looked down at her. "No, really. I'll be fine."

"Okay. Take your time." He stepped away, straightened a few tables, turning his head now and again to look at her. His shoulders were hunched as if too used to bending, like a gardener, Iris thought. With the sleeves of his shirt rolled up just past his wrists, he lifted a napkin from a willow basket and folded it into a fan.

Iris breathed in slowly and imagined white light from the tablecloths filling her chest. She breathed out and imagined it turning gray and smoky and dissolving into the dark walls of the restaurant. Somewhat composed, she said, "The lady in the little shop across the way said you opened for lunch."

"Megaira? She doesn't know anything. We open for lunch, like I said, like the sign says, but not on weekdays. If you're looking for a nice place there's one over—"

"No, I'm not actually."

The waiter crossed to a tall cabinet and pulled some napkins from a drawer.

"I'm looking for someone."

He didn't respond. He kept his head down and brought some

of the fanned napkins to the table beside her. She wasn't sure he'd heard her.

"I don't want lunch. I'm not hungry."

He stopped folding and moved nearer.

"I'm actually looking for someone."

"Aren't we all, lady?" A kind of impatience was gathering and she felt ready to burst.

"I'm looking for Hilary Barrett," she blurted.

Having said it—the name out loud—was like some deep secret was finally revealed. But with the revelation something had to happen, either the world would stop spinning and one of its doors would spring open and maybe she wouldn't have to look any further and she could keep her promise and everything would be just the way Luke wanted it. Or . . .

"Hilary Barrett," she said again.

The man thought for a moment. (Or so Iris thought.) He looked at her with narrowed eyes, then over her right shoulder, as if he was remembering something or was he looking where Hilary was about to enter. Iris couldn't breathe.

"I knew a Hil—"

She gasped.

He came and placed his hand on the table. When he'd leaned in, Iris saw the hearing aid behind his left ear. "You sure you're all right."

"Yes. I'm fine. I'm fine." Instinctively she placed her hand on her breast. "You said you know a Hil—"

He straightened up and took one step back. "Well . . . I . . . what do you want her for?"

"It's . . . personal." Iris stood up. Face-to-face then with the person who might be one degree of separation from her daughter's birth mother, she suddenly could think of nothing more to say. Her mind went blank. So she extended her hand as if presenting herself. "I'm Iris. Iris Bowen. From Ireland."

It took a moment for the man to smile. But he did. Wrinkles creased in his tanned face. "Thornton Pletz. Polish. Shortened on the boat from 'Plezinski,' a generation back." He took her hand. "You're a long way from home."

She looked out the window just as a bird swooped from a rooftop. "I am." Iris paused a moment. "About Hil . . ." She half stumbled on the name. "Hilary . . . where do you think I might find her?"

"Ah. You see . . ." Thornton Pletz said. "I don't, is the answer."

"Is . . . is she the owner?"

"Owner? Of Botolph's? No, ma'am. She's not. I've been here since the restaurant opened. Let me think. Fifteen or so years ago." His brows lowered.

"But she used to live here . . . at 99 St. Botolph Street!" Iris reached into her purse for the envelope. She showed it to him. "This is her handwriting. See . . . ? See the return address?"

Thornton fingered the worn envelope carefully, as if it were a thin piece of cracked porcelain that had been glued back together. His brows lifted. "Barrett? It says . . ."

"Barrett, yes, Hilary Barrett, that's right."

"Sorry. Barnett, Barnett. I thought you said *Barnett*." He pointed to his ears. "Sorry, ma'am, I'm a little hard of hearing. I once knew a Hilda Barnett. I thought it odd you asking me that. About Hill. She's in Pittsburgh now."

Iris stared blankly back at him.

Mr. Pletz from Poland checked his watch, adjusted his hearing aid, which was suddenly buzzing, and waited for Iris to speak, his whole face holding an expectant pose.

"The flowers . . . they're cosmos," Iris said finally.

"Huh?"

"I remember now. The name of those flowers."

"Right," Thornton said and looked at them, too. "Cosmos. What do you know?"

Iris tidied her chair into the table and when Thornton walked toward the doors she followed. He held the door open. She had that vacant feeling in her legs, again. They felt hollow and yet she was trembling.

At the top of the steps, Iris hesitated. It was hot and cloudless outside. She sensed Thornton Pletz's eyes upon her. "You know," he said, touching her arm as he held the door, "there's a nice place to sit not far from here, across Huntington." He pointed through the building. She imagined he had more to say to her but for some reason hadn't. So she looked at his eyes to check. They were gray. But no, he wasn't saying anything more. She went down the steps to the sidewalk and didn't look back. The door closed behind her.

Around the corner, at Huntington, a woman about her age with three small girls in dresses was stopped at the traffic light beside her. The girls each had a balloon tied on their wrists, and when the light turned Iris watched the balloons bob up and down as they crossed the busy street. She stood still. She let the light go red and waited until it was green again before crossing to the other side.

She turned left and walked in the direction of a great, domed, churchlike building that rose at the far end of a plaza. Bordered on one side was a complex of sand-colored buildings, and a long avenue of linden trees lined the other. Groups of people crossed the plaza. Some tourists. Some shoppers. Some stood watching a group of children chasing each other beneath jets from a circular water fountain that shot up from a flat surface of concrete. Beyond the fountain, running nearly the full length of the plaza, was a shallow infinity pool.

Iris could go no farther. She sat on the curved, hard edge of the pool. An elderly woman in a blue suit and white shoes walked by, holding something that Iris thought looked like a Bible.

Iris was still holding the envelope. She folded it and put it back into her handbag. (She'd seen that handwriting before. A few months after the official order to adopt had been made, a letter from Rose's birth mother had come from the Adoption Board. Iris knew what it said by heart: *Always remember you are doubly loved. By me, forever, and by your parents.*)

Iris sat on the curved, hard edge of the infinity pool and dipped in her hands. Then she saw the sign, NO WADING. Reading it made her want to do just that, to lift her dress knee-high and walk the full length of the pool and out the other side. As she stared into the water the glint of copper pennies on the tarred bottom caught her eye. She took off her heels and a moment later stepped into the pool. She toed the pennies with her foot and, for one long moment, stood in the cold, shallow water holding her dress just above her knees. She wished she were standing far away from there, at the edge of the sea at Doughmore with Rose. Standing with their feet in the freezing sea and giggling as they watched Luke dive into the waves and reappear, howling from the cold. She wished the world wasn't so hard. She wished she didn't have a sense of failing Luke and failing Rose. She wished she didn't have the dread of the callback at the Breast Clinic, that she didn't have this question mark stamped on her chest, nor the feeling that everything resisted her. She drew a line with her foot under the water, moving the pennies, and wishing that this time things would work out.

Out of the corner of her eye, a man in a uniform at the other end of the plaza was motioning to her, but Iris didn't move. He started toward her then with a purposeful stride and just as she was stepping out she heard an accent familiar to her.

"Mother of God, I hope it's cool in there, Francis. I'm roasting!"

A pink-faced foursome, sweltering mother and father with two boys in green-and-white soccer jerseys, was passing. Iris stepped out of the water and into her shoes and followed them, tagging along, her legs itching as the water evaporated. The family was heading toward the front of what Iris soon understood was the granite dome of the mother church of Christian Scientists, and the complex, which she later learned housed not only the church but a library and conference rooms. The world headquarters. And over there was the Mapparium, a sign said. Iris followed behind the family like she was one of them.

She needed a still moment in her spinning-out-of-control world. Entering the magnificent building, into which the whole of her village back in the west of Ireland could fit, there was silence. Cool and deep.

The door to the Mapparium was modest, and yet what it opened into was anything but, as if she, along with the Irish family, had landed somewhere over the rainbow, arriving into the middle of a stained-glass world, a giant, three-dimensional Technicolor ball of the globe. The world had swallowed her whole.

Billy from Grace Hale's was right. It *was* awesome: There was no other word for it. A floating bridge of glass swam across eye level with the equator. France was green. Spain was orange. Alaska was yellow. Africa was huge across its northern half and taper-

ing down to the Cape of Good Hope. And surrounding everything was the blue-blue air-water of the Earth.

"Hey, Colin, look!" whispered the smaller boy of the family,
"the North Po—" He stopped suddenly, startled by the sound of
his own voice booming across the world to the other end of the
bridge, where his parents were observing the bluey glass of the
Atlantic Ocean.

"Yeah! Brilliant! Can ye hear *me*?" The taller boy's voice
boomed, too.

"Shh . . . Robert!" the father said. His whisper traveled
around behind and flipped back at him, loud and clear. The
mother's laughter broke, burst like glass bubbles.

As Iris stood looking up at Ireland, blood-red and tiny against
the sea, she invited their laughter into her heart. The man named
Hector said it was a whispering gallery. She smiled at them as
tears wet her cheeks. When she reached into her bag to grab a
tissue, the thing that often happened to Iris happened then. All
sorts of paraphernalia—boarding pass, lipstick, her Irish passport, the T receipt, the scribbled note from Hi-I'm-Kerry-
Welcome-to-Boston's pad, Hilary's envelope, and her map—spilled
out. She quickly bent to retrieve the contents that had made a
map of their own on the floor of the glass bridge.

"Here, love. Let me help."

In the middle of the world, it was the pink mother speaking
to her. She'd bent, too, and patted Iris's arm, handing back the
map.

"Thank you."

The bizarre synchronicity of two Irishwomen in the heart of
this crystal-like world briefly comforted Iris. The pink mother
smiled. She picked up the Welcome-to-Boston note, but as she
did she knocked the envelope with Hilary's address off the edge

of the bridge. Iris let out a small cry, an aching sigh reeling from her throat. It echoed around them as the envelope, floating and winging its way, like a pale yellow butterfly—passing San Francisco and Mexico and the Bernardo O'Higgins Region of central Chile—finally landed in the glass ocean somewhere near the bottom of the world.

Seven

Hector Sherr had first seen Iris Bowen when she came in for breakfast that morning, in the second week of June and the start of a heat wave. Unusual, so early in the summer. He was deep into his composition and didn't acknowledge her, but later he would remember a scent of apples in the air. Even though he was engrossed in his work, he sensed something about her. That something was troubling her. It was in the way her dove gray eyes darted about the room. Like a wary bird, he thought. He saw her from the corner of his eye. She didn't know he was looking at her. And, even though he liked to think he was the kind of person who could walk up to a total stranger and say, "Hey, can I help?" this wasn't that day.

Anyway, Billy was doing the talking, chatting away like some overenthusiastic tourist-academy graduate about the Mapparium over on Mass Ave. Mrs. Bowen, as Billy called her, was listening politely. Hector put his head down and tried to get back to work, but two minutes later he got up and left. Truth was, he was a bit rude in his departure and regretted it the minute he'd left. He wasn't really that kind of guy.

He was a last-minute kind. That night he would be performing one of his own compositions in a concert at Titus Sparrow Park and he still hadn't completed the final riff, *and* he was already late for his students over at Berklee College of Music. (For the past ten summers he'd been teaching a class there and staying with his friend Grace whenever he came from his home in California.)

Grace and Hector went back to the days when he was a college music student at Berklee two and half decades ago. She'd been his landlady then. Grace had inherited her grandparents' home on West Newton. He'd met her by answering a "room for rent" ad, and ever since then her redbrick town house had been his home away from home. He was so sorry for her when Bob died. In fact, it was he who'd convinced her to open her house to the occasional paying guest. He was pleased she'd gone with his suggestion and was now considering going into the hospitality business full-time. ("Good God, Grace. What a great idea," he'd said when she starting planning, forgetting he himself had planted the seed.)

The piece unfinished and the students waiting, Hector left Grace's and crossed Huntington. Something has happened, he thought. *Something.* Out of nowhere there was a new rhythm shaping in his head and the image of the lady in the blue dress was spread out against the sky. But it was the last thing he needed today. He needed to finish his piece. He needed to get to his waiting class. He stood at the intersection of Mass Ave. and he tried to concentrate on hearing *Sparrow in Summer* in his head. But there she was. She was like some walking bass line. A blue note. A blue flower. Suddenly, in the middle of his piece, the Bowen lady was an improv all her own.

What was it about her? Her hair—that was like, like what? Cinnamon.

He raced up the stairs ten minutes late. The students were all there. They were used to seeing him a bit tangled, and used to him going into the wrong classroom, getting their names mixed up, calling them "Clarinet One" and "Sax Two." It didn't diminish their respect. He was Hector Sherr.

"Okay," he said, and pushed his hands along his thighs. "So. You know I've played the park before, right? In '99 and '04, both times as part of a trio: sax, bass, and me on piano. And it was cool both times. But this is the first time I've decided to invite two students to join me on stage." He watched a little flicker of nervousness run through them.

"But it's improv, guys. So don't sweat it." He relaxed now, getting into his role as the offbeat professor. "The way I see it, there are three groups of people in the world. Those who rein in their creativity because they're afraid to express themselves, those who just express themselves without thought or form, and those who follow their creativity and listen to it, without restricting it, allowing it . . . personal feeling. And that, that's jazz, baby. That's what I'm looking for. Can you guys deliver?"

He broke his students into groups, gave instructions, the major chords and key signature, and sent them to work on their improvs in practice rooms. Alone in the studio then, he sat down at the piano, a Boston upright, and worked on the final chord progression for *Sparrow in Summer*. (Turned out allowing personal feeling wasn't so easy.) He worked until one, taking breaks to check on the students, and coming back with a kind of punchy electric urgency. Just before lunch he cracked the tune.

"Got it! That's it," he said under his breath. "Yes yes yes," and he played the piece again to secure it. "Thank you. Mrs. Bowen!"

After a quick lunch of an apple and a yogurt he'd taken from Grace's refrigerator, he went to audition the students. He had an extra bounce in him now. The students could see it. They knew his piece must have come together. He chose Casey and Belletti for the concert that evening, told them they'd be sensational and told the others he wished they could all be on stage, that he was that proud of them all.

When he came out into the sunlight, he had the elation of completing the composition and the brief glory of thinking it was great. He was light-headed and his heart was jumping. If you saw him coming, then you'd say he almost *shone.*

He crossed Mass Ave. and continued along and before he knew it, or before he'd admitted it to himself, he was heading for the massive doors of the Mary Baker Eddy Library and the Mapparium to see if, maybe, she, Mrs. Bowen, had taken Billy's suggestion and gone there. It was unlikely, but so was the world. He'd dip in anyway. The Mapparium was one of the old haunts of all the students at Berklee.

The fact was, she *had* helped with the piece. He wanted to find her to thank her for that. Maybe he could even thank her *and* apologize for his brusqueness that morning.

That was what he told himself. That was the reason. It was nothing to do with the fact that she was beautiful and he just wanted to see her again. See that red hair, those cinnamon curls.

He found the entrance to the Mapparium and walked in through the Indian Ocean. Two boys in green-and-white soccer jerseys with the numbers 6 and 8 were whispering.

"Hey Colin, look! The North Po—" whispered the younger boy of the family. He stopped suddenly, startled by the sound of his own voice so loud, so bright, so booming around the world.

"Yeah! Brilliant! Can ye hear *me*?" the older boy whispered. Their laughter bubbled, like a cascading waterfall, like the sound of Art Tatum's fingers running the keyboard playing "Tea for Two."

"Shh . . . Robert!" said the father, trying to keep his voice quiet without success, then he, too, was laughing, and so, too, was their pink, sun-flushed mother.

And at the end of the glass bridge, nearly thirty feet away, blue on blue, was Iris. Her back was turned and she was busy with her handbag. She didn't see Hector. As she fussed, the contents of her handbag spilled out. The pink soccer mom stooped to help her and from the opposite side of the world Hector heard them whisper—a soft murmur that was a loud murmur in the whispering gallery.

"Here, love. Let me help."

They gathered the contents and the soccer mom feather-touched Iris's shoulder. But as she rose, her left foot moved a last piece of note paper or something that had lain on the bridge. The paper was moved to the edge, and as the woman stepped away it slipped though the gap off the glass walkway. Iris gasped, her hands outstretched to it. And then she, like Hector, watched the falling note drift like a tumbleweed, down Central America, past Costa Rica, past Peru, then Chile, riffing along the curve of the blue Pacific, until it stopped thirty feet below, somewhere west of the South Pole.

When Hector looked up, Iris was hurrying out.

Outside in the blinding sunlight he stood scanning the crowds for her. The pavement scorched the rubber of his shoes. She was gone. After the blue cool, the heat was a shock and he went across the plaza straight to the splash fountain. The water was rising and falling in arcs from its flat concrete base, and into it Hector stepped, triggering an eruption of whoops and glees in the children as he crossed through the fountain in his own kind of cool, and coming out the far side.

Something was happening, something was definitely happening, but he hadn't the words for it yet. Shaking the water from his hair he suddenly remembered. "Jesus, Hector," and from the back pocket of his shorts he pulled the envelope she had dropped. (He'd had the attendant retrieve it from the bottom of the glass world.) It hadn't got wet in the fountain. He shook it in the air a moment just in case. Although it was just an empty envelope, yellowing, with a handwritten address on the front, he wanted to deliver it back to Iris intact. He took off, heading over Huntington and back to Grace's, and without needing to pause he plucked a daisy that poked through the park railings. He had a sense of propulsion, of things moving forward without his wishing or planning, and he was just going to go with it. He hadn't felt this way since . . . since . . . He wasn't going to think about that.

By the time he got to Grace's, he was nearly steaming, so when his wet clothes hit the a/c he felt chilled. He took the stairs in leaps. He needed a shower and a nap, but he needed to calm down first. He rang Billy and asked for coffee and lemonade. Then he put the daisy in a glass and the envelope on the desk and looked carefully at it. It was addressed to the Adoption Board, Merrion

Square, Dublin, Ireland. In the upper, left-hand corner was the sender's address: Hilary Barrett, 99 St. Botolph Street, Boston, MA. Postmark: August 21, 1991.

What was the story here? What was the connect? Had there been more than one thing lying in the bottom of the glass sea? Maybe this wasn't Iris's. Had the guy fished out the wrong thing?

There was a knock. He opened the door to Billy, who was smiling. Hector was down to his boxers. The tattoo of an eagle on Hector's right arm caught the sunlight. "Hey, Professor." Billy put down the lemonade and coffee. "Mrs. Hale said she'd see you later. She hopes you got a ticket for—"

"Of course I did. Two, in fact." Hector winked.

"Right. She'll be pleased."

"Hey. Has the Mrs. Bowen lady returned? I mean, she staying here tonight?"

"No, she hasn't and yes, she is. I told her about the Mapparium. And I told her where the public library was. She wanted Internet. So maybe—"

"Gotcha. She's here but not here." Hector didn't exactly push Billy out, but he held the door for him and closed it quickly. He drank the lemonade first, then the coffee, then he lay out on the bed, but couldn't nap. He sat up, lay down again, but still couldn't nap. His head was buzzing between *Sparrow in Summer* and Mrs. Bowen. There was no way he was going to be able to sleep.

He woke with a start when a door closed. It was 5:27. The students expected him to join them for special supper at Botolph's at six.

He shaved, calmed his hair, threw on his blue Hawaiian shirt, the one with the white hibiscus, and bolted downstairs. There was no sign of Grace in the front room. He checked the kitchen. No sign of her there. Nor Billy. Nor Mrs. Bowen. By the side table in the front hall, he found a brown envelope and stuck two tickets inside, scribbled *For Your Grace and Mrs. Bowen,* and left.

He hurried along West Newton and when he reached the corner, he stopped dead, as if for the first time noticing the street number of Botolph's restaurant. He'd been coming here for what? Fifteen years or so. Since it opened. But there etched in white fancy numbers was 99, in the glass above the door. What do you know? How many times had he been there? With Grace, with students, with colleagues?

Now he noticed—99.

What it meant he had no idea, but it didn't take a rocket scientist, he thought, to know something here was of concern to Mrs. Bowen. It was the *something* troubling her which he'd sensed that morning. He had no words for his thoughts, only feelings, and those feelings in one intense flash of inspiration had already found their way into *Sparrow in Summer.* But there was more, he was certain.

After a light supper, rambling monologues, sudden silences, and nervous jokes from Casey and Belletti, Hector walked with his students to Titus Sparrow Park. A large audience had already gathered with picnic baskets and rugs and multicolored nylon beach chairs. The summer concerts always began just at twilight. Hector looked around him, at the light tumbling down, disappearing into the trees and across the flowerbeds. Layers of different hues of blue cloaked the sky. Soon, the other musicians would appear and the evening would become magical.

But before the magic could begin, the musicians needed to warm up. Backstage, Hector's mind was gliding and humming, running through riffs and runs, swings and syncopations. He was bounce-walking up and down, rolling his shoulders, loosening his neck muscles, looking up into the night sky, getting ready for the music, but all the time, playing like a thumb line, was something he wanted to say to the woman named Iris: that blue in all its splendid dynamism was the color of hope. He couldn't articulate it any better than that. He peeped through the curtains. Grace wasn't there yet. He'd left reserved seats for her in the front row.

Hector finished his warm-up, then he gathered Belletti and Casey, brought them over to meet the man sitting in the corner cradling his guitar. "And here's Amos McGee, the one and only. Best bass guitarist there is. Close your eyes when you hear him play and it sounds like a horn has slipped in. Amos, meet Casey and Belletti. And guys . . . meet Amos."

"Hey, kids, welcome aboard," Amos said. He tipped his baseball cap back on his head one second and lowered it again. He stood up then and walked out on the stage. The clapping began right away because Amos McGee was a legend in Boston. His name stretched back into the days when Dizzy Gillespie played in the South End. In his Red Sox cap, he strode smooth and cool, paused a moment, and then did his customary pirouette.

The rumble of applause rose up from the grass into the gloaming sky. Hector stepped to the microphone and introduced the band. "Mr. Amos McGee, you all know." More applause. Amos bowed just slightly, his hands moving over his guitar. "And, here, now, are two of Berklee's finest, Mossy Casey and Gino Belletti, who'll back up Amos and maybe . . . let's see how it flies . . . maybe they'll have a riff or two of their own—to take us higher."

He paused for effect, let the evening gather its breath. "Ladies and gentlemen, on this bee . . . u . . . ti . . . full night, I give you, *Sparrow in Summer.*"

Hector sat down, summoned that still place inside, and then broke it open, playing the black and white notes fast and free, sounding like a bird jam, like a sparrow sings. Sharp notes. A succession of warbles and trills. *Chimp. Tsip. Tsip. Tsip.* He nodded to Amos and his thumping and plucking sounded like the repeated chattering of a sparrow Hector had imagined. Then he and Amos held back while Casey and Belletti stepped forward, showcasing the slap bass improvisation they'd worked on earlier.

Hector looked out at the crowd and breathed it all in. At the piano he was fully alive, and the thing that was happening inside him fused with the music and he knew he was playing better than he had in a long time, and he looked up into the dark blue sky and he thought, Man, this is a little like paradise, this is jazz as it is in heaven, sound upon sound with no boundary, mingling, colliding, harmonizing, blending, melding, balancing, clashing, fusing. An acoustic Arcadia, smooth and easy, head-buzzing, heart-stopping, and goddamn transformative.

He looked out and there was Grace. And, sitting right beside her, some kind of illumination, was Iris Bowen. She looked up at him with the saddest-looking eyes he'd ever seen. And he knew. He knew right then with perfect clarity that this was the something that had changed, had changed utterly, and although he still didn't have the words for it, he had the notes.

And, for Iris Bowen, he played.

Later, after the final encore, after the sparrow had flown, but still in the high of performance, still in that particular mindscape that jazz brings, out of the seeming chaos of chords and rhythms to a place of harmony where things fit together and the world seems to make better sense—or at least it did for Hector—he went back and found Grace sitting in the kitchen. It was after midnight.

"Hello, Your Grace." He bowed exuberantly and looked around expectantly.

"Hector. Hector. Hector. That was wonderful." She jumped up and hugged him. "So wonderful, right? I'm so proud. I'm sitting here thinking about how Bob would have loved it, too. Yes?"

"Yeah, Grace. Thanks. I'm flying high."

"Something to drink?"

"No. No. I'm buzzing."

They stood silently for a few moments; Hector judging whether he could mention Mrs. Bowen.

"Mrs Bowen—" Grace started to say.

"I was just about to ask if—"

"Iris loved it, too."

"Yeah?"

"Oh, yes." She looked at him and knew. Something was different.

"Great." That's all he had. Just the one word. He turned to go, but Grace wanted more.

"I'm so glad you left me *two* tickets. You must meet her."

"I'd like to meet her." He didn't exactly blurt it. But he nearly did. Then it was confirmed for Grace, too: something *was* going on.

"Maybe in the morning, then, although . . . she's not . . . what can I say . . . ? I think she's been upset by something today. She didn't say. When I told her there was a second ticket for the evening's concert she wasn't going to take it. But I knew she needed something. And Hector, I can be persuasive."

From the pocket of his shirt Hector took the envelope and handed it to Grace. He'd kept it all night like it was a talisman. "She dropped this in the Mapparium." He looked down as if to shield his face from Grace's. "I was there, but she didn't see me.

115

She ran off before I could help her get it back. But I got someone to fish it out."

"I see." Grace took the envelope, turned it over. "Just an envelope." Then she read the addressee, then the sender. "Adoption Board?" She paused. "Well, I wonder what that means." She tapped the fingers of her left hand on the table. Her nails made a *tat tat tat*. "That's odd," she said then. "Hector, this is quite odd." She looked to the right, absorbed in a memory, then said, "Hilary Barrett. I know this name. Don't I?"

"Really?"

A memory began to play on Grace's face. Lines of wrinkles bunched across her brow. Her mouth tightened. But then it faded.

"And 99 St. Botolph?" Hector asked.

"Well. I just can't say. It wasn't always a restaurant. That much I can tell you." She fell silent again and after a moment she stamped her foot. "Oh, I can't remember."

"Okay. No worries. I'm going to bed."

Grace Hale didn't move. She stood there trying to think, then shook her head. "Sorry. Sometimes I think I remember everybody."

Eight

In a blue Lucky Express Town Car, Rowan Blake was sped away
from New York City into Westchester, into the landscape of his
childhood. An hour north he looked out the window when the
suburbs eased into a forest of maple and birch, oak and pine, and
yielded to lakes and black reservoirs. Granite stone glinted. Now,
in nearly mid-June, an occasional dogwood still illumined the
wood. How stunning their white-leafed petals, how strong and
vibrant against the gathering dusk. Westchester always did this
to him, made him sentimental. He'd lived on Long Island Sound
ever since he'd started a small landscape architecture firm in the
city, twenty years ago, but whenever he returned to Westchester
there was always the sense of a flowing return, of coming back
into a newly awakened memory.

Sometimes it hurt.

As the car edged into northern Westchester closer to Heri-
tage Hills, Rowan tried to shake off his disquiet. He'd been

entertaining clients in the newly opened Standard Grill and their brunch extended to late afternoon. Mimosas gave way to martinis. He'd closed the deal on a large project in Sag Harbor, but by the time he'd finally looked at his phone there were five missed calls from his mother and one stinker of a text from his brother telling him to answer his goddamn phone. It was urgent.

He didn't feel sober enough to maneuver from the lower West Side up to Grand Central—just the *thought* of a taxi was making him nauseous. It was the second Thursday in June, the traffic would be hell. Plus, he'd miss the 4:57 and couldn't wait another half hour longer. Considering the windfall of the Sag project, he'd sprung for a car and driver. The Standard hotel, where he had been brought in as a consultant when designs for the High Line were being finalized, had helped him arrange it. He remembers now how his grandfather Burdy had encouraged him to "go for it" and, although his own submission wasn't accepted, he'd facilitated some important design changes and now remained a special guest. The park, built along the railway line above the streets of the West Side, thrilled him. It was one of the things he loved most about New York City. He and Burdy had joined the Friends of the High Line and volunteered for spring and autumn cleanup.

Rowan Blake was forty-four years old. If you saw him being driven up I-684 you might think power and privilege, and to an extent it was true. But behind the tinted glass of the town car the handsome man was sitting alone. He had no wife, no partner, and few friends. Not exactly one of the Masters of the Universe, he was a successful "producer" with his own firm and half a dozen employees. Because of his grandfather, he knew a lot about a lot of different things and could converse on many subjects, from good opening bids in bridge to why Jack Nicklaus was perhaps the greatest golfer of all time. He had read *The Fountainhead* and Joyce's *Portrait of an Artist* and was a weekly recipient of *The New Yorker*. But in the last few months these last lay unopened on his coffee table and the one by his bedside, the one with Obama dressed as Washington, was four months old and had wrinkled waves from when a glass of Hennessy had toppled. He was a man on the edge.

Winding up through the hills, past the golf course and clubhouse, Rowan's heart sank. When the driver pulled into Greenview Drive he saw his mother pacing outside her two-bedroom condo holding the portable house phone. It was unlike her to be so visible. He wondered if all the neighbors knew before he had about Burdy. There she stood, loafered feet, bare, tanned legs showing beneath a flared print skirt. She was the kind of woman who wore a short string of pearls with everything, even when she played golf, always a badge of elegance about her.

"Mother . . ." Rowan's voice broke as he exited the car. Louise Blake ran and with a perfumed embrace slumped her petite frame against him, her face warm on his chest,

"Mother . . ." It was all he could say, his voice thickened by the afternoon of alcohol. He held her while the driver pulled the car around the small cul-de-sac of condos burrowed against the hill and drove quietly away.

"He was playing golf this morning. Just fell. That was it. Gone. Like that. On the seventeenth."

Rowan knew Burdy wouldn't have wanted it any other way, but he didn't say so. His gut twisted. He wished he'd been there. Somehow. Had one last putt or something, with his grandfather.

As if she'd heard his thoughts, Louise pulled back. "Honey, it's all right. You couldn't have known. It was too sudden."

119

"I know, but I missed our golf date last week. I had to cancel. I had something on. And . . . and . . ."

She looked up into his tearing eyes, brown, like his father's, and saw how tired he was. Rowan led his mother though the front door, his arm cupped around her, and into the immaculate white kitchen, its hanging ferns curtaining the window.

"I tried to reach you." She looked at her son the way some mothers do, as if his was a story only she could read. "Was your phone off? Did you get my messages? I had to begin the arrangements. Kings' have already taken the body—"

"Please, Mother . . ."

She sat at the table with a look he knew well. "I worried when I couldn't reach you." She forced a pause. "That's all."

"I'm sorry. I'm sorry you had to do that on your own." They sat in silence for a few minutes. Rowan's hands lay crossed on the table. He closed his eyes and dropped his head. He was still in his work suit, a dark blue fine wool, his white shirt opened at the neck. The tie stuffed in his pocket. His mother reached for a pack of cigarettes, fished one out, and snapped into flame a silver lighter.

She hadn't taken three draws when she stood and said, "Coffee." She crossed the kitchen to the sink and ran the water. While she did, Rowan left the room.

Pierce Blake, Rowan's older brother, an entertainment lawyer, was on his way from Los Angeles. Louise had sent a car to the airport for him. After a failed marriage he, too, was a bachelor now.

Louise planned to make her boys dinner (filet mignon, baked potato, and a citrus salad with Bibb lettuce), "like in the old days,"

she told Rowan when he returned to the kitchen. It had been Burdy's favorite, too. He'd washed his face, his dark hair, smartly
cut, was combed, and he'd taken off his jacket. His sleeves were
folded midway up his forearms. A large mug of black coffee waited
for him on the table.

"There, that might help. I've made a pot."

Rowan ignored the pointed tone in her voice, but picked up
the coffee. "Mother, what can I do?"

"Nothing now . . . dear. I've a list of people we need to call.
Let's wait for Pierce." Her back was to him.

"Sorry. For earlier, I mean. My phone was on silent. I was entertaining clients—"

"Yes. I know. When I spoke with your intern"—she paused but
didn't turn around—"he said you weren't there." Louise said it
like she was leaving a door open for him, even though she knew
he wouldn't walk through it. She knew her son by heart. She was
certain he was on his way to becoming an alcoholic, if he wasn't
one already. She'd seen something like this coming for months.
She'd seen it in her own mother and sisters and knew the signs
well. She stopped fixing the salad and began to thump one
small-fisted hand on the counter, muffled but insistent, as if to
squash her rising grief into a pulpy mash and dispose of it in
the garbage disposal.

Rowan said nothing. He took the coffee, came toward her, but
stopped midway, then walked out. Everything about him was
tired. He opened the patio screen door and was soon on the edge
of the golf course. He stood on the trimmed rough of the 16th
and wished himself back into an earlier time when his life seemed
full of promises and innocence.

"It's all about balance, Ro," his grandfather said. "Relax your
grip, son. Swing easy. And mind the rough." It was a spring

afternoon. He was twelve years old. Burdy was wearing his gold ochre sweater and linen golf trousers, his silver hair soft like silky milkweed threads, explaining the rules of putting, angles, and imaginary lines and how to read the green. "If you get your putting right, you're halfway there. Putting is the foundation of building your game. The trick is to focus on the line of the putt. Visualize it moving across the green. View the hole from different aspects, Rowan. You've got to *feel* the move of the green."

He stood in behind Rowan. "That's it, Ro. Line your foot up to the ball. Keep the club square to the line. Now, let your shoulders hang loose. Hands level with the ball. How does that feel?"

"Okay. I guess?"

"Good boy." Burdy laughed and stepped away. "You're a natural. Remember, a perfect putting stroke resembles a pendulum."

Rowan had stopped and turned around to look at his grandfather, puzzled.

"No. Keep your eyes on the ball. Remember, like a pendulum. Keep your putter on the line, square with the target."

Burdy had a special marker, an old Irish coin—a nickel three pence picturing a hare and a harp. That was also his lucky piece. "Here, let me show you." He picked up Rowan's ball and put down the coin, dropped his own ball beside it. He stepped up and with his feet in place, he shifted easily back and forth, looked from the hole to his ball, his grip as light as a feather. He pulled back and through, stroking the back of the ball. Soft like a puff, the ball poofed along the imaginary line, following the lay of the land before dropping, *plonk,* into the hole.

"It's all about balance, Ro."

It's all about balance, Ro. But Burdy was dead and balance was the last thing Rowan Blake had in his life.

Half an hour later, another car pulled into 316 Greenview Drive. A man in his late forties got out and paid the driver. He was tall and straight, had a long but handsome nose, full lips, and brown eyes that resembled his brother's. He carried a bouquet of peonies and a leather suit bag. Louise, seeing him from the kitchen, rushed out to meet him.

"Honey! Pierce . . . dear. You're here." As she'd done earlier with Rowan, she now clasped onto her eldest son, more like a child than a mother.

"It's all right. It's all right, Mother." He held her close and patted her back. Both sons were a foot taller than Louise. "It was Burdy's time. He'd a great life."

"I know," she said. "I know. But . . . it was so . . . so sudden. I wasn't ready." As she partly spoke, partly wept, Rowan appeared at the door and came toward them. "I'm so glad you're here," she whispered to Pierce.

Over the top of her head, Pierce's deep voice called, "Rowan! Hey! How are you, brother?"

Louise released her hold and moved aside. The brothers hugged briefly but warmly. Like Rowan, Pierce was wearing a white shirt. It was how the Blake men always dressed. Crisp white shirts. They were the kind of men you'd look at if they passed you in the street—perfectly groomed and full of the quiet self-assurance tall men often have. "It's just us now against the world, hey?" Pierce said gently and they stood a moment. All three looked in different directions to the hundreds of trees that sheltered them, not touching but close enough so the space between them was as intimate as a whisper.

"Ah," Pierce said, coming into the kitchen, "pink grapefruit and blue cheese!" Louise had set the table and placed her famous salad on place mats. "No one does it like you, Mother." He winked at Rowan and handed her the flowers. "I don't suppose you've prepared the mignon and the Idaho, too?"

"You're too much, Pierce. You make me laugh." She was on the verge of tears.

"You shouldn't have," Pierce said, picking up her hands and holding them in his own. "We could have ordered in—"

"I needed to do something while I waited for you. . . . For you both."

Pierce "at home" had revived Louise, Rowan observed with some regret as his mother steadied the bouquet into a glass vase. Then she broiled the steaks under the grill. The potatoes, wrapped in tinfoil, waited on the plates. For a few minutes they made small talk like nothing had happened. Both men leaned back on the kitchen counter, side by side, arms folded across their chests. Pierce asked Rowan how the landscaping business was going.

"In L.A. it seems every other house has a fancy tree lit up with soft lights and smart water features and minimalist planters. What's it like in New York? Still doing those brownstone gardens in Brooklyn?" He seemed truly interested. He was, after all, the older brother. Rowan said he was working on a redesign for Paley Park on East Fifty-third, in fact.

"Dogwoods and box and a few multistem Himalayan birch."

"It's time you came out to Brentwood, buddy, helped me with my ten-by-ten gravel backyard. What would you say to a swimming pool?" Pierce chuckled and gave his brother a soft thump on the back.

Their conversation seemed to settle Louise. She asked them then to sit down and they held hands across the kitchen table, as was customary in the Blake household. Louise looked to Rowan. "Will you say grace, please?"

After the dinner, which none of them could really eat, some of Louise's neighbors stopped by; it was late, but Pierce and Rowan pretended it was polite to slip away. They stepped outside onto the deck. Fireflies flashed with silent electricity. A breeze stirred the trees and offered some relief to the hot night.

"We could take Mother's car down to Muscoot's?" said Rowan.

"That old haunt? Doesn't have this fresh air, Ro." Pierce slapped his hands together and laughed his big, deep laugh. "Let's just walk a bit. We're past those days, don't you think? Beer joints?"

They walked in silence with the crickets sounding. A few stars hung above the 16th fairway. Rowan said nothing, although he ached with emotion. And he wanted a drink. From time to time he glanced over at Pierce and wondered if his brother thought him much altered from his visit last summer.

"Come on. Cheer up, and tell me, how's it going down there in the Big Apple? You seem a few bites short? Is it just Burdy, or something else?"

It wasn't something else. It was that, and, *everything* else. Between bidding for projects, executing accepted ones, and training new staff, he was keeping late hours. It left little time for leisure or dating and he ended up exhausted at night but also wired. It was a balancing act but the seesaw of his life catapulted him, more often than not these days, through intoxication, landing him on the flat of his back, inches away from the proverbial gutter. But each day he got up and was back in the game, although each day a little more bruised.

Rowan leaned nearer. "You wouldn't say no to a martini, would you? Back at the house?"

"Once Mother's in bed I've got to phone some clients back in L.A."

"Sure," said Rowan. "I've got some calls to make, as well."

When the friends had left, Louise found her sons out on the back deck sitting in her Adirondack chairs. "You boys are terrible," she said, "deserting me," but her eyes understood. She knew Pierce was assuming his big brother role. She kissed their heads. "Good night."

When Louise was in bed, the brothers came inside and Rowan mixed gin and vermouth. (Louise always had a bottle of Bombay and one of Jameson in the cabinet.) He'd finished his second before Pierce returned from his phone calls.

"So, tell me," Pierce said, "what's up?"

Rowan followed his brother's eyes, which went to his empty glass, but he looked directly back at Pierce, challengingly, and Pierce shrugged. "Just go easy on that stuff."

They talked instead about Pierce's latest project on a copyright infringement case. And after just one martini Pierce went to bed.

Rowan drifted like a buoy lost of its mooring. The night closed in like a dark ocean, his head barely above water. No land in sight. In which direction he should swim, he'd no idea. Just thinking about it disabled him moment by moment. (And fuck it, he was a good swimmer.)

It was because of his grandfather, Burdock Emmet, that Rowan had become interested in architecture in the first place. Burdy had taken him under his wing after the boys' father had left, moved away, and remarried a woman from Singapore who had an export business, leaving Louise embittered for years. The boys had taken it hard and they hardly ever saw him now. Stepping, as best he could, into the hole left by Rowan's father, Burdy had parceled encouragement in little chunks and had weaved the glory of architecture into Rowan's mind. Under the tree at Christmas were books like *Great Moments in Architecture* and Wilde's *Michelangelo: Six Lectures* alongside an essential something from Ireland. "You mustn't forget your Irish roots, Ro. And you know, if I were you," Burdy had said as they walked along the putting green, "I'd be thinking seriously of becoming an architect when I grew up. Building good buildings is good citizenship. What do you think of that?"

Rowan thought for a second. "I'd like to be a musician. But Mother says I should listen to you."

Burdy laughed. His eyes glistened. "And so you should, lad, so you should. Keep up the saxophone playing, and the golf practice, and your studies, and you'll be a proper Renaissance Man." He put a light hand on the boy's shoulder. It was a hand that felt like a father's might.

Now, alone and the only one awake in 316 Greenview, it was that hand he missed. Outside the dark grass sloped away. The crickets, or the peepers as his mother called them, were chirping a very quiet song. In the Bombay there was one measure left. Rowan turned the bottle in the half light. In it was mostly a pale emptiness.

Louise and Pierce, as the executors of Burdy's affairs, decided on a private cremation with just the three Blakes at the funeral home. Neighbors and close friends were advised of a memorial service being held at the golf club two days later. The Hills, as it

was known locally, was a close community and many of Burdock
Emmet's friends, and Louise's, were expected. And after the service they'd planned to spread Burdy's ashes on the putting green.
Because his mother had asked him to please play, Rowan had
taken her car to his apartment in Stamford and spent a few hours
practicing his saxophone.

"Early summer," Pierce said, gazing toward a grove of sugar maples burnishing in the late afternoon, "is a perfect time to celebrate a life well lived." They were sitting, mother and sons, over
iced Arnold Palmers—half lemonade/half iced tea—on the open
deck of the golf club while the Healy Room was being set up for
the memorial service.

"The obituary was in the papers this morning," Louise said.
Her shoulders had a slumped look and her grief was palpable.
She had changed into a black dress for the service. "People will
have read it. . . . Did we ask the Wilsons? And the Morgans? And
his old secretary? Dad had so many friends." She fingered the
string of her pearls. Rowan realized suddenly how hard this was
going to be for her, how much she was going to miss her father.
He'd been selfish, thinking only about his own sorrow and how
Burdy's death was going to impact *his* life. He reached over and
grabbed her hand. She smiled weakly. "Thank you, dear. I'm all
right." Pierce looked to Rowan and nodded his head.

The likelihood of there being guests whom Rowan had long
forgotten now struck him. Not being an ace at chitchat like Pierce,
he thought about it just long enough to shrug it off because in
that moment he didn't care about them. It was Burdy and his
mother and the hole opening larger in his life that consumed

his attention. That, and how soon he could have a martini. Just one. He'd promised Pierce.

The Healy Room's fourth wall opened onto a terrace overlooking the putting green. With the short service completed, the staff mingled with trays of drinks and finger sandwiches among the large crowd who'd come to pay their respects. The Arnold Palmers turned into Leland Palmers (added gin and Limoncello) and the twilight scattered across the course, hitting every blade of grass. Given the occasion, Rowan wasn't expected to be entertaining. He'd already done his bit. He'd managed to play "Amazing Grace" and his playing had taken the mourners beyond the place Pierce's moving eulogy had brought them.

"Thank you," his mother had said. "It's all I want for you, you know?" Her eyes stayed fixed on his face long enough for Rowan to feel her meaning. She didn't need to say the words: amazing grace.

Rowan leaned alongside the iron balustrade that supported the glass roof of the conservatory and surveyed the gathering. Burdy was there in the faces of all his friends, his aging golfing buddies, his bridge partners, and his fellow hospice volunteers. Rowan recognized many of them, even some of his father's old business associates. (Because of such short notice, his father was unable to come from Singapore, he'd said, but he told Pierce, who'd telephoned him with the news, that next time he was in New York he'd be sure to be in touch with Louise and Rowan. Living on that side of the world Pierce saw him more than Rowan did, although not regularly. The boys had pretty much dismissed their father and his lackluster attention.)

The music for the service had been left up to Rowan and as he listened to the violin trio, a woman in her seventies dressed in a pink two-piece suit with black trim weaved her way through the crowd toward him, carrying a silver purse in one hand and a drink in the other.

"I love that old spiritual," she said, stopping in front of Rowan. "You played it well."

"Thank you."

" 'I once was lost and now I'm found.' " She gave her glass a little swirl, ice cubes, lemon, and mint colliding. "It's a pity we didn't have the words to sing along with you," she said. "I love a good old singsong. But that wouldn't do now, would it? No. Not at all, at all. Not appropriate. What was I thinking?" She pronounced "what" with a breathy H. "Too much Leland and not enough Arnold." She laughed at herself, her white permed hair bouncing as she did.

Rowan shifted and looked toward Pierce. Who was this woman? But his brother was deep in conversation with some people Rowan didn't know. He looked to his mother, but she was surrounded by a group of women, members of her yoga class or creative writing group, or something. They had that intimate posture about them—a posture women of a certain age have who know each other from a "shared experience." There was no one to help him recall the name of the woman before him. So he went with it, took another sip from his glass, and smiled, hearing Burdy's voice in his ear saying, *This woman is a flibbertigibbet.* Rowan watched her thin, disappearing lips move sideways as they opened and closed and made sounds. For a few moments he just watched them. How sweet the soundless, he thought, and laughed. He'd had three martinis and was just beginning to float. He motioned to a waiter.

"Oh, I know. One does tend to drink too much on these sad occasions. But this isn't really that sad. Is it, do you think? Mr. Emmet's was a full life, God bless him and save him, and may he rest in peace."

At the mention of "Mr. Emmet," Rowan suddenly remembered. "Mrs. Dillon! A full life. Yes. You're absolutely right. Forgive me for not recognizing you."

"I was wondering if you had forgotten me." She sipped her drink rather coyly.

"Momentarily." He smiled. "Momentarily. But a laugh as jolly as yours is hard to forget. I *am* sorry. How have you been?"

"Not too bad. Although I was sad to hear of my dear Mr. Emmet. Will you miss him terribly?" Subtlety was not her forte.

"Yes." What more could he say?

Burdy had schooled him: always be a gentleman when speaking with your elders. Suddenly he felt like a twelve-year-old again and then he recalled Mrs. Dillon had been Burdy's secretary. When Burdy retired twenty years ago, so had she. Originally from Ireland, she was interested in, what was it? Something? What? Reading the tea leaves! When he visited Burdy in his office, occasionally Mrs. Dillon would make him a cup of tea and then "read" the leaves. Afterward, she'd say something enormously positive about the loose leaves left in the cup. "You're going to grow up to be an astronaut. Or maybe an architect. Something that begins with an A. And you're going to be rich and famous. Oh yes, and of course one day you'll go to Ireland and find a nice girl. And it will change your life." It took a long time, but Rowan eventually figured out that her fortune-telling was always the flowering of some seed Burdy had planted earlier.

"It's been years since I saw you, dear. I didn't really expect you to remember me, although I hoped you would."

"I do remember. Of course. You were Burdy's 'Galway Gal Friday.' Isn't that what he called you? And, I remember you were at my graduation." Rowan was pleased; his memory had returned and the moment unveiled like a curtain drawn back upon a stage.

"That's right. But that was a long time ago." She finished her drink. "I think that was the last time I saw you."

Across the putting green in blackness a bank of trees was silhouetted against the sky like a ship harbored in a dark sea.

Peggy Dillon licked the remnants of the gin and Limoncello on her lips and seemed to drift away in thought, but then her eyes returned to anchor on Rowan's face. "Whatever became of the child?"

Rowan stared at her.

Her eyes widened and squeezed, closed briefly, as if she were having a dialogue in her mind.

Rowan took her arm. "What child?"

She saw the shock on his face and spoke quietly. "You know I saw her. That time in Dublin. I was there with the Friends of St. Patrick. For the parade. We were in Trinity to see the Book of Kells and I saw her passing. I waved. But she didn't see me. I said to my friends, 'There goes that sweet girl young Rowan Blake is engaged to.' "

"You must be wrong. She didn't have a child."

"Nooo . . ." she replied slowly. "She didn't. Not then. But . . . I mean . . . she *was* pregnant. You could see, I mean there was no doubt she—"

Rowan was no longer listening. He was getting around the canapes table, pushing his way past the Wilsons and the Morgans, getting to the French doors and, watched by Pierce, bolting across the terrace onto the golf course, so he didn't hear the Joyces asking Louise if he would play again and he didn't hear her say he's going to miss Burdy so, and he didn't hear Peggy Dillon turn to the memorial picture of Burdoch Emmet on the table and say, "All right, Burdy? I told him."

Nine

Rose is woken by the seagulls, or is it her phone squawking? She gets up quickly. What time is it? What *day* is it? Her head hurts. Pages of sheet music on the music stand turn, others on the floor scurry, stirred by the wind as she opens the curtains and the door to a bright blue noon. Her phone beeps. She's had several missed calls from Roger. Feck. She doesn't want to speak to him.

Rose steps out to the balcony and her phone rings again. She lets it, considers letting it ring out, then snaps it on.

"Rose! I'd tried to reach you all day yesterday! Are you all right?" She hears Roger's exasperated breath. "I was about to phone your mother, but I didn't have her number. Where have you been? I need to explain. I need to apologize . . ."

The sun is bright in her eyes and she winces, then thinks of the lyric about the sun and lemon drops.

"Rose? Rose, are you there?"

Her eyes drink in the trees and redbrick buildings in front

of her. A barge cuts along through the film of silken green algae on the canal. "I'm here," she says quietly.

"The master class. It's important that we straighten this out."

Rose doesn't say anything. She watches the wake of the barge, the ruffled silk return to smooth.

"It's my daughter. Victoria. She came to see me in London. Her mother and I, we're divorced. Victoria's a musician, too . . . in New York. She came to tell me she's quitting. Quitting! I tried to talk her out of it, yesterday. But she wouldn't hear of it. She says it's too fucking hard. After all that work, she wants to toss it away. She's not like you, she has to *work* for her talent. You've got heaps of talent. A gift that can't be taught."

Rose listens but says nothing. *A gift that can't be taught.*

"Rose? Are you hearing me?"

"Yes." The canal is sour this morning. It happens in the heat. Effluent waves lap at the brickwork.

"I was hard on you, I admit. I'm sorry, Rose. Really sorry, hey? It wasn't you. I was thinking of Victoria," he says. "Listen, I'm taking a cab to Primrose Hill. Meet me at The Engineer in an hour and we'll have a proper chat about it. Okay?"

"Okay, Roger. Maybe."

On her small smartphone, Rose presses "End." The phone in her hand feels heavy and she wants to drop it. She lowers her arm over the balcony but as she does, just seconds later, the phone rings again and she speaks, "Roger, I said I'll think about it, o—"

"Rose . . . Rose Bowen?"

Rose doesn't recognize the man's voice.

"This is Conor. Conor Flynn."

Her chin tucked, her eyes closed, Rose loses her concentration. "Conor?"

"Yeah. How are you?"

"Um . . . not great actually. I can't talk now."

"I thought not. I had an idea you might be feeling . . . well, pretty shit—"

"What?"

"Because, like, maybe, you *lost* something?"

"Oh God . . . !"

"Only you didn't exactly lose it, is how I heard—"

"Conor, tell me." Rose spins around on her balcony, loses her balance, and nearly drops the phone. Her left hand comes to join the right one holding it. She's trembling.

"I got a call from this guy. A *really* nice guy, apparently, who saw you on the tube Tuesday night. He said you left your violin case on the seat and walked off. He said you stood watching as the train pulled away. He got off at the next station and went back to your stop. And—"

"Conor!"

"It's all right . . . he's got it. Or he did have it, I mean."

"What . . . ?" Rose's voice skirls an octave higher.

"Easy . . . It's all right, Rosie."

He calls her Rosie. It registers like harmonics in her head. *Rosie.*

"What do you mean . . . he *had* it?"

"Well . . . he had it, and now . . ." Conor pauses. "It's like this, if you want it, you have to come back to Clare. It's on its way home. I asked him to courier it back, back to the *wesshhtt*, as we say. Like an Irish boomerang. It should arrive by Friday."

Rose is silent. Tears fall down her cheeks, slipping down her chin. She slumps to a chair.

"I'm sorry," Conor says, feeling her upset, "it's not funny."

For a long moment neither of them speaks. Finally Conor asks, "Rosie, what's going on?"

She can just about get the words out. "I'll come home." She falls silent then. The Canal Club below at the Pirate Castle is setting up for the trip to Little Venice farther down the canal. Life jackets adjusted, the group assembles and slips into colored canoes. As they paddle away, Rose thinks about the man who saved her violin. He'd have found Conor's cards inside the velvet box in her case.

She whispers his name. "Conor?"

"Yes?"

"Thank you."

On Saturday, Rose is in Heathrow about to board the midday flight to Shannon. She rings her mother, again, for the third time that day, but doesn't get her. She leaves Iris two messages, on cell and home phones, then she texts her mother's friend.

Hi Tess, Can't reach Mum. Pls, PLS, can u pick me up @ SNN 4 2day? :-)
xx Rosie

She briefly thinks of how she had stood Roger up, sees him sitting in The Engineer waiting for her. One part of her would have liked to have left him there forever, but in the end she had done the right thing and texted him to say she'd gone home to Ireland and she'd be in touch next week.

And PS . . . good luck with Victoria. And PPS . . . Trust in the universe, Roger.

She'd left him a smiley face. :)

When Rose walks through the arrival doors, Tess is there waiting. Two of her boys are with her, but the smile on Tess's face isn't in sync with her eyes.

"There's Rosie! Hey, Rosie!" The boys run when they see her and she greets them each by bending to their height, letting go her bag, and hugging them gently. She says, "Thanks for picking me up!" Then, standing to face Tess with her back to the boys, who scramble to take her bag, she says, "Where's Mum?"

"A bit of a mystery that, but listen, pet, don't worry. I'm certain she's fine."

"What do you mean? Fine? Is she not at home?"

"No."

Rose stops. "I don't get it. Where is she?"

"I don't know." Tess puts her hand on Rose's back and guides her forward. "But knowing your mother, she could be off visiting some garden in Dublin or up north for a few days, and has forgot her phone."

Rose isn't convinced.

"Don't worry. I saw her on Monday night. She was fine." They walk out into the windy parking lot of the airport. "Was she expecting you home?"

"No. She thinks I've been preparing for a master class with my tutor."

"Oh. Right." Tess gives her a doubtful look. "Well, then, I hope it's going well."

Rose precludes further conversation on the subject by turning to the boys and asking how their soccer training is going.

They reach the car and load up, boys in the back, suitcase in between, Rose in front. In a panic, Tess shouts, "Where's your fiddle? Oh God, did you leave it on the plane?"

"No, no. I didn't. It's all right."

Tess glances at Rose, her eyebrows raise, her mouth opens about to say something more but then stops. "O . . . kay."

"It's a long story," Rose says.

"Fab. I love long stories. So, will I take you home, or do you want to stay with us?"

"Home, please. Okay?"

Driving from Shannon to Ashwood under the ceiling of the western sky, violet blue and cloudless, Rose looks to the hills, green and rolling and dotted white with sheep and brown with cattle. They're all moving in one direction, like followers congregating. Clare is a place Rose realizes she misses only when she returns. Then it hits her. Home. She carries it deep inside and, like a singing bowl, it rings in her whole being once the western wind strokes her face.

When they pull into the drive, Cicero meets them. The cat seems hungry and meows loudly. Tess retrieves the hidden key under the blue pot and lets them all in. The boys run into the kitchen and out again and Tess switches on the heat. Even though it's summer, a two-hundred-year-old cottage with three-foot-thick walls is cold when it's been vacant for more than a day. Rose opens the window to feed the cat on the outside sill. The flowers in pots along the front of the house are wilting. What the hell? She's looks with fear to Tess, who's listening to a message from a missed call on her cell phone.

"A client, Rose, not your mum. Sorry, pet."

"Tess?"

"I know . . . I know how it looks, but—"

"But nothing! She should have rung by now. I've left her half a dozen messages since Thursday."

Rose walks toward the doors that lead to the garden.

"Where are you going?"

"Check the post. See how many days she's been gone."

In less than a minute Rose returns. "What's this?" she asks. It's an envelope with a Breast Clinic logo. "What's going on, Tess?"

Tess is skilled at therapeutics and doesn't rattle easily but now, as Rose watches, the face of her mother's best friend reveals concern. In a firm voice, Tess tells her sons to get back into the car and wait for her there. "I'll be along in a minute." They obey and the women watch from the window as the boys run to the car, chasing but without fuss.

"It's probably nothing. Probably just a routine letter suggesting your mum make an appointment for a mammogram."

"Will we open it?"

"Um . . . I don't know, really. It's . . . it's addressed to your mum—"

Rose tears the envelope and reads:

Dear Mrs. Bowen,

We would like to remind you of your follow-up appointment at Breast Clinic on 12 June. We were unable to reach you by telephone or e-mail to confirm. Please contact the department to reschedule if you were unable to attend. As stated in the previous letter, in the majority of cases, women have nothing to fear, but it is vital you undergo an ultrasound, results of which the consultant will discuss with you on the day. But nevertheless, it is important you attend in the event you need a biopsy procedure . . .

Rose stops reading and looks to Tess. "Did you know about this? Is Mum all right? The appointment was for yesterday. Look at the date."

"I see." Tess shakes her head. "The truth is, I don't know. I mean, I did know she had a follow-up appointment." Tess takes Rose by the arm and leads her to the sofa, the one that faces the back garden where an iron table and two chairs cast shadows in the fading light. "Sit down. Let's talk this through."

"Just tell me." Rose's lips tremble.

"Two weeks ago, Iris went for a routine mammogram."

"Go on."

"That's it. She was called back for a follow-up. They sometimes do that. That's all. From that letter it seems she didn't confirm her follow-up—"

"Confirm her appointment? She missed her appointment!"

"I know. She missed it. But I trust her. Really, I don't think there is anything to worry about. Something must have come up. I know your mum won't ignore it."

"Then, where is she?"

Tess looks backward through the kitchen window to where the boys are chasing the cat around the car. "Listen, pet, I'll pop over home quickly and drop the boys. Then I'll be straight back. I'll bring some groceries." Tess rises and places her hand on Rose's and kisses the top of her head. "You'll be all right till then?" Tess gives Rose one long look. "Okay?"

Rose wants to believe everything is all right. It must be. If not, that would be too cruel. God isn't like that. Tess is right, her mum probably forgot her phone. Right? And the follow-up is routine. That's it. It's so like Iris to neglect herself, she thinks. Ever since her father died. She walks into her mother's garden, intense with twilight. She's almost forgotten how bright it is in the evenings in the west of Ireland. She gets the hose and traipses across the front of the house to water the flowerpots for something to do while she waits. Iris's garden is aglow with color. Names escape her, but there are blue, star-shaped flowers and red, pokerlike flowers and flat discs of yellow on silvery stalks. Cicero paces across the uncut lawn and nudges her. Rose picks him up and they watch the swallows dart in and out of the stone cabin's doorless doorway. She sits at the wooden table under the porch for a while.

Then from a distance the sound of a motor rumbles on the narrow lane that runs in front of the garden. That was quick. She's dying for a cup of tea and something to eat. And maybe Tess has news. Wherever Iris has gone, she's taken the car. A blur of red breezes past the gaps in the hedgerow. A motor stops, a door clunks open and closes, and in the cabin's dark doorway a figure stands.

Conor Flynn is carrying a violin case. He walks straight toward her, holding the violin over his head. "It arrived yesterday, safe and sound, Rosie girl."

Rose reaches for it. Her hair brushes his face. He holds it a moment higher, then lowers it a bit over her head as if he's about to embrace her but loses confidence at the last moment and gives it to her.

"Thank you," Rose says and holds the case against her chest like it's a baby.

He seems different, she thinks. He's grown older, but still wearing that funny wooly hat. Then she realizes. "You cut your hair?"

"Yeah, too many bad hair days. Always bringing too much sea home with me. The wood didn't like it."

Rose doesn't understand.

"Surfing was playing havoc with my hair *and* my workshop." He laughs, big and open and musical like a major C.

Rose sighs.

"What?" Conor asks. "Tell me you don't like surfers."

"I've only met one and the jury's not totally in on him yet."

"A heartbreaker?"

"Something like that."

The sun has sunk below the tree line and half the garden is in cool shadow. Midges emerge from the grass. Rose and Conor stand like strangers on a train waiting for that moment when a jolt will throw them together or apart. It's Rose's move. It's her house. It's her violin. The least she can do is invite him in.

"May I?" he asks once inside the kitchen, and takes out the violin before she can answer. He tunes it, takes the bow up, and begins to play an Irish reel. He ornaments it like a seasoned player with slides and rolls and triple notes.

"You never said."

"What?" He stops.

"You're a *good* fiddler."

"There's lots about me you don't know." Blue eyes dart from his bow hand to her face, then he continues playing. Music fills the room. It feels like the old walls resonate and release stored memories of *bodhráns* and spoons and ancient sounds of *céilis* and *seisiúns* that happened in the old cottage long before Rose came.

"A gift that can't be taught," she says quietly.

"What?"

"Nothing."

Conor hands her the violin. "Why did you leave it on the tube?"

She stares beyond him and out the window to the blue-flowered vine climbing on the cabin door. She remembers when she and her father painted that door. "To see if it would come back to me."

"Why?"

Rose's voice quivers when she says, "I was thinking of giving up."

He takes this in but doesn't say anything. The evening is gathering into night outside.

"I'm tired."

"Sure," Conor says. "I'll get going, then." He rises.

"I didn't mean that. I mean. Oh. How come life can be so messy all of a sudden?" Her face is flushed and she pushes back her dark hair with both hands. Today it has a bit of a curl to it. She flops down into a chair.

"Tell me," he says.

She looks at him, she looks at the blue eyes that seem full of understanding then, and so she does. She explains it all to him. The master class. Roger. Her mother gone missing. The letter. "Tess thinks that she's gone visiting a garden somewhere and doesn't have her phone with her. I don't know. I thought she'd have rung me by now. It's just not like her."

"I'm sure it'll be all right," he says.

Rose rises quickly. "Why does everybody say that? How do you know? How does anyone know?" She paces. "And where's Tess! She said she'd be right back!" She crosses to the counter and sees for the first time shriveled petals of red poppies and the naked stems with their bulbous seed pods. She bursts like a rain cloud and cries.

Conor goes to her, holds her, and she drops her head against his heart.

A little later Tess does arrive. Rose is standing, playing her violin, and Conor is beside her. A swath of light from the window catches them. Tess looks at Conor, who rises and introduces himself.

"Any news?" Rose asks. The anxiety makes her eyes look frightened.

"Actually, yes," Tess says, still looking at Conor, trying to work out who the stranger is. "Your mum's in Boston."

"What?"

"I know. Crazy Iris."

"A long way to go to visit a garden," Conor says. He takes a sudden in-breath and turns to Rose. "Her phone mightn't work there."

"Right. I told her you were home and—" Tess says.

"Is she okay?"

"Oh yes, Rose. Sorry. She's fine! Absolutely fine." Tess takes her hand. "She's going to ring you now. On the home phone from her hotel. When I told her you were home she was quite worried. Something about a *big* master class you are due to have next week?"

Rose nods. "Yeah, it was Tuesday. It got moved up and I didn't tell her. But *what* did she say about the letter? And the appointment?"

"She didn't and I didn't—" Tess is cut short because just then the phone rings.

All three look to it.

Ten

The next time Hector saw Iris it was the morning after the concert and she was sitting on a bench in the community gardens of
Titus Sparrow Park. Sunlight was hitting her hair. Hector noted
that she looked sad, but he was so wrapped up in figuring how
best to present himself that he didn't quite register the white in
her hand was a tissue. He wasn't ready to officially introduce himself and so crossed the street and kept walking. His pace quickened. When he reached the end of the block, he veered right
toward the river.

The words to "Down to the River to Pray" were running in
his head. After about ten minutes he arrived on the banks of the
Charles. He stopped, faced the river, sank back into his heels in
a sort of Standing Tree meditation, and closed his eyes, needing grounding and inspiration and awaiting it like some thirsty,
rooted thing. A breeze blew hard.

He thought about his vision the night of the concert of

returning the fallen envelope like some knight in shining armor and how it had not in fact materialized. In meditation, more visions of himself, winged and angelic, appeared. And why not? he suddenly thought. Why couldn't he have the angel's part? Calm down, Hector. Breathe.

It was like the start of a new composition where he had a musical phrase, a cluster of notes, but no idea how to continue or in which key to begin, although he knew it was a minor, maybe D or G. Finally, he broke his pose and jogged along the esplanade. Sailboats on the black ripple water circled every which way, their white triangles flapping like swans' wings. The heat of another scorcher sucked up into itself the cool greenness of the grass and in the sky bunches of clouds, staccatolike, shielded the sun periodically. He jogged for about a mile but when he couldn't discharge his restlessness, he decided to return to the South End to discuss it all with Grace.

Grace, dressed in her tennis gear, met him at the front door. She spoke first. "Hector, Hector, we've got a problem."

"Tell me about it!"

"No, really. It's Mrs. Bowen . . . Iris."

"Yeah, I know. I saw her in the gardens sitting—"

"No, she's back. She's in the kitchen now. Her cell phone isn't working so I told her to use my landline. I've just heard her speaking with someone. Someone named Tess. When she hung up she was pacing around the kitchen. I'm afraid whatever this Tess said has upset her." Grace looked at him with those nut brown eyes and whispered, "I think she's crying, Hector."

Grace led him into her office where there was a second door into the kitchen. Iris was on the phone again and they could hear her clearly.

"Hello, honey."

There was a long pause.

Then they heard a kitchen chair scrape against the floor. "Oh, Rosie . . . honey . . . I'm so sorry. I thought your master class was next week. Why didn't you tell me it was changed? Honey? How awful. I would have come. I wanted to come. Rose . . ." Several long silences followed, punctuated by Iris's sighs. "Tell me what happened."

"She's speaking with someone named Rosie," whispered Grace.

Under the circumstances it wasn't right and Hector knew that, but to relieve his own tension he chuckled, "You're a supersleuth, Grace."

She shushed him. "Who is Rosie?"

"Sounds like . . . her daughter?"

Grace's face lit up in a brief register of understanding but suffused quickly into a frown. Grace and Hector sat side-by-side, listening and half hearing; they were like an old, childless couple, strangers to the language of parental discourse.

From snippets of conversation over the next ten minutes, they pieced together that Iris hadn't told her daughter she had come to Boston. And that Rose had some kind of master class that seemingly didn't go well.

"What's a master class?" Grace whispered.

"*Shh.*"

"Doesn't sound good, though, right?"

Hector remembered how Iris had looked the night before, like she was bathed in a quiet sadness, and now whatever was going on was only adding to it. He stood, peeked in through the crack in the door. Sitting, her hand like a vise gripping her forehead, shielding her eyes, with her elbow on the table as a fulcrum, Iris rocked from side to side. She was explaining in that soft Irish cadence—music to his ears—that she was in Boston on a gardening gig. She'd got hired last-minute on an assignment for a UK newspaper, so she said, and she'd tried to ring yesterday but her cell phone wasn't connected to a network. "As soon as I realized I rang you from here where I'm staying, but it didn't connect. Yes. That's right, honey. That's why I rang Tess at home."

"Gardening assignment? Hector . . . ?"

"I know. I'm thinking, Grace." A musician friend of Hector's once told him that it's the silence in between where the real stuff is going on.

"Oh . . . you opened it?"

There was silence.

Then Iris said, "I didn't tell you because I didn't want to worry you. Honey? . . . Don't cry. Please . . . Rose? I'm sure it's nothing. Absolutely. Really, I'll be fine. I will, I promise. Dr. O'Reilly said I shouldn't be worried. Honestly. Please don't worry. Rose?" Pause. Sighs. Iris's voice dropped lower. "I know. I know it was yesterday. I'll reschedule as soon as I get home. No. It's the weekend, I can't ring now. Okay. Okay. I will. I'll be home in just a few days. I promise."

Grace's mouth dropped open, but she covered the startled sound it made with her hand. She whispered, "Oh dear, this—"

"This is no ordinary conversation between mother and daughter," Hector said.

"I love you, sweetheart." Another scrape of the chair sounded against the floor, then a clunk of the phone receiver being replaced. Iris passed by the office on her way upstairs, as if she was trying to be invisible. The sound of her footsteps disappeared and a door closed.

"I should go to her, right?" Grace said.

"And say what? 'I was being nosy and listened to your conversation'? I don't think so. No. No, Grace. Here's what we do. I'll knock on her door under the pretense of returning the envelope. And see how she is."

After a few moments Hector went upstairs, but just short of reaching the top step he stopped when he heard weeping. It took him by surprise. It was thoughtless of him, perhaps. He was acting from a cavalier notion that he could rescue Iris. But her crying made it suddenly real. He stood a few moments in the hallway outside her door, the green walls, like a forest, closing in on him. He was lost. Way out of his comfort zone.

He tiptoed on by Iris's door and went to his own room down the hall. He got a blank piece of staff paper from his sheet music and wrote:

Dear Iris,

He crossed that out and wrote:

Hello Iris,

Crossed that out and wrote:

Dear Mrs. Bowen,

Unsure how to put his feelings into words, he put down the pen. He was a musician, for cripes sake, not a man of letters. Like a tourist in lovelorn territory, he was finding his way alone. He got a fresh piece and started again.

Mrs. Bowen,

Hope you enjoyed the concert last night. Thanks for coming. I was happy to see you there.

    Here's the envelope you dropped in the Mapparium. It fell from your bag. I was just arriving as you were leaving yesterday. I saw it. I saw you.

    I hope I'll see you later . . .

Hector Sherr

Room 12

P.S. I hope everything's all right . . .

He folded the letter around the envelope and held it to his chest. He wanted to kiss it and for a moment he was eleven years old on Valentine's Day in Woodside Elementary School in California, where he grew up.

Outside Iris's door Hector stood, listening to the quiet on the other side. He brought his fist to within an inch of the door several times, but in the end lost his courage. Finally, he slid the letter under her door and went downstairs, quickly, blushing like a schoolboy, and flew out onto the street.

Had he been too blunt? *P.S. I hope everything's all right?* Would she know they had overheard her? Oh. Now he wished he hadn't added the P.S. Did he always have to go one step too far?

He crossed the plaza. The splash fountain was turned off but a small crowd sat on the gray lip of the reflecting pool and cooled their feet. Thinking about Iris, about *Sparrow in Summer,* and listening to the summered voices mixing with the midmorning traffic, he stopped and closed his eyes. There was a kind of odd harmony to it all, rainbow-colored even.

"Mr. Sherr?"

A voice, breathless, was calling from behind him. At first he thought he'd imagined it.

"Mr. Sherr?" He turned. His heart, as if separating from springs, leapt from its held place and zipped toward her. Iris. She was holding his letter.

"Thank you. For your note."

"Anytime."

She looked at him with surprise.

"I mean—"

"And for . . .' She stopped. Iris smiled weakly and what followed was a long pause when neither of them seemed to know what to do. It was the first time Hector was close to her. Her eyes were very clear, with tiny lines that stretched from the corners to her temples. The crying had only just left them. She had a pale patch of freckles across the bridge of her nose. Her hair had been quickly tied up, but strands fell in twirls about her face and neck and she tried to fix them behind her ears. She was in a white cotton blouse and blue jeans. She was gorgeous, he thought. As he looked down he saw she was barefoot.

She turned to go but he caught her arm and blurted, "Stay. Let's walk. Get a coffee. See the river." His hands flung to the sides of his head as he stuttered.

Iris didn't seem to notice his gawkiness, or if she had, it didn't matter. She looked down to her feet and Hector put his hand on her back and, to his great surprise, she let herself be guided back to Grace's. While Iris went in to get shoes, Hector waited outside, not wanting to dilute the spell he felt cast under. When she reappeared she was wearing sandals. Sunglasses nestled on top of her head. They walked north and cut through the Prudential Center Plaza, and continued on a few short blocks. Neither of them spoke. They passed onto Gloucester with its ornate streetlamps and old Victorian brownstones with their ancient lead-glass windows and black window frames. Crossing over Comm Ave., the street widened into two-way traffic and was divided down the middle by a tree-lined pedestrian walk. Iris looked into the shaded tunnel carved by the trees.

"Can we sit?"

"Great idea." Hector swung around, looked for an empty spot, and strode to the nearest bench, landing with a thud as if in being able to claim it for her so solidly he was gallant. And just like that there she was, Iris of the blue dress sitting right there beside him. Her hands were folded in her lap. She looked up and down the tree-lined mall and across the avenue at the redbrick buildings.

"Magnolias," he said.

"What?"

"Those trees you're looking at. They're saucer magnolias. This place is famous for them. In early May the streets are lit up like little pink and white balloons." He was chuffed with himself and hoped he'd impressed her. If truth were told, everyone in Boston knew that about the magnolias in spring along Comm Ave. He didn't know a thing about trees.

After a few moments she said, "I enjoyed the concert last night. Hearing you play—"

"Thank you," he said. "That was a great audience." He relaxed his tall frame, unfurling like a fern, fanning out across the bench, his arms abreast along the top rung.

"We don't have too many outdoor concerts like that but we—"

"Ireland? Right?" He'd cut her off with his enthusiasm and immediately felt sorry.

"We do have a music festival every summer."

"Yeah, of course you do. Everybody's heard of the Cork Jazz Festival. I mean, anyone in the jazz world."

"Actually we have one near where I live. Doonbeg."

Hector raised his eyebrows with a look that said, *Wow*. But before he could ask her more about it she added, "My daughter's a musician, too."

"I'm sorry," he blurted (thinking back to the morning's phone conversation). "I mean, what does she play?"

Iris looked at him quizzically but continued. "The violin. Classical violin."

"Double wow." Suddenly it was impossible for him to know what more to say because he felt guilty and thought it must be written on his face. Next she would tell him her name.

"Her name is Rose."

He wanted to say something. But what? *Say something supportive.* "I like the way you wear your hair."

Iris looked at him and then couldn't help herself, she laughed. Really laughed. It was as if a river rippled from her and spilled onto the path and climbed up the trees, a sort of tintinnabulation. And Hector felt it, too, and laughed with her. Didn't hold back.

Hector jumped up and held out his hand. She took it briefly, then let go. Then, as if feeling less cautious, she walked forward. After a few blocks, they'd crossed onto the footbridge over Storrow Drive, then down to the Charles, where they walked along the esplanade. Hector felt surprisingly jaunty and began humming. Iris's footfalls were soft and she picked a long blade of grass and swung it around in the air. It was one of those near perfect days of summer, blue sky even though hot. And for a moment, Hector imagined they were just two second-chance lovers sauntering·on a midsummer's morning along one of the finest promenades on the eastern coast of America.

"Hector?" Iris said at last, her voice a different tempo and thinner. "Can you show me where the public library is?"

"The library? Sure. Yeah. It's not too far, but we have to cross back over."

She stopped. "I need to find someone."

"In the . . . library?"

"Billy said I could use the Internet there. Isn't that right?"

"Oh, right. But you don't *need* the library. I have my laptop with me back at Grace's. We can go there if you like and you can use mine."

Iris considered. "All right," she said at last, and they turned back. She told him then that her daughter, Rose, was studying at the Royal Academy of Music in London.

"Well, now I'm impressed." Hector said most Americans probably wouldn't have heard of it, but he had because he taught music composition at Berklee. "I mean, we have Juilliard, and Oberlin, too, and right here . . . well . . . over there"—he pointed as they crossed back over Huntington—"is the New England Conservatory. But the RAM? Wow. She must be *really* good." They kept walking, but Iris had picked up the pace.

Hector at last orchestrated his thoughts about Hilary Barrett of 99 St. Botolph Street and now Iris's promise about rescheduling some appointment. A further thought struck him. A discordant note. How had he not heard it before? Because he was a selfish so-and-so.

He looked quickly to her hand.

"You and . . . um . . . Mr. Bowen must be truly proud of her."

"Yes. Very. Very proud of her."

"I mean, sure—"

She stopped. Hector thought he'd insulted her. She looked away. "Luke, her father, died two years ago." Then she walked on.

It's a terrible thing in a man when half his heart is going one way, feeling sad, but in the other half, the strings of joy are playing full on. What could he say? "I'm sorry."

They walked the remaining few minutes in silence, then once back at Grace's went upstairs to their rooms, having agreed to meet in Grace's old parlor in half an hour. Hector wasted no time, changed his shirt quickly for another of his Hawaiians, the olive green one with blue flowers, got his laptop, and raced back down.

Billy appeared from the kitchen. "Hey, Hector?"

"Billy." Hector had arranged two armchairs around the coffee table. "Is Grace around?"

"No. Playing tennis with the seniors."

"Good! I mean, good for Grace. Mrs. Hale. Her enthusiasm is a lesson for us all, hey? Listen, kid, me and Mrs. Bowen will be working in here."

"Oh?"

"Mrs. Bowen needs to send some e-mails. I'm letting her use my laptop."

Billy gave Hector a knowing look.

"I'm hooked. What can I say? But that's between you and me."

When Iris eventually appeared she'd changed clothes, too, and had washed her hair. It was still wet, the ends curving into scrolls, and dampening patches on her cotton blouse. Billy reappeared and she asked him for a pot of tea.

Hector turned the open laptop toward Iris. "Here you go." The cursor beat in the search bar.

"I've never done this before."

"What?" He pulled his chair closer to hers. She was still cool from showering and her hair smelled like apples.

"I've never 'searched' for a person before."

Iris typed in "Hilary Barrett." Hector didn't say a word.

A 0.16-second search yielded nearly six million entries. She turned to him startled. "There can't be *that* many people with the same name! I'll never find her."

"Try 'Boston phone book,' " Hector said.

Her face reddened. "What? Why Boston?"

Hector stammered. "It . . . it was on the envelope . . . 99 St. Botolph Street. Right? I'm sorry. That's around the corner?"

She thought about this for a second. "Right. The envelope. Of course." Those gray eyes closed for a second.

"I'm sorry. It's none of my business." Hector looked at her, but she was looking out the window toward the park. After a long pause, she said, "It's complicated. And . . . she wasn't there. I went yesterday. It's a restaurant, you know?" Back at the screen she typed "Boston phone book." Her eyes scanned the first page of results. Top was White Pages.com.

Just then Grace opened the door carrying a tray. She was still in her tennis shorts. A gold chain was half hidden beneath her polo shirt.

"Iris! How are you? Billy said you'd like some tea. Here you go." As she laid down the tray, her face obscured from Iris, she looked at Hector, thin eyebrows raised.

"Hector—"

"Gracie, Gracie, Gracie. Good match?"

"Wonderful . . . So you've finally met our Hector? Is he behaving himself? He's a bit of wild card. Isn't that right, Hector?"

Grace edged closer and squinted to see what was on the screen, but couldn't. As she turned away, her red lips quivered, twitching to say something.

"I'm trying to locate an old friend," Iris said at last. "Someone I met a long time ago in Dublin. She used to live in Boston."

"Oh?"

"A Hilary Barrett."

"Hil—"

"We're searching the White Pages on the 'Net," Hector interrupted, his tone suddenly harsh, cocked, and aimed at Grace. Iris seemed to sense there was a subplot, or so Hector feared, so he smiled at Grace then.

"Right. Yes. Of course," Grace said. "Good idea. The White Pages. Well, you never know. Right? Always a good place to start, with the telephone book." Grace walked toward the door but turned before leaving. Iris couldn't see that she held her hands open as if ready to catch something. Like an answer. Eyes so wide that if they had been speaking they'd have been saying, *Hector, what have you found out?* Hector shushed her away with a small wave of his hand.

In all, there were thirteen search results for Hilary Barrett in the White Pages for Massachusetts. But only one in the age bracket that matched Iris's guesstimation: Becket, MA.

"It's probably not her." She thought a moment. "Where is Becket? Maybe she moved there?" She fell silent again. She shook her head. "Anyway. I just can't ring her up—"

"Sure. Sure you can. She'll remember you. I mean . . . yours is not a voice one easily forgets." *Hector, Hector, Hector. What are you saying?*

Iris paused. She stared at the screen. Her face flushed as she took this in. "No, I mean. I don't even know her. She's not an old friend," she said at last. She bit her lower lip hard. Looked around the room and at the closed door. "She's my daughter's birth mother."

Hector sat back and inclined his head forward and his mouth formed an "oh." He looked surprised because he was. The missing piece had fallen into place, but it wasn't what he'd expected.

"Rose is my adopted daughter." Iris closed the laptop. Her hands lay on her lap and she made small fists with them. And then she explained: the promise she'd made to her husband before he died but had never carried out; how she'd "stolen" the envelope just a few days earlier from the Adoption Board and got the name and address; and that yesterday when she visited 99 St. Botolph Street, the man there had never heard of a woman named Hilary Barrett.

She explained it all except for the now missed appointment and the reason for it.

"So you see, I can't just ring her up, even if this Hilary Barrett in Becket *is* the woman I'm looking for."

She was elegant in her distress. She held it together. There was strength in this woman; Hector wondered if she knew she had it. Her story was breaking his heart, but his heart had a mind of its own and, to paraphrase the great Irish singer/songwriter, his heart was doing his thinking and it was leading him into a danger zone. He needed more time. More time to get to wherever this was going and to figure out some way to help her, and so in a flush of feeling he found himself saying, "Why don't I drive you there?"

"What?"

"Sure. Why not? Plan B. You could get out of the city heat and see some country."

"Is it far?"

"Becket? Not really. About two hours. West across the state. Into the Berkshires. Part of the Appalachian mountain range and really—"

"I don't know."

"I'll ask Grace if we can borrow the car."

"Please! Please don't tell her—"

"No. No. Of course not."

"Why," she continued, "it's probably nothing. I've been pretty unlucky so far."

Hector laid his hand on hers. "Sure. I understand. Your secret's—" Iris looked at him. She pulled her hand away like it'd been stung by a bee.

"Sorry, I'm not good with words. What I meant was—"

"It's okay. I think I know what you meant."

"I just want to . . . you know . . . help." He reached for her hand and held it firmly for a second, then let go. "I meant to tell you last night before the concert, but you weren't around. I want to help you because . . . you helped me."

"What?" Her eyes widened.

"Yeah. Yesterday morning. I finished my piece because of you . . . *you* were my inspiration."

A group of young teenagers cycled past the window, their voices loud and happy. He watched her watching them until they cycled out of sight. Iris stood and went to the window. After a few moments, she walked toward Hector, put her hand briefly on his shoulder, and said, "Okay," and then went out the front door and crossed the street to the park.

Christine Breen

Hector found Grace and Billy in the office and when he told Grace that he wanted to borrow her car to take Iris to the Berkshires, she gave him that mother of all looks.

"What have you found out? What's the appointment? And who is she looking for? Is it the name on the envelope? Have you found her?"

"Nothing about the appointment, and not exactly."

"Hector! Tell me."

"It's a needle in a haystack, Grace. We found one Hilary Barrett in Becket, Massachusetts. What are the chances? Right, Billy?"

"Hilary Barrett. Hilary Barrett." Grace mused and screwed her round, dolphinlike eyes closed. "I *know* that name." Billy and Hector waited. Waiting for Grace to clarify, but she kept shaking her head and closing her eyes. "I can't remember. Oh . . ."

"I might be able to help," Billy said at last. Grace and Hector looked to him. "I mean. I am in *computers*. What do we know?"

"Of course. Billy. Computers! Now." Grace spoke excitedly, her voice rising.

"We only know that she is Mrs. Bowen's daughter's birth mother," said Hector.

Billy raised his eyebrows. "That's a mouthful."

"And, that this Hilary Barrett *once* lived at 99 St. Botolph Street. That's about it. Right?" Hector looked to Grace. "She'd be around . . . I don't know. What do *you* think? How old is Iris?"

"Oh my. She's so pretty. Um? Early forties?"

"Yeah, that's what I'm thinking. So her daughter is . . . like . . . twenty?"

"No. Nearly nineteen," Billy said and Grace and Hector looked

160

to him. "Yeah, she told me yesterday morning when we were talking at breakfast and—"

"Right. Okay." Hector was nodding his head up and down in
a kind of staccatolike beat in double-time. "That makes this Hilary anywhere from forty to forty-five. Ish. Yeah?" Hector was
bouncing on his toes now. Rocking back and forth. "Okay. See
if you can find anything out, kiddo."

"Will do."

Then, as if in silent consent, they left in separate directions.
Grace to the kitchen to plan that evening's dinner, Billy to his
laptop to see what he could find out. And Hector to his room,
where he lay down and waited for the sound of Iris's footsteps
returning.

Eleven

The thing about Iris Bowen was she liked to talk to people, even strangers. Like a few days earlier with Thornton Pletz, the Polish-American waiter at Botolph's. If it hadn't been for the dead-ended conversation about Hilary, she would have gone on and asked him about his family in Europe. Had he any relatives still there? Did he have children? Or, with Kerry at the airport the day she arrived, if she hadn't been so overwhelmed with the sense of arrival and her mission, Iris would have asked in what village in County Kerry her granny was born.

At home in Clare, she struck up conversations with the people behind shop counters, too. With the man who sold her flowers on a Wednesday afternoon at the street market in Ennis, with the fair-haired fishmonger from Slovakia, who had developed a habit of asking each time he met her, "When is Rose due back?" To which Iris usually replied, "In a few weeks." Her answer, too, had become a habit. Their frequent exchanges (Iris always bought a piece of halibut from him on a Friday) had turned to repartee, which made the Slovakian and other customers in the fish shop smile.

A few things like that, little anchors, helped her cope with loss. And, it made her feel less lonely.

Before flowers and fish, Iris would often meet Tess for lunch in Ennis. In winter they sat in old feather-stuffed chairs beside the fire, just inside the front door of the Old Ground Hotel. In the summer they sat in garden chairs under the ancient beech tree on the moss-lined patio. They became regulars among regulars and the owner, an art lover named Allen, got to know their names. He never failed to ask how Rose was getting on. He'd known Luke because Luke often lunched there on his noncourt days and they'd become friends. When Luke was in hospital, Allen would send meals from the hotel's kitchen. One day he had driven all the way out to Ashwood to deliver a bread-and-butter pudding, which was Luke's favorite.

All of this Iris thought about the following morning as she stood at the bedroom window upstairs in Grace Hale's house, wondering if she should phone Tess again. She was sure Grace wouldn't mind if she used her phone. She listened to the unfamiliar sounds of Boston's early morning traffic, of buses and cars and garbage trucks. American cities woke so early. She was used to birds and tractors and, at this time of year, the disappearing song of the cuckoo.

Her hands were restless and she kept fussing with her hair. Twice since rising, Iris had changed her clothes. Nothing looked right. Sitting on the bed fastening her sandals she recalled the dream she'd had early that morning. Luke was in it.

He was walking out of the sea holding a box. He walked toward her but the tide kept coming with him and he made no progress to the shore. He wasn't struggling, just walking in his suit, ankle deep in the tide pools. He smiled. She couldn't see what was in the box he carried from the sea.

She missed her garden—her own garden—where things had a way of working themselves out. A knock on the door made Iris jump. She opened it to find Hector, who had a tray that held a teapot and some toast and a daisy in a water glass.

"I thought maybe we could get a head start on breakfast and hit the road when you're ready," he said and he put the tray down on her made-up bed. He stood back as if somehow proud of himself. "You still want to go, don't you?"

She nodded. "I'll be down"—she hesitated—"in a bit. Five minutes."

"Great." He clapped his hands together. "I'll get the car ready."

Iris looked at the daisy. Some of its petals were missing. As if someone had plucked them.

Grace had agreed to lend Hector her old Jaguar so he could drive into the Berkshire Mountains to show Iris some of America. Or at least that's what Grace had thought the previous night when they met for meat loaf and salad in her kitchen.

"To see some of my great state of Massachusetts, right?"

The table was laid with bone china and linen napkins and an assortment of lit candles. "I asked Billy to tidy up the car for your little road trip tomorrow," Grace had said, pulling her muumuu that had gathered tight beneath her gold belt. She'd looked at Hector, whose teeth slightly eclipsed his bottom lip. His eyes seemed charged with some meaning Iris didn't understand. Grace returned his scrutiny, then turned to Iris and went on. "Bob loved that car. You'll like it. Drives like a dream. I couldn't give it up when he died. I know it's old—"

"Gracie, you're a visionary," Hector had said promptly, and pulled the chair for her to sit. He'd poured her wine and given her a look, which Iris found puzzling. Grace drank half the glass in one long sip.

"You'd better watch him, Iris, he's a charmer." Her voice had a curious undertone, Iris thought, as she watched her cut the meat loaf into slices.

During the supper, Iris succeeded in not having to talk about herself. Grateful the subject of the phone calls to Ireland was not referred to, she had instead asked questions. She'd learned about the renovation of the South End, which had been Grace's passion for twenty years. Learned how Hector had answered an ad for a spare room and how he ended up living with Bob and Grace when he was a student at Berklee, and how long ago the neighborhood around St. Botolph had been populated by jazz musicians.

"Hector wore his hair in a ponytail those days," Grace said distractedly.

Hector glanced sideways at Iris.

Grace continued, "You know, Botolph is the patron saint of Boston. It was named after him when the Pilgrims came here in the early 1600s. Right, Hector?"

"Something like that, Gracie."

With a twinge of regret that here she was sitting, listening to something she knew Luke would have been more interested in than she was, Iris recalled when he'd told Rosie that a Bowen ancestor had been a passenger on the *Mayflower*, survived the journey, and landed at Plymouth Rock. Rose was doing a genealogy chart in primary school. Iris remembered because Rose was distressed about it. "Are they *my* ancestors, too?" she'd asked.

"Of course! What's mine is yours, *ma petite chou*," Luke had said.

And with that Rose was happy. If she ever struggled about her biological connections, she hid it well. Maybe she'd locked it away in a box. Iris could never be sure.

"Yes, I remember now," Grace said. "Something about a stone and a monastery and a Benedictine abbot named Botwulf in England. English Pilgrims landed here and called it Boston. I can't quite remember the connection. I have it written down somewhere." She paused. "If you're interested I can find it. You know—" Grace stopped suddenly and looked directly at Iris. "You know, I never asked you what brought you to Boston."

"Grace! None of our business, I think."

"I'm doing a gardening piece on Boston city gardens," Iris said. She said it quickly, and she didn't look at Hector.

"Oh?" Grace turned the wine in her glass. "That's nice."

They ate in silence for a little while.

"Enough for me," Hector said, his hand covering his glass when Grace attempted to fill it from a third bottle. She looked to Iris, who shook her head gently.

"But thank you. It's been a lovely evening."

"Pleasure, I'm sure," Grace replied with a just little too much emphasis on her Ss. "Sorry it was only meat loaf. Not much of a cook since Bob . . ." She paused and spoke pointedly to Iris. "It's never the same. But we manage. We get on with it." She rose and stood for a moment and looked toward the door. Hector got up then and put his arm around her, kissed her cheek, and led her out the door, his hasty movement making the candles flicker. For a moment then, light mottled the room and Iris had sat alone, feeling guilty that she had lied and wondering what she was going to say to Hilary Barrett in Becket, Massachusetts, the next day.

Now, in the sun-drenched morning, Iris locked her bedroom door and went downstairs. She looked into the breakfast room for Grace, but only Billy was there, serving a table of two young couples. More of Kerry's special people? she wondered. He was telling them about the Mapparium.

Hector appeared at the front door. "Ready?" A swish of heat rushed in as he held the door open. His tall frame blocked the light coming through the doorway.

"Yes."

"Wait!" Grace called when they were in the hallway. She came, still in her white terry-cloth bathrobe, carrying a basket. "I've some chicken sandwiches and lemonade. For your journey."

"You're too good." Iris took the basket, gave Grace a half hug with her free arm.

"Thanks, Gracie." Hector stood at the door and opened it wider, an edgy look raising his eyebrows.

Iris moved past him, down the steps to the car.

"Oh . . . wait! I remembered something," Grace called.

"What?" asked Hector.

Ignoring him, Grace looked to Iris. "About St. Botolph . . . he's known as the patron saint of travelers and wayfarers."

Iris gave the basket to Hector and went back up the steps and hugged Grace with both arms. "You're a pet, as we say in Ireland. A real pet."

"Ohhhh," Grace said, teary-eyed, adjusting the belt of her

robe. "I do hope everything works out. It can, you know. Sometimes. Right?"

How suddenly surreal Iris's life felt then. So unfamiliar was the blue day, the heat, the fancy car, and, not least, the man sitting beside her, humming. His quirky manner mystified her. Even excited her. She hadn't been in the solo company of a man since her husband died. Not really. Not like this. Hector's eyes shot from the rearview to the side mirror as he pulled the car quickly away from the curb. He wasn't a smooth driver.

As they passed along St. Botolph, she noted the dark windows of the restaurant. It was Sunday, Thornton would be opening for brunch soon. At the corner of her mind was the look on Grace's face as they pulled away. It was a look of a thousand words, none of which Iris understood, and she wondered if she was meant to.

"Is Grace all right?"

"Grace? Sure, fine. She's probably a little under the weather. You know? Too much vino. No need to worry." Hector drove the car west along Huntington. It seemed like he wanted to hurry. He pressed and released the accelerator as if pumping the car forward. She found it a little disturbing. After a few moments he turned the car right onto a larger road, and, as if she could hear his thoughts rummaging about in his head, flicking through his repertoire of suitable topics for discussion with a woman he hardly knew, but was trying to impress, she awaited his conversation. She looked out the window as they passed the Mary Baker Eddy Library and recalled the pink Irish family in the Mapparium and wondered where they were sweltering today. She hoped for their sakes they were at a beach. And for one brief moment, she wished she were there with them, safe among her own.

"That's Berklee," Hector said finally, and pointed. "Over there. Some of my happiest days—"

"Is it?" Iris said with a little more gusto then she'd intended, turning her head toward him but regretting her enthusiasm immediately.

What was she doing? She grabbed her hair, which uncharacteristically, she had braided loosely that morning. Like a schoolgirl's. She began to untie it. She was looking for Hilary Barrett—that's what she was doing. Focus, Iris.

A horn blared from behind. Hector's eyes darted sideways and his head turned over his right shoulder. He was in the wrong lane. He flicked on the indicator, veered sharply off under the large green sign, MASSACHUSETTS TURNPIKE, and swung the car down the ramp onto the highway. It had happened too quickly for Iris to be scared. Hector was shaking his head and mumbling. Iris rubbed her elbow, which had struck the window.

"You hurt?"

"No. It's okay."

"I'm really sorry. God. I'm usually a good driver. Just a bit out of practice." He slowed and settled into the middle lane. "I usually bike to work from where I live."

"Oh?"

"Yeah, I teach composition at the conservatory in San Francisco. I'm just here in Boston in the summer." He looked at her like he was going to say something more, like he was searching for words to explain himself, but he didn't.

They drove west on the interstate, cutting through an abundant landscape of cedar trees at the edge of the city. And because she didn't want only Hilary Barrett running in her mind, Iris said, "Tell me about Berklee?"

Hector hesitated only for a moment. "Really?"

"Really. I do know a little bit about music schools."

"Of course you do. Right. I forgot. Rose. Well . . . for me, jazz is the thing. Not classical. Sorry. I eat, drink, sleep it. Berklee's like the best jazz place for students in this country. Maybe the world." He paused, but only for a second. "Ever hear of Quincy Jones? He was there before my time, but what an inspiration. 'Dream a dream so big that if you just get half of it, you'll still do okay.' Pure Quincy. When I was a student"—Hector laughed—"actually . . . when I was at Grace and Bob's, in the room you're in, I'd lay awake at night and think what was the biggest dream I could dream."

"Why don't you teach there all the time?" As soon as she'd said it, the penny dropped. Oh God, he's married. She turned to the window. That's what the look on Grace's face was about! She turned back. "Are you—?" She stopped herself, then realized she had to ask. "Are you married?"

"No. No. I'm not." He glanced across at her. "I was. Once."

"Children?"

"No."

Iris didn't want to know anymore right then, although his "once" lingered on the air like an echo.

Hector turned on the radio. Jazz with Eric Somebody or Other and soon he was drumming his fingers on the steering wheel. Inside the music, his driving improved. The Jag's old air-conditioning made spurting noises so they turned it off and opened the windows. Iris's hair curled about her face and she reached for it, tying it back again.

"In answer to your first question"—he looked over to her—

"I love teaching at Berklee and a lot of great things happened there and came from there, but I love California. More." His face was tan and nearly handsome but his eyes were timid, shylike. In having returned his gaze Iris sensed he was infatuated with her. She could feel it in her body, somewhere in her center, and it sent signals up and down, like sunrays lighting the dark.

Sitting as a passenger in a car gave her more comfort than just about anything else. Responsibility deferred to the driver and all other thoughts adjourned. She missed that—being a passenger. Such a simple thing. A thing you never think of when there's two of you. Now she had to drive everywhere herself. When Luke was alive, Sundays saw them driving with Rose to the sea and up the west coast to Blackhead.

Iris let her hand extend out the open window. Her fingers felt the air, like she was combing waves.

"Ever heard of the Real Book?" Hector said after they'd been driving a while.

"No . . . but sounds *real* interesting." She laughed. She'd made a joke. An actual joke. Something about Hector was bringing out a side of her that had gone underground. Okay, he was a bit eccentric, but she had to admit also there was a vibrancy in him that energized her. And although part of her resisted it, and even felt guilty, another part of her welcomed it. "Sorry. Tell me more."

"Yeah?"

"No."

"Oh."

"Kidding. Go on."

"Jazz isn't like anything else, right?" he began, glancing at her to make sure. She nodded. "In the old days we used to play tunes from lead sheets, copied from old Tune-Dex cards. But these were full of mistakes. Then the tunes were compiled into the Real Book, because before that there was . . ."

"Don't tell me," said Iris, feeling irrepressibly girlish, "a fake book."

Hector had relaxed. His laugh said so. Big and staccatolike and far removed from the brusque figure who'd stamped from the breakfast room on her first morning, just a couple days earlier.

"Seriously . . ." he went on.

Iris pretended to look serious.

"At the tail end of my years at Berklee, I sort of got myself involved with two guys, teachers, who put together—what became famously known in the jazz world as the Real Book. Every jazz player had to have one." Hector's eyes were alight and his voice quickened. "There are *hundreds* of tunes out there, but nobody was keeping track of them—exactly—I mean except for what came out in the Fakebook—"

"So . . . there *were* fake books?"

"Oh yeah. And just to confuse things, the Real Book is actually a Fakebook." He laughed.

"I see." She didn't, but she admired his enthusiasm.

"It's too confusing. The dudes whose songs were in the Fakebooks weren't getting royalties. But there was no other way for young jazz musicians to learn, so it became the reference for every jazz song there ever was, the main link for students to jam and practice. It was called 'fake' because it was illegitimate." Hector paused. "Get it?" But Iris had turned away. She was looking out the window. Somewhere between the "illegitimate" and "fake" he'd lost her.

"I'm rambling. Sorry. Once I get started on the Real Book . . . it still blows my mind." Hector drummed his fingers on the dashboard of the Jag like it was a keyboard and he was playing the melody to the song playing on the radio.

Iris stayed looking at the Massachusetts countryside from the passenger window. *He* doesn't get it, she thought. Illegitimate. Fake. Real. Come on. But as hurtful as it was, Iris didn't blame him for cutting too close to the bone, or for being unaware that he had. It was something she had been dealing with her whole mothering life. Feeling like an imposter.

When they had been driving for about half an hour deep into western Massachusetts and were into the Berkshire Mountains, Hector pulled off the interstate at an exit called Lily Pond and explained it was where he used to stop on his way to Tanglewood. "There's a jazz festival there in September," he told her. "Maybe it's a good idea to stretch our legs, or something. Have Grace's picnic. Okay?" He pulled the car into a parking lot by the pond.

"Okay, Hector," she said, hiding her apprehension. The more she thought about it, the more she felt she had no reference point for this sort of thing. None of it felt quite right now, standing in the open New England air in her summer dress, holding a picnic basket. The girlishness she'd let herself experience earlier was lost. The flirtation she'd allowed herself stung. The noon sun intensified an immense guilt.

In the trunk Hector had found a blanket. "Grace thinks of everything." Facing the water a few meters from the shoreline he considered where to put it. The ground was hard and stony where it slipped into the brown mountain lake. A breeze blew feebly. It wasn't enough to cool Iris, who stood holding the basket.

"Here, Iris. Shade. Over there." Hector had found a wooden table a little way back from the water's edge. Into the pine woods of white, filtered light Iris made out a stone shelter. Hiking socks hung along a rope tied between two trees, and beach towels and T-shirts draped over bushes like scattered flags. A young woman in a bathing suit came from behind the cabin, chased by a young man in shorts. Sidestepping rocks as she reached the water, the woman dove and swam in strong strokes.

Hector brushed pine needles away and laid the blanket on the bench and the basket on the picnic table. "Madam," he said, and gestured theatrically.

Iris sat facing the water, her back leaning against the hard edge of the table.

The man at the water's edge dove in loudly after the girl and when his head surfaced he shouted. "Fuck! It's cold!" He swam wild, jerky strokes with his head out of the water, not a match for the woman he was chasing, who had reached a floating platform a short distance out and emerged up the ladder like some water nymph. It was a summer's scene worthy of an American movie, but it only made Iris feel worse.

Hector emptied the basket and came around to face her, offering a sandwich. "Has Grace told you yet she makes the best chicken sandwiches?"

Not looking at him, she unwrapped the sandwich and left it open on her lap. She wasn't sure what to say. They sat in their silence together while the untroubled voices of the two swimmers echoed across the pond.

"Tell me what you know about her," Hector said at last.

"About who? The *real* mother?"

Stunned, he looked at the ground, shifted his weight, and his shoulders rose to his ears. "It was all that dumb talk. What a jerk I am. I'm sorry."

"It's not your fault." Iris put her uneaten sandwich on the table and stood up abruptly. "What am I doing here?" She turned around as if ready to go. It was as if her feelings had finally caught up with her thoughts. "I don't even know you." She smoothed the linen dress, which was wrinkled in lines across her thighs. "I'm in the middle of nowhere with a man I've only just met on my way to talk to a woman who might be the mother of *my* child. How un*real* is that?"

Hector just looked at her, eyes of a wounded child who'd just been scolded.

"I've got to calm down before I lose the run of myself." She sat again and started to take off her sandals. She had it in her mind to cool down by standing in the water, but changed her mind midway and restrapped them. She turned to Hector and said, "Can we go, please? I don't want to be here."

"Yeah, sure, Iris. Sorry. My fault. I thought it would be nice to come here. But it was wrong. I'm sorry. I—"

"Hector! Stop saying that. It's not your fault. It's mine. I let myself be persuaded this was a good idea, to go looking for Hilary Barrett . . . with you. You're just trying to help me." She sat down again and, looking to the two swimmers in the pond, she said, "I did meet her once, okay? But I can't tell you anything about her except what she was wearing. And that she was quiet. And very pretty. Young, in her early twenties. She seemed really nice, but it was extremely awkward. You get one chance at a thing like that. You hope for the best. You hope everyone is doing the right thing. The right thing for . . . for . . . for Rose. That's what we all felt. And now, now. Oh! I don't know what I'm doing!"

"Let's go back to Boston." Hector had jumped up and was already packing up.

"No." She looked out to the swimmers on the float. "Take me to Becket."

175

"What?"

"Take me to Becket."

"Are you sure?" He stood his full height and came toward her. He put his hands on her shoulders.

She looked up to him and nodded. "At least I can feel that I've tried. I know it's a long shot. Part of me feels now that I'm just going through the motions. On a quest that I already know will end without an answer."

She felt it again. That buzz in her center, but she eased herself away from his gathering embrace. Now Hector seemed very unsure of himself. "Lily Pond was a bad idea," he said.

"I felt trapped."

"Sorry."

"Stop apologizing. Please."

His phone rang. He looked at the number. "I'd better take this," he said, and while Iris put the basket and blanket in the car he walked back to the water's edge with his phone. The call lasted only moments, but when Hector came back up and got into the car he seemed distant. He drove in silence. Lily Pond vanished behind them and the road flowed away ahead. Now as he drove, one hand on the wheel, he fussed with his hair with his free hand. The man who'd earlier been joyfully engaged in explaining the difference between Real Books and Fakebooks had become subdued. They were another ten miles farther on before he said, "Iris, we should talk about . . . Hilary."

"There's nothing more to say until I meet her. If . . . I meet her."

"She . . ." He hesitated. With his right hand he pulled on the cords of his throat. He pressed his lips together, released them. "She mightn't be there," he said.

"I know."

Approaching Becket, they came through a forested landscape: firs, birch, and beech, oaks and chestnuts. These were more trees than she'd seen in her lifetime. Quieted by the greenness of it all, the manicured, tree-shaded lawns rolling under sugar maples, and charmed, too, by the wood-shuttered windows, she said, "Everything's so pretty. Anyone would want to live here."

"*Why* exactly do you want to meet her?" His question stung and she knew he felt it, too. "Forget it, Iris. I'm sorry, it's none of my business."

Had she *not* told him about her breast cancer scare? No, she hadn't. All she'd told him was about her promise to Luke, but not why he had asked it. It had all happened so fast and now here they were.

Well, anyway, he was right, it was none of his business.

"What are you going to say to her?" he asked.

"I don't know." She reached into her bag for a hairbrush. "I haven't thought about that. I mean, I have. A hundred times. But not really, as in, what I would *really* say if I met her face-to-face. I know it's right that no one thinks about how the adoptive mother feels, but I have thought about her, I mean, Hilary, a lot. Down through the years. Mostly, I wished I could tell her how well Rose was doing."

The truth was that in the last few days she had thought about nothing else—what she would actually say when she found her.

"Thank you," Iris said very quietly. "*Thank you*, that's what I've always wanted to say, *Thank you, for Rose.*"

Hector slowed down and eased the Jag alongside a footpath in front of number 43 and parked. "This is the street. Valley View Terrace."

She glanced quickly at him and then up toward the small,

gray-shingled house with a white porch. A row of trimmed,
ball-shaped boxwood lined the path and house front like green
rosary beads.

"Should I come in with you?"

"No. Thank you. I have to do this by myself."

Iris got out of the car. She shook her dress and smoothed her
hair and walked toward the house. At the front door she looked
back. Then she stepped up under the small porch and pressed
the doorbell.

After a few moments, a tall woman, early forties with very short
dark hair, opened the door.

"May I help you?"

Iris could barely breathe. "Are you Hilary Barrett?"

"Yes."

Iris's hand went out to steady herself against the nearest support, the upright of the little porch, which was just behind her.
She nearly fell off the short step. The woman looked guardedly
at her. "I wonder if I might speak with you."

"If it's about my yoga class, I'm not teaching from home anymore. Did the hotel send you? I've told them I'm not doing pri-
vates anymore."

She doesn't recognize me. But I don't recognize her, either.

In a strange way, Iris was relieved that she could say she didn't
want a private class. "The hotel didn't send me."

"Oh. What then?"

"I wonder if I can come in."

The woman had been standing behind a screen door so her
face was visible only through a mesh, but Iris could see she was
dressed in workout clothes, black, like her hair.

"It won't take long."

"You're not a Jehovah's Witness?"

"No. I'm not. I'm from Ireland and—"

"Are you looking for a place to stay? Is *that* what the hotel said? They're always sending people here if they're full. I used to do rooms during the Tanglewood concerts, but not anymore, I'm sorry. I've got to talk to them—"

"I'm sorry . . . Ms. Barrett, I don't want a room, either. I just want to talk with you . . . to ask you . . . I want to tell you . . ." Iris faltered. This was hard. This was impossible. "May I please come in?"

Hilary Barrett opened the screen door then and came out and stood beside Iris. She'd closed her front door behind her. There was barely enough space under the small porch for the two women to stand. Iris could see the color of her eyes. They were brown like Rose's but not quite the same almond shape. The woman squinted into the sun and put a hand up to shield her eyes. Her fingers were long like Rose's but, unlike her daughter, she wore several silver rings. Was this the same woman she'd met in Dublin over twenty years ago? Iris couldn't decide.

"What's this about? You're scaring me."

"I really am sorry to disturb you," said Iris and she looked quickly back to the car where Hector was no longer sitting. Where was he? She hadn't heard the car door open or close. She felt dizzy. "This is awkward," Iris said. "I'm not sure how to put this."

"You're Irish, you said?"

Iris pulled down on her shoulder bag for support and crossed one leg behind the other.

"I've always wanted to go to Ireland."

"What?" Iris said quickly.

"I hear it's really nice. The people are supposed to be real friendly."

"You've . . . never been?" she stammered.

"No . . ." the woman replied with her head cocked slightly. "I've been to Europe. You know, Eurailing, college days. But . . ."

Iris shook her head. What was she saying? *She'd never been to Ireland.*

The woman waited for Iris to explain herself. She even smiled and looked around as if maybe this was a joke and someone was going to pop out from behind the car and shout something surprising.

Finally Iris said, "You're not the real Hilary Barrett, then."

"Excuse me?"

"I mean . . . you're not the person I'm looking for."

The woman said nothing.

"You never lived on St. Botolph Street in Boston?"

"Now look, this is getting weird. Either you tell me what you want, or—"

Iris made no sound, but her eyes teared and she looked helplessly around her.

"Iris?" Hector's voice sounded from the sidewalk. He was standing on the driver's side of the car.

"Is that your husband?" the woman asked.

Iris shook her head. "Sorry" was all she managed, then she turned and stumbled down toward the car.

Hilary Barrett peered after her, bewildered, and took a stance with her hands on her hips as if ready to adopt a Warriorlike yoga pose, then she started down the path toward the Jag, but Hector held out his hands like he was stopping traffic and motioned for her to stay. He went around to the passenger side and opened the door for Iris. When she sat in she collapsed forward. He came around to the driver's side and sat in, too. Hilary Barrett stood where she was, midway down the path.

"She's not . . . the Hilary Barrett I'm looking for," Iris said, her breath choking on words between sobs.

"I know," Hector said.

"What?" Iris turned to him.

"The one you're looking for is dead."

Twelve

Rowan lay on the night grass of the seventeenth green, his shoes off, his tie loose. Several hours after the mourners had departed the memorial service, Pierce had found him, the blue-flowered urn with Burdy's ashes lying beside him. Above them, a crescent moon formed a triangle with Venus and Jupiter.

For a few moments, neither of them spoke. The bentgrass cushioned Pierce's shoes as he rocked back and forth on the flawless green. "I thought I'd find you here. Burdy's Last Stand, hey?" Pierce wasn't the sort to lower his tall frame onto the now damp grass. Not usually. It was too awkward, but eventually, seeing that his brother showed no signs of getting up or even acknowledging his presence, he sat down beside Rowan.

After a few moments, Pierce indicated the urn. "Is he still there?"

"All there," Rowan said.

With one arm resting on his bent knee, Pierce peered into the darkness, gauging his brother's state of mind. Finally. "Come on, Ro. Get up." His bother nudged him. "Time to go home. It's nearly over."

Rowan shifted his weight and turned to look at him. "Is it? Or just beginning?"

"Ah, brother," said Pierce, "School of Life rulebook? Very deep." He laughed lightly. "Come on now. Enough's enough." Pierce stood. He bent toward his brother with an outstretched arm. Rowan hesitated but Pierce kept his arm extended until his brother grabbed it and helped himself up. Rowan picked up the urn. The night air thrummed with crickets. Pierce stood for a moment on the green and pretended an air swing.

Rowan started walking away, and then, because there was no other way to shed the thing that was weighing him down, he turned back, and said, "She had a baby."

Pierce stalled midswing. "What? Who?"

"Hilary." Rowan stopped. "Hilary Barrett." There were no lights along the fairway. They could barely see each other.

"What are you talking about?" Pierce seized hold of his brother's arm. "Hilary?"

"Burdy's old secretary told me."

"*That's* who that was? Peggy Dillon? I thought I recognized her. *What* did she say? *Exactly?*"

"She said she saw Hilary in Dublin. Pregnant."

"God! When?"

"St. Patrick's Day."

"No, I mean what year?"

"The only year she was in Ireland. The year before she died. Do the math!"

Rowan walked away carrying the urn. The grass cooled his feet but his head was hot. Pierce went after him. "I don't want to say this, but what makes you think it's . . . ?"

"It was six months after I broke off with her is why."

"Still . . . it mightn't—"

"Still. Nothing." He put down the urn, swept his hands along the grass, then ran his wet fingers through his hair. Pierce waited and then they linked forward in the direction of Louise's house, as if following an invisible ball. The moon had moved and was hidden by the trees bordering the fairway. The course was patterned in light and dark, white metal signs indicated the directions to tees and gleamed low in the grass.

All the lights were on when they reached the condo. Rowan hesitated. Pierce placed a hand on his brother's shoulder. "You go in, Ro. I'll walk back to the clubhouse and settle up."

"I'll come with you."

"No," he said firmly. "You need to go in to Mother."

Rowan looked at him. "What have I done?" he said quietly.

The kitchen table was set for three, ready for morning. Louise, in a pink cotton bathrobe, the top of her hair in rollers and the remnants of five cigarette butts in the glass ashtray in front of her, gauged her son's intoxication as he laid down the urn.

"Sorry, Mother. Something came up."

"Is that all you can say? Then *please* . . . explain why you weren't there to say good-bye to the guests."

"Sit down, Mother."

"I don't want to sit down. I've been sitting down since ten waiting for you to come home. I sent Pierce to find you. I thought . . . I thought—"

Rowan interrupted her sharply. "Stop." He held out his hands toward her. "Please. There's something I need to tell you." Rowan sat and took the glass in his hand. "I think I'm going to need your help."

It was the thing she was most hoping to hear. She sat down beside him and took hold of his hands. "There's a meeting every other night in the community center."

"No."

"Rowan, dear, come on. It's the only way. One day at a time."

He paused. "It's not what you think." He withdrew his hands.

"Don't be dismissive. That's the thing I hated most about your father!"

Rowan looked at her. That hurt. He rocked his head side to side in sadness. His eyes watered, and he gulped to stop himself from crying. It seemed they sat a long time, neither of them speaking, Louise opening and closing her mouth forming words she didn't speak. Louise got up from the table and walked to the sink. To the refrigerator. Back to the table and sat. Rowan didn't see Pierce, but he'd heard the screen door open and knew his brother stood in the hallway, waiting.

Finally Louise said, "Tell me! What's happened?"

The look on Rowan's face startled her. "Oh God," she said. "What have you done?"

"Mother—"

"Tell me!"

"Calm down, please."

Pierce came up behind Rowan and put a hand on his shoulder and shook him gently. "Hey, buddy. It's going to be all right." He left his hand there and, after waiting a few moments, in case Rowan would explain to their mother, Pierce turned to Louise. "You might be a grandmother after all."

Louise's eyes quivered. Stunned, mouth fully agape, she looked first to Pierce, then to Rowan. Fluorescent light showed the full weariness of her face. "I don't understand."

"It's late. It's been a full-on day," said Pierce.

"Hilary?" she said softly, her voice waning like light rain falling.

Pierce went to his mother and bent to kiss the side of her face, which was turned to Rowan with tears in her eyes. "And enough's been said for the time being, I think. Rowan will tell us all about it in the morning." Pierce's commanding voice quieted them and in a way gave them permission to be silent. No more talking was necessary, his look told his mother. "You need to sleep. And so does Rowan. Nothing can be achieved tonight."

It was as if all at once in the silence of the bright kitchen all three received, individually, a kind of blessing from Burdy. The urn with his ashes, bathed in a kind of blue aura, seemed to radiate. It was like a key turning the plot of a life, Rowan thought. He went to his mother then to assist her to stand. Despite the occasion and the enormity of the disclosure, Rowan somehow now managed a smile, albeit weak. His wasn't a tortured face any longer, just drained and tired. With his help Louise stood and she took hold of him, and for the first time in a long time Rowan let himself be held.

In the morning Louise went out early and came back with a box of pastries, and over coffee in the kitchen her sons puzzled together the scant information they had. "If Hilary *really* had a child," she said, "her parents would know."

"Maybe. Maybe not," Pierce said.

"But if they knew, why wouldn't they have told me?" Rowan fidgeted with his coffee spoon.

Pierce said he remembered attending her funeral. "What? Twenty years ago?"

"Seventeen. She died on February 15, 1992."

It had been a cold February day when a snowstorm threatened to disable the service. Louise remembered Hilary's grief-stricken father, Jack, and the seething anger that was clearly directed at her son. Rowan had been forced to consider that Mr. Barrett's anger was in some way justified. He'd broken the engagement rather unchivalrously. He'd been too young. They'd both been too young. In the years since there had been no further contact, but every February 15, in that place inside him where he had left his love for her and where once the world had been full of the possibility of marriage and children and happy ever after, Rowan thought of her. And as the years went on, he knew he had made a mistake.

He'd met Hilary at a house party of a mutual friend, Scott, somewhere off Harvard Square. Scott played electric guitar and Rowan played tenor sax in a jazz ensemble. Scott and Hilary were in their senior year at college in Boston and Rowan was completing his MLA nearby in Cambridge.

She was tall with shoulder-length brown hair. She wore a sheepskin jacket that cold night, and a blue-jean skirt with frayed edges she'd fashioned herself, and lace-up boots with black tights. She'd come to the party on her own because Scott told her there was this guy he *really* wanted her to meet. She moved on the edge of the party with a kind of confidence that showed she was comfortable in herself, and even proud, and she spoke with Scott without needing to look around the room for the person he'd proposed for her to meet. When Scott finally brought them together he'd said, "You two have a destiny. I can feel it."

Rowan had found out much about Hilary that first night. She

came from the same part of New York State. It was this that got them talking so easily. They talked about places they visited in Westchester and found they had a mutual partiality for the old Bedford Village Playhouse and an Italian restaurant called Nino's. They agreed right then and there that the next time they were both "home" they'd catch a film and dinner. Maybe Scott was right. Maybe they had a destiny.

Hilary lived in Brighton in a studio apartment. She cycled everywhere, she'd said. And she loved Bonnie Raitt and Bruce Springsteen and an Irish singer called Elvis Costello. Half a dozen silver bracelets on her arm made a kind of music, like cymbals proclaiming the arrival of royalty, Rowan had mused, every time she moved. He liked that she wore mismatched earrings, and liked the color green, and Irish poetry, and that she hoped to do a master's degree in Ireland at Trinity College in September. Rowan told her about Burdy and his own Irish connection.

He remembered that in the dark, crowded room of the kitchen when someone had dimmed the lights he'd kissed her suddenly and said he wanted to take her back to his place. If Rowan closed his eyes, even now, there she was, waving good-bye to him as she went down into the station at Harvard Square to catch the T back to Brighton. She hadn't accepted his invitation to spend that first night together.

Now, twenty years later, midmorning, Rowan was driving down the Saw Mill River Parkway. Louise had checked the phonebook—the Barretts still lived at 57 Cedar Lane—twenty minutes away. Mother and brother had wanted to go with him.

"Moral support, brother?"

"Pierce, thanks," said Rowan. "I need to do this on my own, though."

A heat wave was folding in over the whole of the northeastern coast, from the Jersey Shore to Boston, but Rowan turned off the air-conditioning and drove with the windows down. He needed a bit of reality. It was Sunday morning and traffic was light. He'd spent many hours up and down this highway traveling by car from the city to visit Burdy and his mother. Or he'd take the train that snaked along the river, a tributary of the Hudson that Burdy had once told him was known by the Native Americans as *Nepperhan*, meaning "rapid little stream." He sometimes felt he belonged more to the landscape than to anything, to the richness of its place names and its flora and fauna.

Hilary had felt the same, and during one of their times together they'd taken a drive on the Taconic State Parkway up through the Hudson Valley to Chatham to spend the night in a country inn. He remembered telling her that the Taconic was as perfect an example of what was meant by a *park*way as you could hope to find. A magnificent blend of highway engineering and landscape architecture. She'd let him ramble on about the designer, whom Rowan had studied at Harvard. "That's the guy that designed the Unisphere," he'd said. "You know the thing . . . the giant globe? You pass it on the way into Queens if you're going to Long Island?"

"I know it. It's pretty—"

"Over seven hundred thousand pounds of pure steel. Biggest world on earth."

Rowan cringed now, recalling how he'd just been trying to boast and hear himself talk. He remembered the weekend because it was the end of September, the autumn leaves were turning. Hilary was leaving for Ireland.

He got off the parkway at Exit 32 and onto Route 120 and drove down into Chappaqua. From memory he knew the house was somewhere near, but made two wrong turns before he found Cedar Lane. He parked the car alongside the curb in front of the mailbox of number 57. A decal of ducks flew across the aluminum box. It was then that Rowan recalled Jack Barrett had been editor-in-chief of *Field & Stream*. An American flag the size of a large beach towel angled out under a black porch of the white, shingled house. On the seat beside him lay the music for his tribute to Burdy.

And grace will lead me home.

He blew a sigh and got out of the car.

The Barrett house was a Colonial Revival with black shutters sitting on a well-manicured front lawn with a two-car garage on an acre of land. To the left, an old red maple rose from the center of a bed of pachysandra. To the right, an old-fashioned rose bed. Simple and elegant and impressive. The front inner door was open and he could see into a foyer through a screen door. A mound of shoes—a pair each of loafers, boots, and running shoes—were piled inside to the left at the base of a stairway.

Rowan knocked on the wooden frame and waited.

A man accompanied by a black Labrador came to the door. He was wearing a Yankees baseball cap and khaki shorts and a black T-shirt. "Who have we here, Bullet?" the man said, looking down to the dog and scratching its head. "Hey, fella?" He turned back to Rowan. "Friend or foe?" He didn't open the screen door.

"Hello, Mr. Barrett."

As Mr. Barrett studied the stranger standing at his front door, his face transitioned from friendly curiosity to vexation. It only took a few seconds. "What do you want?" Bullet's back stiffened and his tail heightened as he responded to the tone of his owner's voice.

"It's been a long time—" Rowan said.

"Seventeen years and a few months. And not long enough."

"I have to speak with you . . . please."

"Whatever it is, I'm not interested." Bullet's mouth curled and he growled. Jack Barrett was about the same age as Rowan's father, late sixties. He stood squarely in the doorway.

"It's important."

"Jack? Jack? What is it?" A tall woman with graying hair tied up in an elegant bun appeared behind Jack. Marjorie Barrett was carrying small pruning scissors and wore one gardening glove.

"Please, Mrs. Barrett, Jack . . . I have to know if. . . . Did Hilary . . . ?"

"Blake!" Jack Barrett raised his voice. "You—"

"Jack," Mrs. Barrett said gently, putting her hand on his arm. "Don't. Please." She stepped in front of him. "I'm sorry, Rowan. It's been a long time." Mrs. Barrett went to open the screen door. "I know why you're here."

"Is it true? Did Hilary? Did she? Did she have a baby?" The words lurched up from Rowan's gut.

Mr. Barrett stayed his wife's hand on the door handle and stared at Rowan a moment, his lips quivering, and then he stomped off, leaving his wife with her head down, staring at the floor, then she, too, turned and walked deep into her home.

If there had been a chair or bench Rowan would have collapsed onto it. Instead his head sunk and he clasped his hands over his head. His shoulders heaved up and down and he sobbed. The energy rising in him, like a tornado, was so intense he had to move so as not to fall. He went around in a small circle on the graveled path to regain his balance.

Inside the house Bullet was barking.

Because he had to do something, because his world was spinning out of control, Rowan grabbed a fistful of gravel and threw it across the lawn. Pathetic. He bent over with his hands on his knees, trying to catch his breath, looking down at the circle of pachysandra around the red maple. He wanted to yank it out.

Then the front door of the house opened. Mrs. Barrett came toward Rowan with slow steps. In her brown eyes he saw Hilary. He backed away as she advanced.

"I'm sorry," he said and let go of the last of the sharp gravel in his hand.

She extended her hand to him. "I hoped one day you would come. I didn't know how or why or when. But I'd hoped you would because I wanted you to know. The birth of a child is a miracle. No matter what. It's a sign that the world goes on, with or without us, it goes on. And you are a part of that." She put her hand on the side of his face and left it there a moment.

Rowan pulled awkwardly on the flagged path. "Why didn't she tell me? Why didn't you tell me?"

"It was too late. There was nothing you, or we, could have done by the time we learned about the baby. It's the way Hilary wanted it. I'm so sorry. It was a mistake . . . not to tell you." Marjorie's eyes teared as she watched him take this in, watched as his thoughts crisscrossed his face, reconstructing the past as if he were adding and subtracting all the permutations and reconciling the past with the present.

"No. I'm sorry. The mistake was mine. I should never have

broken it off. Fact is, Mrs. Barrett, there hasn't been anyone like Hilary in my life . . . since."

"Here," she said. "We found this after . . . after . . . here . . ." The words choked her throat. She handed Rowan a neatly folded piece of notepaper. It was inside a sealed plastic bag. "Hilary meant for you to have this. It tells you everything."

Thirteen

When Pierce arrived at the White Horse Tavern in Chappaqua it was empty except for Rowan. He was sitting near the front window, staring at the piece of paper in his hands. He folded it when his brother approached. Pierce came over quickly, sat down opposite. They stayed like that a few moments, Pierce watching Rowan, and Rowan watching three small boys sitting on a bench across the street. They were horsing around and laughing.

"What's happened?" Pierce said.

The bartender, a young woman in shorts and a polo shirt, came to the table.

"I'll have another," Rowan said. And to his brother, "You want something?"

His brother looked at Rowan's empty glass, then to the bartender, and said, "No. No, thanks. I'm fine. Maybe water." Then to Rowan, he said, "Buddy? It's early for that. Let's wait till we're back at Mother's." The woman shrugged and went away.

Rowan didn't get angry. He might have, but he didn't. Something was happening to him. He wasn't sure what. He said, "Allow me to quote the proverbial words of the great Irishman Edmund Burke," he said, "I may be turning over a new leaf."

"What?"

"It's a Coke. I'm drinking Coke."

"Good. That's good." Pierce paused. "Sorry." And then, as if unable to remain patient any longer, Pierce shifted in his chair and made to get up. Half sitting, half standing, he said, somewhat exasperated, "Are you going to tell me what happened?"

"Yes. Sit down."

"Will *I* need a drink for this?"

The bartender laid the Coke in front of Rowan and raised her eyes. When she was out of earshot, Pierce said, "Okay, tell me."

Rowan recounted the entire incident. The barking dog, Jack Barrett, the red maple, the American flag, Marjorie Barrett, and the letter. He showed the letter, but didn't give it to him. "Hilary had written this but she never sent it. Her parents found it among her things."

"Oh, Jesus. It's addressed to you."

Rowan looked again out the window where a woman, about the age of their mother, was tying the shoes of one of the little boys. "Yes, it's addressed to me."

After a time he turned back. "She *did* have a baby. A girl."

Pierce might have prepared for something like this, but the look on his face showed his shock and his hand rose instinctively to cover his brother's outstretched hand.

"Jack blames me for Hilary's death."

"So they kept it from you? And . . ." Pierce paused briefly. "I'm so sorry, Ro. But it's . . ." He looked at Rowan. "It's kind of . . ." He didn't say more but surveyed his brother's face to calculate how he was taking this. Rowan was oddly calm. There was a sense of determination about him that hadn't surfaced for a long time. He'd spent too many years ignoring the insidious way alcohol had crept, like a slowly growing fungus, into his life. He had fooled himself, but all the time there was a part of him that understood if only he could . . . if only he could kill the rot, his life would be better.

"I'm going to Ireland."

The next afternoon, Pierce drove Rowan to JFK for an evening flight to Dublin. Rowan had phoned his office to say he was taking a week's vacation. It was last minute but he'd be contactable by cell phone.

"I wish I could go with you. Here," Pierce said. "Mother gave me this to give to you. Put it in your suitcase."

"What is it?"

"Don't ask." Pierce rolled his eyes. "Just scatter them somewhere."

Rowan registered with a similar rolling-eyed expression. He understood. Burdy's ashes.

The only tickets left to Dublin that night were in business, but Rowan didn't want to wait a couple of days for a cheaper fare. When he'd settled in and was offered complimentary champagne, he chose orange juice instead. One day at a time, he thought.

Rowan had never been to Ireland. Burdy had always meant to take him on a golf trip and to show him the statue in St. Stephen's Green of his great-great-great-grand uncle, the Irish patriot, Robert Emmet. But it never happened. Why was that? Rowan had been too busy. That's why. It was his own fault. Another lost opportunity. The road to regret is paved with inaction. When he stopped long enough to think about it his regrets were many. After it had ended with Hilary there had been other women but nothing amounted to anything lasting or meaningful. He couldn't say why, really. He regretted that he hadn't tried harder. He regretted, too, that he hadn't spent enough time with his mother. For too long all his regrets had been absolved by alcohol.

Burdy had warned him that it was in his genes, this alcoholic inheritance, and there was only one way to beat it. "I'll only say this one time because I know you will find your way. You don't have to hit bottom with this thing. It's an elevator going down, you can get off any floor you want."

In his pocket, he fingered the Irish coin with the harp and the hare, the threepenny piece, Burdy's lucky golf ball marker.

Seven o'clock in the morning, steady rain falling, a Turkish taxi driver dropped him at the Merrion hotel in Dublin's city center. Emerging from the car, Rowan tilted back his head and let the rain fall on his face. He looked around at the pale gray granite columns and gated entrance of a large, lead-domed building across the wide street. Government buildings, the taxi driver told him. Even though the driver was a foreigner he pointed out all the cultural sights. Croke Park. The Custom House. The Liffey. The Bank of Ireland. Trinity College.

"Good morning, good morning. May I take your luggage, sir?" An elderly porter in top hat and tails said. He'd been standing, waiting at the hotel's discreet front door.

Rowan wasn't normally a guest at hotels with porters in top hats but he'd chosen this one because it was around the corner from the offices of the Adoption Board. His credit card would take another hit. "No, I can carry it. Thanks." He looked up and down the street but didn't move.

"Will I get you an umbrella, sir?"

"Is Merrion Square that way?" Rowan nodded to the right.

"Yes. Right there, sir. And the National Gallery is just across the street. But it's not open yet. Are you sure you're not wanting me to take your bag, sir?"

"No. Thanks. I'll check in now." Rowan followed the porter into the front room of the hotel, where a tall, blond receptionist named Sabine checked him in and a few minutes later a young man with a middle-European accent showed him into a garden-view suite. (Thus far the only Irish person he'd actually encountered in Ireland was the old porter, whose brogue was strong, maybe by way of compensation.)

"We have upgraded you sir," said the young man. "May I show you the room's amenities?"

By the time he was shown into the marble-floored bathroom, Rowan said, "Thanks. I think I can manage from here," and handed him a five-euro note.

In a tangled mixture of grief, shock, and a jet-lagged trance then, he looked down at the enclosed garden, the reflecting pool, clipped boxwood hedging, the blooming campanula and white calla lilies and a very old magnolia tree. He wished in a way he'd said yes to his mother's offer to accompany him. But it was too soon after Burdy. He was grateful Pierce was able to stay and attend to her as well as to Burdy's estate.

Rowan leaned against the window frame and looked down at the order of the garden, and in his mind he laid out the distorted architecture of what he now knew: Hilary *had* had a baby, a girl, and placed her for adoption. In Ireland. He was now in the category known as a "natural" parent. He had learned on the Adoption Board's Web site that he could officially sign up as such, the natural father, with the "National Adoption Contact Preference Register." In one fell swoop he was a father, if only in the literal sense of the word. He had called the Adoption Board and explained that he was arriving in Dublin from New York the next day and needed an appointment. Urgently.

After a brief nap, mainly to clear his head of jet lag, Rowan accepted an umbrella offered by the gentleman porter and walked out, turning left outside the hotel, into a cloudburst. A few yards farther, he turned right onto Baggot Street. Place names suddenly jumped out at him as he passed along: O'Donaghue's, Doheny and Nesbitt, Toners. Names on a postcard Hilary had sent him after arriving in Dublin to attend Trinity College. She'd been *doing the pub crawl with the other American exchange students,* she'd written and invited him to come visit. It panged his heart to think about it now.

Rowan hadn't told Hilary before she left for Ireland that their relationship was over.

Nor had he told her straight off when she came home for Christmas, even though he had several occasions to. They'd gone out a couple of times. Muscoot's, the White Horse, once to Nino's. He hadn't told her it was over until just before she returned to Ireland after the holiday. He'd met someone else. He was sorry. It was just the way it was. He wasn't ready to get married. They were parked outside her house, the car running. Snow covered the lawns and white lights decorated the bare tree outside the Barretts' house, he remembered. She got out of the car without a word. Midway up the path, she turned and came back. She opened the door and dropped the engagement ring on the seat and walked the path to her parents' house.

Remembering now the look on her face, Rowan felt sick. There was something about the way she reacted. He'd been too indifferent to consider how deeply it might affect her.

Along the north side of St. Stephen's Green he passed the Shelbourne Hotel, crossed the street, and walked along the outside railings of the great square, which, the porter had told him, was once the oldest urban space in the world. Opposite the top of Grafton Street, Rowan continued along the edge of the green and within a few yards pulled up short. There, posed as if in mid-speech, stood the tall, thin statue of Robert Emmet, arms free at his sides, one palm open and turned toward the sky. Rowan was struck by the likeness to his grandfather. It was in the nose.

Rowan walked around the green and back past the hotel. The old porter waved a white-gloved hand as Rowan passed. When he reached the address on Merrion Square just before two in the afternoon the rain had eased. He stared at the blue door, its glass fanlight reflecting a bit of sky and marshmallow cloud and a little green from the trees in the gated park across the street. People passed as he waded in a pool of uncertainty, anxiety, and immense regret. He drew in a long, deep breath, like a swimmer on the starting block. He sucked and held his breath and, in one long whoosh, let it out: *Whoosh.*

Inside, a tall, thin woman in a black cardigan sat at a desk. She was on the phone and motioned with her hand for him to wait. His breath quickened.

She soon hung up and stood. "Mr. Blake, isn't it?"

"Yes." Rowan put out his hand.

"Sonia McGowan," she said, taking it lightly. "Come, this way. Please." She started walking and Rowan followed. "You're just arrived from New York? You must be tired." Without waiting for him to answer, or looking back, she continued. "How was your flight?"

She led him through an open door into a small room with a corner window that looked out onto a gray wall, and indicated an old armchair. Rowan sat and the woman took the seat opposite. There was a small table between them with a box of tissues, a pen, and a clipboard holding paper. The linoleum floor was so polished his shoes squeaked when he shifted position to recross his legs.

"How can I help you?" she said.

Rowan thought she sighed before reaching for the clipboard. He didn't think he could begin.

"Go on, please."

"Well . . ." He ran his fingers through his hair. He looked around the room a moment. "I think I've just become a father."

She didn't say anything right away but a minor smile softened her face. It was brief. "Tell me whatever you know. You've requested a meeting with the Adoption Board, presumably because there's some connection to us—"

Rowan interrupted and spoke quickly, "I found out two days ago that a young woman I was dating over twenty years ago had a baby, and she gave her baby . . ." He paused, searching for the right words. He didn't want to say them.

"She placed her baby for adoption?"

"Yes." Rowan nodded. "That's right. I believe." He sat back in his seat and let out a long, soundless whistle. He put his hands on his knees and clasped them and shifted his weight forward.

"I see," Sonia McGowan said, "and just to be clear, Mr. Blake, you're questioning whether the baby was adopted here? In Ireland?" She was writing on the form held by the clipboard.

"I'm not suggesting it, Ms. McGowan. I know it to be true. I have a letter from her, the baby's mother, telling me that she did." He reached into his pocket and withdrew an envelope and eased the letter carefully from it. He looked once more before handing it over. It was folded in four and well creased.

She read it.

Dear Ro,

A year ago I had a baby. A girl. She was born in Dublin. I gave her up for adoption a couple of weeks after I gave birth. She was placed with a very loving couple in the west of the country a few weeks later. I've had confirmation from a social worker at the agency that an adoption order has been granted to her new parents. So now it's legal. That's why I'm writing.

Our daughter is now someone else's. I met them, Rowan. They will give our baby everything we couldn't. A home, and parents. Plural.

I'm sorry I didn't tell you. I needed to wait until it was too late for you to do something.

I was excited to tell you I was pregnant when I came home that time at Christmas. Excited to be starting a family. I'd meant for it to be a surprise. I was three months then. You didn't notice.

I went back to Dublin after you broke our engagement. I didn't tell my parents I was pregnant. I'm sorry about that, but it would have made them too sad and they would have tried to stop me.

I just wanted my baby to grow up with a mother __and__ a father. With parents who lived together and loved each other.

I hope you will forgive me . . .

Love,
Hil
P.S. Her name is Rose.

The social worker's head was tilted as she read and Rowan noted the dark circles under her eyes. She was older than he'd first thought and there was something deeply melancholic about her. She looked up suddenly and said, "When was this?" There was an odd urgency in her voice.

"About twenty years ago," Rowan said. "Why?"

"It's just—"

"What?"

"Nothing." She looked down at the box of tissues. "I'm . . . I'm not sure *what* I was thinking. Sorry. I was reminded of something." She paused another moment. "It's signed 'Hil,' " she said, returning the letter to Rowan.

"Short for Hilary. Her name was Hilary Barrett. She's dead now. She died—"

The clipboard slipped down Ms. McGowan's lap. It hit the linoleum floor with a sharp *clack*, a sound as if something had snapped or been freed, or, as in an old lock, a key had been turned. Her face paled. Her lips pressed into a thin line as she retrieved the clipboard. "Sorry."

"Ms. McGowan, what's wrong?"

"She's dead?"

"Yes. She died before she could mail me the letter. Her parents kept it and for their own reasons didn't tell me. That's why I only just found out. Purely by accident. If I'd known—"

"I'm so sorry. I'm so sorry to hear that. Poor girl."

"She was . . . lovely."

"No. I mean—"

"What?"

"I mean, of course. Poor girl. I hope she found comfort in knowing she placed her baby with a loving, adoptive couple. A very courageous thing to do." Her voice had changed. It was like

Sonia McGowan had momentarily gone on autopilot. "It seems you have all the information already, Mr. Blake. I'm sorry to tell you that adoptions made legally in this country are closed. You know what that means?"

"It means all identifying information is private. Yes. I checked your Web site. I understand I can join some contact register."

"Yes. That's true. You can register as the natural father."

"I'm not a natural father!"

"You're not the natural father?"

"No . . . I mean, yes I am . . . well, according to Hilary. And I have no reason to question that. But it's a distortion, there's nothing *natural* about it."

Sonia performed a minor smile again. She'd recovered her color, and now unclipped some papers from her clipboard and handed them to Rowan. "The terminology *is* unfortunate. We often hear that from adoptive parents who prefer the term 'birth parent' to 'natural parent.' But, well, we're all in the same—to use your word—distortion," she said. "Here's a form. Take it with you and look it over. You can decide what level of contact, if any, you're open to in the event the adopted person in question is also registered, and, more importantly, also open to contact. Although I have to tell you it is entirely her choice to be contacted. Or not. And if she has requested no contact, we must all abide by that." She looked down. "I hope you understand. Sometimes it turns out adoptive children, when they become adults, are open to being approached by members of the original birth family. I've known of several cases where it has turned out well. But also, I'm sorry to say, I've known cases, in my personal experience, where it hasn't."

Rowan accepted the form and folded it without looking. He kept his eyes on Sonia. His eyes teared. She lifted her eyes and noticed. He'd previously noticed she wasn't wearing a wedding ring.

"Is there anything more I can help you with, Mr. Blake?" she asked. "I'm so sorry you've come all this way. And I can only imagine the state of shock you must be in. I wish, really, there was something more I could do for you. Is there anything else?"

Rowan noted the shift. Sonia had returned from autopilot and was back in manual mode. He studied her a moment because he imagined Sonia McGowan was trying to tell him something. "I'm sorry, Ms. McGowan, but do I get the feeling that you know something you're not saying?"

"There is nothing I know of that I can share with you," she said, looking away. She closed the file. She straightened the line of her cardigan. She took a tissue from the box and tucked it into her sleeve.

"Nothing?"

Not for the first time, it seemed to Rowan, Sonia McGowan fought with herself. In that small room off the square where each day the light and shadow crossed a gray wall she was struggling with something. She pushed back a strand of her hair at her temple. Her voice broke as she began to speak, quietly, haltingly, "Her name is Rose—"

"I know that!"

She hesitated, then she looked at Rowan Blake. "What I mean is, well, adoptive couples often change the name that the birth mother has chosen because, obviously, it is fully within their rights as the legitimate parents to chose a name of their own."

Rowan showed in his face he didn't understand.

One more time, she said, "Her *name* . . . is . . . Rose."

Minutes later, Rowan walked down the steps of the Adoption Board and hurried along the southern side of the square. Sonia had told him nothing more, but somehow he felt she'd told him everything. A missing piece? He felt a connection he couldn't explain. He heard children calling. Beside the railings an openair art exhibition was taking shape. Rowan walked the perimeter of the square, passing the impressive Georgian row houses with their twelve-paned windows. Wall plaques marked the residences of famous Irishmen. Wilde, Yeats, Synge, O'Connell, Russell, Le Fanu.

What must it have been like for Hilary in the midst of all this greatness to bequeath her baby, their baby, to Dublin?

He stopped dead and hung his head. She had done the right thing. He wasn't a natural father. It was just a word and the word was false.

When he returned to his room at the Merrion there was a message. Pierce had discovered that Irish birth records are recorded in something called the "Register of Live Births." "Furthermore," the voice message said, "they are *public* records, Rowan. And, therefore, accessible to anyone!" Pierce advised visiting the research room—ASAP—in the general registrar's office at the Irish Life Centre on Lower Abbey Street.

Rowan returned quickly to the lobby and asked the porter to direct him. He hurried down Grafton Street to College Green, passing the front arch of Trinity College, and onto Westmoreland Street. He was surprised at the heat of the Irish summer now that the sky had cleared of clouds. As he raced along he took off his jacket. *Her name is Rose* became a refrain that kept repeating, keeping time to his steps.

From Westmoreland Street he crossed a busy junction with Japanese tourists in green hats, and backpacking youths in shorts, and middle-aged American tourists in white sneakers. He crossed O'Connell Bridge, wider than it is long, side-stepping pop-up stalls selling postcards and earrings and scarves and pashminas. An old Romanian Gypsy, holding a paper cup, squatted on the bridge's middle point. TELL THE FUTURE read the card at her feet. He stopped and fetched a coin from his pocket and dropped it in the cup, but did not wait to hear his future as he quickly crossed over the black River Liffey.

Two streets farther down he arrived at Lower Abbey Street. He pulled his jacket on, finger-combed his hair, and entered.

A porter directed him up to the third floor to the research room. It couldn't have been any easier. He stood outside the door and peered in, not knowing what he expected to find but imagining there would be something discreet or inaccessible or something. Maybe he needed a letter. Some legal document? A permission slip? But no, it was just a librarylike space with about forty individual wooden desks lined up like a classroom. A young man with short hair, wearing glasses and a rugby shirt, sat at one of the desks, like a student studying. A large book lay open in front of him and beside him was a notebook and pen. Another youngish man behind a counter fronted by shelves of books looked up from a computer screen when Rowan approached. He was wearing an oatmeal-colored sweater vest. They were the only people in the room.

"Can I help you?"

"I'm looking for a birth record," Rowan said hesitantly.

The clerk smiled and replied in the most neutral-sounding voice Rowan had ever heard, "No problem. What year?"

"What year?" Rowan said. "Um . . . 1990, I think."

"You can look through a couple of the indexes if you're not sure. From 1990 to 1995?"

"No. I'm pretty sure. It's 1990."

"Right. Just a minute. Take a seat, I'll bring the index over to you."

He was dumbfounded at how simple this was. Rowan's heart pounded. Was he doing the right thing? He reasoned he had to know more. But this was too easy and something about it seemed wrong. Maybe once he knew more, then . . . well . . . then he'd know if he *was* doing the right thing. Either it would feel right or it wouldn't. His gut would tell him. Either he'd make the putt or the shot would go wide. *Follow the line,* Burdy would have said.

After a few minutes the clerk placed a large red book—the index—in front of him. "There you go . . . 1990. Do you know the name?"

Rowan nodded.

"Great. Then this will give you the reference number for the complete entry in the register. The surname is recorded in the name of the mother," the clerk explained, "if the father's name is not known." He looked deliberately at him and Rowan felt as if he'd just been poked in the chest.

He opened the book and let it fall open in the middle. He side-glanced, as if too guilty to look, at the names:

Murphy. James. 1 November 1990. Murphy.
Murphy. Kieran. 16 May 1990. Godkin.
Murphy. Leah. 29 September 1990. Flynn.

The book was organized alphabetically. Surname. First name. Date of birth. Mother's maiden name. He allowed himself a small chuckle. My Rose here amongst all these great Irish names. Safe here among her own. Rowan thumbed backward to the Bs.

Barr. Liam. 5 July 1990. Barr.

His eyes scanned quickly down the list. He was looking for Barrett. She'd probably used her name.

And there it was. *Barrett.* That was easy.

He looked around the room quickly, furtively even. Then he stared at the entry. His breath stopped.

Barrett. Rose. 30 June 1990. Barrett.

June 30th? She's going to be nineteen at the end of the month!

He stood up and brought the book back to the clerk. His mind was racing. He needed air. The fluorescent lights were painful. A surge of guilt ripped through him.

"Find what you were looking for?" There was that calm voice again.

"Yes. June thirtieth . . ."

"Do you want a copy of the original?"

The original? "The original? Um . . . actually . . . I wonder . . ."

"You looking for something else?"

"I was wondering . . . you see. I'm looking for . . ."

The clerk watched Rowan as if he knew exactly what he wanted, like he'd known from the minute the tall, smart-looking Yank in his tweed jacket entered his library. He spoke with the same air of neutrality as before. "Adoption records?" he said.

"Yes," Rowan said, surprised. "Is that possible?" He felt accused.

209

"Yes. *Public* records are open to the *public*. You can look in the index of the Adopted Children's Register. If that's what you want? You said 1990, right? That'd be the second volume."

Evidence of how easy this was turning out to be left him reeling. Sweat beaded on his forehead.

The clerk, whose ID tag said LIAM, looked at him impassively, but knowingly. About thirty years old and tall like Rowan, but that's where the comparison ended. This guy was nice. He probably had nothing to hide. Nothing to be ashamed of. He probably has a wife and two kids. And they were happy kids, a girl and a boy. And they were lucky to have a father like Liam, and, as if in testament, a tissue paper flower, a lemonade-colored sunflower—the handiwork of a child—adorned the left pocket of Liam's sweater vest.

"I'll bring it over," Liam the father said.

Rowan returned to the desk he'd been sitting at, but he struggled to settle down and kept making small adjustments to his hair and shirt collar. He took off his jacket. Finally he rolled up his sleeves, carefully, slowly, to his elbows.

Liam appeared moments later and landed a large black book in front of him. *Thump.* "The records are logged alphabetically by last name of the adoptee," he said. He looked down at Rowan, who forced himself to meet the man's steady gaze, full-on. "It could take you a good few hours to find a match, though. The adoptee's *real* name now is what you're after," he said pointedly. "You're looking first for the birth date. Then you find a name. But be aware there might be more than one entry on the same date. Just because you have a name from the index doesn't mean the same name will be in the register. Only the birthdate will be the same."

Rowan now had two clues. He opened the volume and started.

He pushed aside feelings that chased his thoughts. This was wrong, blatantly wrong. This information should be private. Isn't that what Sonia had said, *information about adoptions in Ireland is closed.* What does "closed" mean if not sealed? Shouldn't it be inaccessible? To the public? Or something?

The first name was *Aherne. Michael James. 16.05.84.* It was going to take some concentration. He isolated the numbers by placing his left hand over the names and using his passport, still in the pocket of his jacket, as a ruler to scan each page for the year '90. At the top of the third page, at *Ballagh. Sean. 23.04.92,* he suddenly closed the book. He couldn't do it—it wasn't right.

Liam approached when he saw Rowan had closed the book. "Are you finished?"

As he reached for the book, Rowan put a hand on his arm. "No. Wait. I'm not."

"Okay. No problem. Just so you know, we close at half four."

Rowan opened the book again and found where he had left off at *Ballagh.* He fingered his way down the years again: *82. 76. 94. 77. 92. 81. 90,* passing names: *Barry Becket Berrigan Bigley Blaney Bonfield Bowen.*

His finger stopped. *30.06.90.*

There she was. *Bowen. Rose. 30.06.90 Dublin.*

Her name was Rose Bowen.

Part III

Rosa

"Moondance"

Fourteen

"Well, that was a right bummer," Conor says when Rose finally tells him why she left her violin on the tube. She talks about Roger and her confusion. About how he'd walked out of her rehearsal. About her humiliation and how she'd bolted from the master class midpiece. About her tutor's bleached hair and the poster on his wall.

"What an arsehole. I promise you not all surfers are like that," Conor says. "You should request a rematch with the Kiwi dude."

"I don't know . . ."

"Finish what you started. We can take Gerty for a spin."

"A spin to London?" Rose laughs.

"Why not? We'll get to know each other. Anyway, I've been meaning to take a few days off. Come on, it'll be a blast, and your mum won't be back from Boston for a couple more days. You don't want to be all on your own, do you?"

After Conor's cajoling and teasing that she owed it to

him—after all, wasn't he the kingpin in the drama of her violin? And didn't he have a vested interest here?—she decides maybe it's a good idea. She's at loose ends and in a kind of limbo. *Okay,* she texts Roger, and writes she's coming to finish the Bach sonata. And she'll be there on Tuesday. *And* she's bringing her own audience.

That Sunday morning, the day after Rose spoke with her mother in Boston, she and Conor set off across the Irish Sea. They drive from Clare to Rosslare, take the ferry to Pembroke, and arrive in South Wales. They talk about all sorts of things. How he likes to get up early and check the surf forecast. How she likes to eat only toast with almond butter in the morning. That he supports Arsenal and she doesn't know anything about football except her dad rooted for Chelsea. That they're both believers in Vitamin D, and sushi, and lovers of beaches, and Munster Rugby, and cats. In the late afternoon, they head for a funky B and B in Llangennith down the Gower Peninsula, a surfing spot Conor knows about from the surfboards.ie forum.

But on that midsummer evening, in high season, there is only one single room left. Conor insists Rose take it. He rightly senses she is feeling anxious about a hundred things: her mother, Roger, him, so he offers to sleep in the van with his surfboard. He's done it before, sleeping up and down the west coast of Ireland, searching for surf. "Not to worry," he says, "I'm kitted out for it." Standing in the room, the window wide open and the curtains letting in a breeze full of sea scent, Conor corners Rose against the wardrobe. He raises his hands to brush away her hair and holds her face. He kisses her. Rose doesn't resist. Her head is against the hard wood of the wardrobe. Her arms go loose and hang at her sides. She holds her face up as Conor kisses her, teasingly at first then temptingly and then no-holds-barred, full-throttle.

Abruptly, he stops and steps back.

"See you in the morning, Rosie." He gives a swift flick of his head and goes out. She hears his footsteps until they disappear. A moment longer, she thinks, and she would have ripped her clothes off.

When she lays her head down later with the surf beating below, Rose thinks about her father. Luke hadn't had the chance to talk to her about these sorts of things. Relationships with men. She is sure he meant to, but . . . she wonders when her parents first had sex. Sex? It's the only thing on her mind. Should she, shouldn't she? He's out there in the van. She could go to him. She's all at sea. Frustrated, she gets up from the bed and takes out her violin. She doesn't play the Bach sonata, or a jazz piece, or a jig or a reel. Nothing fits her humor, so she practices her scales, pianissimo, in three octaves in the minor keys until her fingertips hurt and her bow arm tires. The scales give her form and content and she can practice style. She starts with single notes, then moves on to double notes. Separate bow. Slurred bow. Spiccato. Vibrato. Fast bows. Slow bows. Marcato in the upper half of the bow until somebody taps on the wall next door. "Quiet." She puts the violin down and falls asleep.

The next morning Rose goes down to the beach. Conor has left a note on his van, he is already surfing. He is so easy in himself, she thinks, watching him ride the small waves into the shore. Calm and patient. Someone whom her father would have definitely called a free spirit. Wouldn't Dadda have liked him?

"I've got an extra wet suit in the van," Conor calls to her.

"I'm afraid of sharks!" she shouts back.

He laughs. "Okay, so, just one more and then we'll get going."

———

The Welsh countryside looks like a green velvet sheet has been thrown over it. Like it's a setting for one of those BBC period dramas.

"Sorry about last night," Rose says, not looking at him.

"No worries. Gerty and I had a lovely sleep." She punches him.

After a four-hour drive, passing Bristol and Swindon and Slough, they arrive in the early evening at Rose's flat in Camden. There is still light enough in the sky to walk along the canal and up into Primrose Hill. They eat pizza outside on a picnic table at the Lansdowne as the sun sets. When they get back to her flat she asks him to sit out on the balcony. She wants to practice, alone.

"Please don't say anything. Good or bad."

"Gotcha. Quiet as a church mouse."

She can't put her finger on it but somehow something about him makes her feel totally free to be herself. She feels like singing and does a little bow to herself in her room in front of the mirror. She plays brilliantly, she thinks. She plays the third movement like a Gypsy. Gets all the dancelike rhythms just right. Take that, Roger Ballantyne, and put that in your pipe and smoke it. She laughs out loud. "Where did that come from?"

When she finishes the sonata, through the open doors of the flat's sitting room, Rose hears clapping.

"What?" Conor says when Rose comes out to him on the balcony, half smiling, half frowning. He leans against the railings. "I didn't say anything." She goes straight up to him and pushes up from her toes and grabs him around the neck and kisses him.

"Now, that's more like it," he says.

That night when they look at Rose's narrow bed, she says, "I'm not ready." She scratches around her eye as if shielding herself from him in some way.

"Me, either. I'm not as easy as I look." He cups Rose's chin in his hand. He touches her birthmark. "Look, I understand. First things first. Let's get that other surfer dude in your life sorted."

Rose sleeps well on her own.

She wakes when she hears talking in the next room. It's Conor talking to her roommate, Isobel.

"Rosie," she says when Rose comes into their sitting room, "you made this poor lad sleep on the couch?" Isobel is wearing her pajama bottoms and a sweater over a string top. She has bleached hair cut to an inch of her scalp. "What's up with that?" She nudges Rose with her elbow. Her socks are mismatched. She is still wearing makeup from the previous night. "I don't blame you, though. He does look a bit rough around the edges."

"Ha ha. Right!" says Conor, rising and giving Rose a big, fat kiss full-on. He dips her ceremoniously and she gives in, her hair falling back and touching the floor. She groans. Conor scoops her back up.

"Oh," says Isobel. "I see." A grin spreads across her face. "So that's the way it is."

Rose looks at Conor blushing and says, "Yup. That's how it is. So rough that if we'd slept together I wouldn't have any energy left for the rematch today."

"Rematch? Huh?" Isobel turns to put the kettle on.

"My master class. It's a long story, Izzy."

The Avenue Gardens in Regent's Park are in full summer bloom and when Rose and Conor pass Readymoney's old drinking fountain in the center of the Broad Walk the clock reads ten past nine. (Roger had texted he'd be in his office at ten.)

"Has your mum been here?"

"Yes. A few times."

"Super gardens."

"She can't pass a flower without taking a picture or taking down notes and making little sketches in her notebook."

Conor bends to a patch of unusual-looking ferns. He reads from the printed sign: "Maidenhair. Species: A. veitchii Hance. Family: Adiantaceae."

"Oh God, my mother will love you!"

Conor smiles. "You nervous?"

"A little."

"Don't be. You played—"

"Conor! I told you not to say anything."

"Sorry, forgot. Jeeze, don't bite my head off. Here, let me take that." He reaches for her violin case.

"No, it'd be bad luck. I'm used to having it against me. It keeps me grounded."

He puts his arm around her and her violin.

Twenty minutes later they are across the park, walking right on Marylebone Road and approaching the wooden doors of the academy. They enter and George the porter smiles his crooked smile when Rose stands before his desk. She signs in.

"I'm bringing a friend in with me today, George, okay?"

"Yes, miss. Nice to see you again."

Rose remembers George had been standing at the front door that afternoon she ran out of the recital hall. "And you, George." She turns and heads up the steps, Conor following, giving her plenty of space. By the time she knocks on Roger Ballantyne's door it's like she is a gathering storm and ready to burst.

"Come in."

She nods to Conor and he holds up the crossed fingers of both hands. Rose hears the words in her head even though he hasn't said them: *Get your Irish up, girleen.* Then she steps into the office.

"Rose! I'm so glad you came back," Roger says. He has on his brown Waiheke Island T-shirt with the wineglass logo and white linen pants and flip-flops. He steps closer, lowers his voice, and says, "I was worried I'd never see you again."

Rose turns to her violin case.

"Listen, before you say anything, let me apologize. My behavior was deplorable. Despicable."

Rose suddenly realizes she isn't nervous, but she pulls a sulky face anyway.

"Can you forgive me?" He shuts the door.

"Maybe." Her pout slowly turns to a smile. "I'm sorry I left, Roger."

"I understand. Don't apologize. No worries. It'll be all right. What do you say we both get a second chance?"

Something has come into her. She doesn't know what. She unpacks her case. She turns her head quickly, swiftly, when she hears a wood pigeon murmuring on the ledge and she hopes Roger won't shoo him away, and when he doesn't, when he just looks too, she feels he is with her and he is ready to listen. She lifts her violin with her left hand and brings it to her shoulder. Her chin senses the known place and nestles into position. She thinks of Conor's workshop and the ginger cats and the winter sunshine on the day they first met. She thinks of the man outside in the corridor who transformed pieces of wood and string into her violin that's about to sing. She hopes he will hear her. She bends her fingers and squares them, places them for the first four-note chord of the adagio. With her bow raised, she takes a moment, counts to three, scans the room: the poster, the morning light angling in from the window, Roger standing by the door. Then, with the top of her bow hovering just a whisper above the strings, she nods imperceptibly to the unseen surfer standing outside in the hall and begins the adagio with a sweeping run into an arpeggio.

It goes like a good dream. She is relaxed, inspired. Somewhere near the end of the second movement, the fugue, Roger nods his head. Then he waves enthusiastically for her to keep going. She does. She plays straight through to the end of the piece and when she finishes with a flourish on the up bow, her chest fills with air and her outbreath releases all her worry in her ability. She *is* good. And now Roger knows it, too. And Conor.

At once the door opens and Conor steps boldly into the room, clapping. "That was mighty! Absolutely one hundred percent—"

Rose shoots him a look and masks her delight.

So does Roger. It takes him a half second before he says, looking at Conor, "Well, your . . . your friend here is right." He eyes Conor as if peering down his nose over his glasses, although he doesn't wear any. To his student he says, "It's great work, Rose. Really great."

Rose is grinning. She thinks Roger is waiting for her to say something. When she doesn't, he asks: "Should you and . . . I . . . go for a drink?"

"No, but thanks," she says, and she puts her violin back into its case. "I'm going back home. I'm going home for the summer."

"Well," Conor says, "that's that, then." And he reaches into his jacket pocket and hands Roger Ballantyne a business card. *Conor Flynn, Master Violin Maker, Kinvara, Co. Galway.* "See you," he says, and follows Rose, who waves to Roger and walks out.

Fifteen

Children are born. They have a life but they belong to no one. This was running through Iris's mind on the long, silent return to West Newton Street. When she and Hector arrived back in the South End early that evening, Grace came out to greet them. She'd heard the car pull in, but as the two soberly approached with a space between them defined as vacant, she stood aside and said nothing. Iris had been crying and when she looked at Grace she shook her head, couldn't speak.

There was nothing and everything to say. Grace stood openmouthed. Hector didn't come inside. He stayed on the sidewalk, not attempting to follow, and watched Iris go in.

In her room Iris began to pack. She was leaving—no matter what—the next day. She'd get on any plane crossing the Atlantic just to get away. It had been a horrible mistake. She was back where she started. She sat on the bed and held her breasts. It was the left breast. It hurt.

"Iris? Are you all right?" There was a soft knock at the door.

Iris didn't answer at first. It was sweet of Grace, but Iris didn't want to have a chat about it. Didn't want to have a sit-down with Grace sitting in Bob's old chair commiserating.

"I just need to sleep," Iris said.

"Of course. I understand. I just thought you might like some tea." There was a soundless pause. "I'll leave it on a tray outside the door in case you change your mind. And I've brought up the phone if . . . in case . . . in case you need to phone Ireland."

Iris heard Grace lay down the tray outside and waited a few moments until she was sure Grace had gone. She listened at the door, wanting also to avoid meeting Hector. She didn't want to see him. Not that any of it was his fault, but her feelings for him were confusing.

Grace had set a tray with a pink rose alongside the tea and a sandwich and the phone. Iris was close to tears upon seeing the flower. Get it together. This is not the time to feel sorry for yourself. She put down the tray and turned to the mirror, remembering Tess's words. "Breathing in, I know I am breathing in. Goddamn it. Breathing out, I know I am breathing out."

It was nine o'clock in the evening, too late to ring Ireland, but she phoned the airline and after a long wait—listening every thirty seconds to the recorded voice: "We are experiencing a high volume of calls and all our operators are busy. Your call is important to us. Please hold the line and a representative will be with you shortly"—a live voice came on. There were seats available for a return flight the next day. She'd only have to pay an extra change-of-date fee. Iris was relieved. She would be in Ashwood in thirty-six hours. She sat against the bed. She didn't want to think about anything else. Not Hilary, not the Breast Clinic, not Hector. She took off her now wrinkled blue dress and folded it, laid it in her case, and put on the bathrobe she'd been wearing the last few nights. She pulled aside the bed covers and slipped inside. She returned to the dream of Luke walking out of the sea toward her. He'd been smiling. Why was he smiling? There was nothing to smile about. There was no one there. Hilary was dead. And as for Hector, Iris wished he'd stayed as he was that first morning. Unapproachable. It would have saved her from behaving like a schoolgirl on a first date and, worse, from feeling guilty that she dared to let herself imagine a relationship. Turning from one side of the old bed to the other, she struggled to get comfortable. She turned around to the foot of the bed, buried her head under a pillow, tried to block out the sound of the irritating air-conditioning vent. She was in that zone she knew well: alert, electric, fully charged, a live wire connected to nothing. She rose from the bed, went to her case and took one of the sleeping tablets Dr. O'Reilly had given her. Soon she was falling asleep, trying to picture Luke coming from the sea.

She woke at six the following morning and went down to Grace's kitchen. She made tea and stood at the window that faced onto a small garden, which she hadn't noticed in the dark the night they'd had dinner.

When she'd finished her tea, she went out the back door in her bare feet and stood on the grass wet with dew. Her feet welcomed it. The as-yet-unlit garden was enclosed with an herb border made with railway ties fringing a brick wall. Peppermint spurted shoots through its gaps. An ill-shaped bed with a pink rosebush, some blue geranium and nepata, and tall white cosmos, which yearned for a good pruning, was dead center in the garden. She moved to it and began with urgent energy to deadhead the spent cosmos flowers. She did it out of instinct because some part of her needed to weed. She moved closer to the rosebush, and with her fingernail, nipped away thin growth along the stem. Iris bent to pull a dandelion sprouting at its base. She made a small pile of weedings and had the oddest feeling that it didn't matter where she was, only that she was *doing something*, and for a moment she forgot where she was.

"Will you stay forever?" Grace came toward her, hands deep into the pockets of her bathrobe, which hung open and showed a knee-length pink nylon slip.

"I didn't realize you had this space out here. It's a little oasis."

"But I could use a good gardener, as you can see. Right?"

Iris smiled.

"Sit down, Iris, please," Grace said, moving to the garden table and its twin metal chairs. "I want to show you something."

Iris thought, Dear God, what now? She sat opposite Grace, who handed over a thing she'd been holding in her pocket. It was a copy from a newspaper dated February 15, 1992.

CAR CRASH CLAIMS LIFE OF YOUNG WOMAN

A woman crossing Huntington Avenue died yesterday morning as the result of a car accident. According to eyewitnesses, the driver of the vehicle, a man in his fifties who is recovering in the hospital, swerved to avoid the young woman when she slipped on the ice. The car spun out of control and hit her head-on. Paramedics rushed to the scene to assist the injured woman but were unable to revive her. She was declared dead at the scene by authorities.

After contacting her parents the police revealed the name of the dead woman as Ms. Hilary Barrett, a local resident of St. Botolph Street and librarian at the Mary Baker Eddy Library across the road from where the accident occurred. Ms. Barrett graduated from Boston University and Trinity College, Dublin. She was twenty-four and is survived by her parents, Marjorie and

Jack Barrett, of Chappaqua, New York. Ms. Barrett was a valued employee at the library and colleagues expressed great regret at the loss.

Authorities have warned pedestrians in the South End to be mindful of icy road conditions at this time of year and have urged residents to use the crosswalk.

Iris couldn't articulate what she was experiencing right then, except she felt a jumble of feelings encircling her, like a tornado, of sorrow, anger, despair, fear, but also an odd, and therefore surprising, sense of relief. There it was in black-and-white. Her mission to find Hilary was at an abrupt and sad end.

So was her promise.

There'd been a very good reason why the beautiful young woman she and Luke had met nearly twenty years ago had stopped responding to queries from the Adoption Board in Dublin. Iris looked down at her hands. Grace sat beside her, and when Hector started to come out she shook her head at him and he turned and went back inside. Iris could have called out to him, but she didn't.

The sun was easing into a space between two buildings and a long, narrow rectangle of light lit up the grass like a neon banner and now it slanted against the wall at the southwest corner. Iris turned to Grace and told her story. The whole story.

Grace reached across the table and laid her hand on Iris's wrist and held it. They sat this way for a while. What was there to say? What was there that could be said? Inch by inch, the narrow rectangle of sunlight widened. Insects moved from shadowed corners.

"I'm sorry, Iris," said Grace finally, "I'm so sorry. *What* you must be going through." She let go of Iris's wrist.

"When did you know?"

"About Hilary?"

"Yes."

"Billy. Billy found out. Yesterday. You'd already left. He's a wiz with computers. You see . . . I remembered the name but I couldn't place it. It was so long ago."

"Did you know her?"

"No. No, I didn't. I mean, I knew *of* her. Afterward. It was in the papers and . . ." Iris watched Grace lower her head and close her eyes. After a few moments she replaced her hand on Iris's. "What did he tell you about himself?"

"Hector?" Iris said and gave Grace a look that showed it couldn't possibly make a difference.

But Grace ignored it and went on. "Probably not much, I'm guessing. The thing about Hector, well, I think I can tell you. It's not a secret, right? He lost his wife to cancer . . . years ago. Her name was Julia." Grace stumbled on the words she spoke. Her eyes darted toward the door of the kitchen and back to Iris, and she dropped her voice. "He thought there was a spark between you. I must admit I saw it, too. So did Billy. I mean, am I right?"

There *had* been a spark, Iris admitted, but today it was too weak to ignite. Today she felt only shame and sadness.

What was she anyway? The collector of lost and dead souls? No. She wasn't going to feel sorry for Hector. Julia was years ago, she thought. He should be over it by now. Isn't that what people said? The first two years are the hardest? For her it'd been, what? Two years and two weeks and a day since Luke died. No. Absolutely not. She wasn't going to feel sorry for him.

But she did. She did feel sorry for him. Maybe he, too, had lost his soul mate. And for a fleeting moment she opened her heart to allow in his sadness.

She looked into the corner of the garden where the sunlight

had widened its netlike cast against the redbrick wall, catching every other leaf and flower bud in a dazzling glare, and now the tiny back garden glowed.

In midafternoon at Logan Airport, standing at the check-in counter, Grace hugged Iris and whispered, "Hector will be sorry you left without saying good-bye. What should I tell him?"

"Good-bye."

"Good-bye?"

Iris nodded.

"That's it? Nothing more?" Grace said.

"I can't, Grace. I'm not ready." Iris gathered her bag and shoulder bag. "Maybe . . . ?"

"Maybe? Maybe what?"

Iris's eyes welled up.

"Okay. Okay. It's all right. I know what to tell him." Grace reached her arms around Iris and held her for a moment. Iris let herself be held but had no strength to hold back. "Let me know how the appointment turns out. I'll be anxious to know. Right?" Grace dropped her arms and took a step back. "In such a short time I feel like I know you. Will you come back? Will you bring Rose?"

Iris couldn't speak. To speak would bring tears.

After she was through security, and her face washed of tears, she looked around for an Internet station and checked her e-mails. One from Tess and garden.ie and Higgledygarden.co.uk and three with unfamiliar addresses. She read Tess's first, which told her Rose was doing well since her "big upset."

Hurry up already and get home Iris! We miss you. And PS . . . What the hell? What are you doing? Missing your appointment? And PPS . . . no need to worry about Rosie. Take my word for it.

Iris wrote back that she was coming home on Flight EI345, arriving at 6:00 a.m., and would explain everything then. But not to tell Rose. And P.S., what did you mean, *Take my word for it?*

The e-mail from an R.E.B. surprised her. She hadn't expected e-mails from blog readers so soon.

Dear Ms. Bowen,

I'm glad to have discovered your blog. As a landscape architect my-self in the heart of NYC, your post on poppies brought a little green into my life.

Kindest regards,
R.E.B.

Delighted, she read the other two. One asked if Iris had ever tried to grow meconopsis. *It's like having a bit of the blue sky in your border.* And the other was a city gardener asking: *Can Icelandic poppies be grown in a window box?* Such simple signposts, tokens, and yet it thrilled her. She *was* connected. Blog readers *were* a link to the world. She'd reply to them all next week and would copy her replies to Arthur Simmons.

A few hours later, she was sitting in an aisle seat in row 37 at the back of the plane near the toilets. When the beverage cart came, she ordered a gin and tonic and two of those plastic quarter bottles of wine to go with her chicken dinner. Her mind pitched back to the South End. Grace would be telling Hector that Iris had been recalled to the Breast Clinic for further tests. She pictured how his face would look. She was suddenly sorry for him. She felt like crying.

The next thing she knew a voice was saying, "The captain has switched on the seat belt sign. We'll be landing in fifteen minutes. The weather in Shannon on this lovely June morning is blustery but the forecast is for sunny spells." Iris looked out onto the clouds scattered across the blue and, below, a little green.

She switched on her phone at the luggage carousel; half a dozen messages beeped their arrival.

From Tess:

Welcome Back!!! Can't b there 2 collect u. Sorry pet. Sendin taxi tho. C u later. x T ps Rose away at music event in London. WITH friend! As promised, didn't tell her u were comin. She'll b back in a few days.

A man holding a placard with her name on it smiled as she approached and he took her bag and said, "Welcome home."

The captain's weather report had been right, there were sunny spells. The sun beamed down on everything, on cattle in the fields, on hawthorn hedgerows, on fuchsia in full bloom. She fell quiet, grateful the driver sensed she didn't want to talk. A little more than half an hour later she arrived home. When she stepped from the taxi, Cicero jumped from the rooftop of the low cabin. He didn't seem to particularly notice she'd been gone five whole days. He gave her no welcome except to jump onto the table where the food was kept. Iris put down her bag and waited until the driver pulled away.

231

Neither did the garden look like it had missed her. It was in perfect order. Did anyone or anything need her?

Getting used to this being alone required a skill she still struggled to perfect. It was on the far side of the road, as if always just over there—the place she couldn't get to, couldn't reach. She had traveled some distance from the initial grief-pain of Luke's death to where she was now—standing still in her garden, listening to the barn swallows' *chideep chideep*—able to somewhat appreciate how far she'd come. This is my life. But she wanted more and it was up to her to get it.

She'd read a novel lately about a man whose wife comes back from the dead. She pops into his life in odd moments, then disappears. Something about unfinished business. One day she came and said, "It wasn't up to you to make my life happy. It was up to me, but your loving helped." Then *poof*! She was gone and returned no more.

Iris wished Luke would appear and tell her something. Tell her how to do it. Without his loving, living was the greatest challenge of her life.

She turned the key and went in.

In the kitchen, the poppies had been cleared away. In their place were two empty mugs.

Tess arrived in the late afternoon and, after hugging Iris a few times, walking around her in a circle and hugging her again, she said, "Poor pet." She stood back and grabbed Iris by her shoulders.

"You ran off to Boston and missed the appointment."

"I know."

Tess shook her head, but smiled. "Here. Where's the phone? I'll ring and reschedule."

"I've made it for Thursday morning." Iris paused a moment. "Will you come with me?"

"Of course . . . but what about Rose?"

"I don't know, Tess. She already has enough on her plate."

"I'll say," Tess said.

It was an odd thing, but Iris didn't read into it. "Plus," Iris said, "I don't know what her plans are. She's probably still upset about that wretched master class."

"Oh . . . I think she's over that."

Iris narrowed her eyes.

"You underestimate her—" Tess said.

"Tess?"

"I just mean, she's more flexible than you realize. Do you think maybe, just maybe, you're overprotective? Just a little? Just a teensy little bit? It's only natural, but—"

"Would you like some tea, Dr. Tess, Medicine Woman?" Iris turned and went to the kitchen. Tess smiled and followed.

"So?"

"So?"

"Yes . . . So? Why did you disappear without a word? To America?"

Iris didn't look up but poured the tea.

"Exciting undercover garden assignment?"

Iris looked at Tess, her eyes betraying her and welling up.

"Oh God. What? Iris? What's wrong?"

When Iris finally told her story, the words burst like a sudden rain shower. "I made a promise to Luke. If anything happened to me I'd find Rose's birth mother. I promised Luke. What if something bad happens? That's why I went to Dublin. Then Boston. She was there, but—"

"She was there?"

"Yes. No . . . I mean she *was* there, but she's not. She's dead."

"Easy, pet. Hold on."

Iris explained about Hilary and how she'd taken the envelope at the Adoption Board and two days later flown to Boston. She told about 99 St. Botolph Street and the waiter. And the Mapparium. And Becket. "It was all for nothing. A big, fat, horrible, stupid mistake."

"Ohhhhh, Iris." Tess put her arms around her.

"I never told you, but Luke and I met her. It was a long time ago . . . I'm sorry she's dead." Iris paused. "Tess, she was the real mother of my child." Iris pulled away and shook herself, circling the island as if to shed the whole blooming thing, like it was something she could shake off and down, like autumn leaves stubbornly holding on to a tree.

"Stop. Iris! Don't say that. You're her—"

"If it wasn't so sad, it'd be funny." Iris raised her hands and held her head, pressing against her temples. "It's so weird to feel sad for someone you never knew." She took her long hair and twisted it around and around and fashioned it into a bun at the back of her head. At the sink she turned on the tap and splashed her face. Take control. Now. With her hands on the edge of the sink she looked out the window. The blue clematis was still flowering.

Tess was at her side and handing her a kitchen towel. "It's all right, Iris. It'll be all right. You'll see. I promise."

Then Iris told about Grace and the odd guesthouse in the South End—"it was rather unconventional"—and she laughed a moment, and about the concert at Titus Sparrow Park, and the Berkshire Mountains.

She left out the part about Hector.

"I'm sorry you've been through all this on your own."

"It's just, I'm frightened, Tess. Frightened of the future. Of death. For Rose. You know?"

They drank tea quietly, listening as a tractor passed below the garden along the road. Iris wasn't ready to tell any more. Cicero appeared and jumped onto the table. Iris picked him up and settled him on her lap. She knew Tess was looking at her, so she returned her gaze.

"So what about you? What's been going on? How are the boys? Sean?" She half listened as Tess gave a rundown of everybody's activities. Boys were done with soccer camp. (A great success.) She'd been at a conference on abused women. (The statistics are alarming.) And Sean was busy planning. (The music festival.) "Oh, that reminds me, Iris . . . Sean's wondering if you could help out, again?"

"Um, maybe. Sure. Remind me when it is?"

"This weekend."

"This weekend? Oh. Right." She'd forgotten about it. The annual midsummer music festival. "What does he want me to do?"

"You know. Your usual. Some flowers. But . . . maybe . . ."

Tess frowned. "Forget it. What am I thinking? Listen. Never mind . . . you—" Tess took Iris's hand, making Cicero jump. "Let's wait and see what we find out at the clinic."

Rose had left her mother a note telling her that she was *sooooo looking forward* to seeing her. And how crazy it was that Iris had disappeared off to America—of all places—and *without me!* Rose wrote she was gone to London because there was something she needed to take care of. Not to worry. And finally, that she'd gone with a friend. A new friend, and she would be home Thursday afternoon. *And P.S. Mum . . . you're going to be all right.*

Tess came at half seven on Thursday morning to take Iris down to the Limerick Regional Hospital. They came in along the corridor and Iris saw the sign for Oncology and felt a sudden chill; it was where Luke had got his diagnosis. Tess took hold of her arm. "Come on, pet." They had arrived in plenty of time for the nine o'clock appointment, but still had to wait, which neither minded because they knew some of the women were exiting having been told *I'm afraid it's not good news.*

In the Breast Clinic ward they sat on hard, plastic chairs set out in rows in a waiting room in the public area. Tess quietly guided Iris in a breathing exercise, but she was unable to settle down. Her heart had a mind of its own and she couldn't stop herself from fearing the worst-case scenario. She might as well have been speaking her thoughts aloud because Tess turned to her and said, "Stop it Iris. Stop thinking ahead. We'll deal with it, whatever it is."

"Of course. I know. You're right. Plenty of women recover from breast cancer."

"Yes. They do. A very high percentage. I know it's because you lost Luke. And you're afraid of the word. Cancer. Say it out loud, Iris. Cancer. If there's cancer we'll beat it."

"Mrs. Bowen? Iris Bowen?"

Iris started. She rose and walked a step away and turned back and held out her hand. "Please come in with me."

"I don't know, Iris," Tess whispered. "They probably won't let me."

"Tell them you're a nurse. *Please.*"

Iris was shown into a small anterior office with a sliding curtain and an examination table and two chairs. And standing just inside the door was L with the magenta hair.

"Oh. It's you," Iris said. She'd caught the woman by surprise.

"Yes, it's me. I work Monday and Tuesdays in Ennis. Wednesday and Thursdays here."

"Nice to see you again. Can my friend come in with me?"

"I'm afraid not, Mrs. Bowen. She has to wait outside. It won't be long."

"Please! She's a nurse, aren't you, Tess?"

Tess reached for Iris's hand in solidarity. "It'll be all right, pet. Really. I'm sure. I'll be right here."

"Well, I'm not supposed to, but you know what? Go for it. You can stay," L said to Tess, "but she has to go in to see the consultant on her own. Mrs. Bowen, if you'd take your top off and your bra and put this on." She handed Iris the familiar blue paper cape. "I'll be back to take you in for an ultrasound. Just a few minutes."

When L left the room, Tess raised her eyebrows. "Now, there's a free-looking spirit. That hair. And the nose ring." Iris nodded, undistracted, turned around and duly undressed and covered up in the paper cape. Then she paced the room. Back and forth, left and right. "It's not me I'm concerned about, you know."

"I know." Tess kept her eyes steadily on Iris. "It's probably not the right time, and, please forgive me, but—"

"I know what you're going to say."

"Do you?" Tess put a hand on Iris's back and made little circles like she was easing an ache. "Rose will be all right. She will be able to take care of herself. She has her own life to live, too."

"But . . ."

"You can't prepare for every eventuality."

"She'd have no family—"

"Maybe . . ." Tess looked at the floor, acknowledging the real possibility of something happening to her friend. She looked into Iris's eyes. "But *I'd* be there for her . . . and, eventually, she'd make a family of her own."

"You don't understand. Rose is my life's work. I can't . . .
leave . . . unfinished. I feel responsible in a way that you don't
understand. You *can't* understand. I've disturbed the natural order of things."

"That's crazy."

"I'm not her real mother."

"Iris!"

Iris resumed pacing. "Have you read the definition of 'mother'?
I have. I know it by heart: 'A woman in relation to a child or children to whom she has given birth.' Why do you think they call
birth parents the 'natural parents'?" Iris's face was flushed. She
lifted her hair away from her neck. The crepe paper cape made
her feel hot and cold at the same time. She had never spoken like
this. Not to Tess, anyway. Not to anyone. No one except Luke
ever knew how Iris felt about being an adoptive mother. She carried on like normal but in her deepest self, she knew she was not
like anyone else. Every other mother she knew was natural. She
believed sometimes she was an imposter. It wasn't organic. She'd
missed out on some essential hormone or something that comes
with being pregnant. Some blueprint that gets downloaded to
your hard drive. An invisible guidebook. Then you know without having to ask when to hold on and when to let go. It's a natural process. You just have to show up and do the right thing. She'd
been showing up and doing the right thing all her life. But as
an adoptive mother she had to go beyond that and yet she was
missing the essential element—the how-to manual. She did her
best to leave no stone unturned and had taken her responsibility as a parent as a matter of life and death.

Tess was stunned. Her eyes glossed. She was usually quick to
respond but not now; now she was speechless. Iris was grateful

her friend didn't rush in to fill the silence with platitudes. She'd heard so many of them down through the years. "You're so lucky you didn't have to go through morning sickness!" Or, "You didn't have to go through the pain of childbirth—you don't know how lucky you are!" To all such comments from well-meaning mothers, Iris simply and slowly nodded.

There were tears in Tess's eyes when she finally spoke. "Iris Bowen, you're the most natural mother I know."

Just then L had returned. "This way, Mrs. Bowen. Please follow me." The nurse held the door open. "I think you'll be fine, Mrs. Bowen. Really. And," she smiled, "it's nice to see you again, too."

A different nurse helped her up onto the examination bed and checked her name and birth date and the file. She patted Iris on the arm. The door opened and a woman dressed in heels and a dark skirt and white coat walked in.

"Hello, Mrs. Bowen, I'm Dr. Browne. I'll be performing the ultrasound." The nurse prepared Iris's breast with gel, then stood by Iris's side and held her hand. The light from the monitor shined on the doctor's young face. Dr. Browne took the probe and rolled it over Iris's left breast with one hand. She stopped and clicked with the other on the keyboard. "Don't be alarmed, Mrs. Bowen, just taking pictures." She stopped the probe, centering in on what Iris imagined must be the distortion, and clicked some more.

Even though the probe was cold, Iris felt as if she were being ironed. The doctor pressed hard and rolled the probe back and forth across her left breast. It hurt. Iris tried to imagine all the badness being pressed out of her, like wrinkles in her blue linen dress being steam cleaned, and all the crinkles and creases, corrugations and distortions being ironed away into faultless perfection. A terrifying few moments ensued as the doctor rolled and stopped and clicked. Iris shivered.

"Just want to make absolutely sure. These architectural distortions can be tricky things." The doctor said nothing for the next little while and looked at the monitor. She replaced the probe and stepped back. She nodded to the nurse, who wiped Iris's breast clear of the gel and helped her sit up. The doctor waited while Iris adjusted the cape and moved to the edge of the examination table. "Let's keep an eye on that left breast." She placed a hand on Iris's arm. "You've got some very busy breast tissue, Mrs Bowen."

Iris began to cry.

"There's a lot going on in there."

It seemed an age before the doctor added, "But I'm happy with what I see. You'll be fine."

Iris looked at her. Then she called out: "Tess! Tess!" And without anyone's say-so, Tess burst into the room.

"Tell *her*," Iris said to the doctor. "Tell her what you just said."

And because Iris Bowen was not, on that day, someone you could deny, Dr. Browne said again: "She has some very busy breast tissue."

"A lot going on in there," Iris said.

"A lot going on in there," repeated the doctor, nodding. "Yes."

"But . . ." Tess said.

"But she'll be fine."

"But I'll be fine." Iris looked to Tess, who was coming to embrace her.

Iris dressed and on the way out of the clinic's waiting room, passing the half dozen anxious women awaiting their turn, she met L and smiled and went on through the door. As they headed along the hospital's wide corridor with its framed artwork on freshly painted honey-yellow walls, Iris said to Tess, "Hold on," and Iris hurried back. She peeked in the door of the outer examination room. L was getting the next blue cape ready. "I'm sorry, but, may I ask? What is your name? It's been driving me crazy."

"Latara. My name is Latara."

"Nice to meet you." And for no reason she could quite explain she grabbed Latara with the magenta streak. "Thank you," she whispered. Iris released her hold and was off and out of the clinic so fast, Tess had to skip to keep up with her.

Sixteen

Rose arrives back home on Thursday. With Conor. She approaches through the gate and up the path that leads to the front door, but her mother doesn't rush to meet her as she expects. Only the cat does.

"Where is she?"

"Your mum?"

"You'd think she'd be here," says Rose, turning the key. "Her car's here." She stops at the door and looks around.

"Not being nosy or anything, but did you tell her what time you were coming back? Did you tell her about me—"

"No." Rose looks at Conor with narrowed eyes. It's a look that stops him, but only for a moment. They walk into the kitchen. Iris's blue Wellies are neatly paired by the back door and propped against a tall vase of flowers on the counter is a note. As Rose begins to read, her face changes.

"What is it?"

"Her appointment. She's gone to the Breast Clinic with Tess. I didn't know it was today."

Conor studies her. Then he waves her hair over her shoulder and leaves his hand on her back. He draws her toward him and she folds into his arms and buries her head. Rose and Conor have been together four days and three nights, but already they are so comfortable in each other's company that anyone seeing them would think they'd been together for years. Conor sits on the sofa in the kitchen and watches her now. "It'll be all right, Rosie girl."

"Yeah," she says, and she walks back the way they came in and opens the door for the cat. She lifts and holds him. "You want some milk, don't you, Cicero? Yes, you do. Yes, you do." The cat tries to climb onto her shoulder while she pours out milk. Rose lets him drink from a saucer on the counter and plays with his tail.

"Breast cancer is really treatable these days, you know. My aunt Fran had it and came through fine. Healthy as a horse now."

"I don't want to talk about it."

"Sure. No problem." He shrugs his shoulders, smiles, pushes back the wooly hat. "But you know—"

"Conor!"

"Right. Got it." He folds his arms. "The girl knows her own mind," he says to Cicero when the cat finishes the milk and jumps down to rub himself against Conor's legs.

Rose says nothing. It's like there's a still, airless place inside her and she's retreated. She tries Iris's phone but it goes directly to voice mail. She doesn't leave a message.

Cicero makes his way to the door and Rose follows and lets him out. Conor rises and reaches in his pocket for his keys. "I think maybe I should get going."

She turns and looks at him. Her eyes are tearful.

"All right," he says, "you've persuaded me, I'll stay."

In the late afternoon light in the Ashwood garden, bathed in a half dozen hues of green, sploshes of color punctuate here and there. Red poppies. Spires of blue. White daisies with bright yellow centers. At the bottom of the garden a bush with long blooms of purple is covered in butterflies. Clouds come slowly from the west, drawing across the sky like a silver wave rolling in.

Rose is awfully worried about her mother, but Conor succeeds in distracting her. He asks her if she will play her fiddle.

"You mean my violin," she says.

"No. I mean your fiddle. The master class was a great success and all, but you're back in Ireland now, girl. We plays da fiddle here, you know."

After a brief pause, she laughs and says, "My dad would have liked you."

He beams, knows it's the best thing she could have said. "I know you didn't want me to say anything but I'm telling you now for nothing—you played brilliantly! You really nailed it."

Rose picks up her fiddle, her bow, and starts tuning.

"You know, Kiwi Surfer Dude isn't a surfer?"

"Yes, he is."

"Nope. He's not."

"Really? What's with the poster, then?"

"Just for show." Conor picks up his fiddle.

"How do you know?"

"A surfer knows a surfer," he says, and breaks into the fiddle with a quick flourish of his bow. "And a fiddler knows a fiddler."

They begin with the "Currach" from "Inishlacken," a concerto for fiddle and violin by the contemporary Irish composer Bill Whelan. Rose has been learning it in her spare time. A challenging piece blending the traditional and the classical. She has only seen and heard it on YouTube when the Irish National Chamber Orchestra played it in Beijing. Conor has played it before with his mother.

"Really? Did she go to China?" Rose asks.

"Yeah."

"I want to go!"

"Just play!"

He gets me, she thinks. He really gets me. Fact is, she likes playing with someone else, she likes being in a group surrounded by bodies pulsing and being in the music, together, one breathing, magical sound. While she plays she thinks of Andreas. *You're in the music and the music's in you.*

"Brilliant," he says. "You know what? My mother will really like you." Conor pushes back his wooly hat and adds, "You'll be perfect for the festival this weekend."

"Festival? What?"

"In Doonbeg. You know? The jazz. I've sort of invited myself and they accepted. Play with me?"

Rose is caught by surprise. "I don't know. I don't know. I'm not good enough for *that* piece." Before Conor can reply she hears voices, she lays down her violin and runs to the sliding glass door. Her mother and Tess are walking up the path but neither sees her standing there. She pulls open the door.

"Mum?"

Iris drops her rattan handbag and runs to Rose, who meets her halfway. The hug they share is deep, silent, and all-encompassing, long and powerful and beyond words. Inside it, they rock side to side. Rose cries.

"No. No. No. Don't cry, honey. It's all right. Everything is all right."

"Tell me. I want to know everything. What did they say?"

"The doctor said your mother has very busy breast tissue!" Tess says.

"What—"

"Seriously." Tess laughs. "It took a good few go-arounds with the ultrasound, didn't it, pet?"

Iris smiles. "The doctor was very funny. Afterward she said, 'You're fine, but you have a lot going on in there.' "

"You should have told me," Rose says, halting between tears.

"I should have."

Relieved, Rose feels like collapsing on the lawn. As they walk toward the house her mother takes her hand. Tess is ahead of them, Cicero behind.

"I'm sorry I worried you," Iris says, taking Rose's hand to her face and speaking softly.

"I could have handled it, Mum," Rose says. "Dad told me to take care of you."

"I know."

"How can I take care of you if you don't tell me what's going on?"

"I know."

Rose stops. "And no more secrets."

Tess goes through the door first. And it startles Iris when she hears her speaking to someone inside. "Hello, *Conor,*" Tess says in a I-didn't-know-*you*-were-here voice.

Rose drops her mother's hand and rushes into the kitchen, landing beside Conor just before her mother enters. Head tilted down but a smile breaking on her face, she says, "Mum, *this* is Conor." She pauses for a moment. "Conor, *this* is Mum!"

Rose watches her mother's eyes dart to Tess, then back to Rose and over to Conor, then onto the stringed instruments lying side by side in their open cases. They are waiting for her to say something. Even Cicero has jumped back up onto the counter and looks around expectantly. Something registers on Iris's face and she walks to the young man she's seen before and says, "Nice to see you again, Conor." He has cut his hair. Now it is short and curly. The ponytail is gone but the wooly hat is still there. She turns and plucks the cat off the counter.

"You, too, Mrs. Bowen," Conor says. He reaches to shake her hand but can't because she is holding the cat.

"So . . ." Iris says, "this is your new friend?"

Rose shoots her mother a warning look. The four of them are standing around the counter and for a second Iris looks like she's the stranger in her own house. Then Tess says, "I think I'd better get going. The boys are hoping I'll take them to Doonbeg this evening, to set up."

"For the festival?" asks Conor.

"Yes," Tess says, raising an eyebrow the way only Tess can.

"Yeah? Cool. Rosie and I are going, too. In fact, tomorrow night we might—"

"I haven't decided yet," Rose interrupts him, sharply, and for a moment no one says anything. "I haven't said yes."

Iris shakes her head. "I feel as if I've been gone a month!"

"That's what happens when you're missing in action, Mum," Rose says, a bit too sharply, and it makes Conor look at her in surprise.

Tess winks at Rose. "You're all right now, pet," she says to Iris as she leaves. "See you later."

"I'm off then, too," says Conor, looking inquiringly at Rose, but she avoids his gaze. "I can be back later if you want to go to the pub session tonight. Or you, Mrs. Bowen? We could go together." Iris looks at Rose, but she's not saying anything. Conor shrugs. "I'm glad you're all right, Mrs. Bowen." He closes his fiddle case and crosses in front of Rose to the door. "Maybe I'll see you later," he says and he hesitates a moment as if for a kiss.

Rose feels Iris's eyes on her as she lets Conor pass. She bites her lower lip, she pushes her hair behind her ears. She glances at her mother, and then outside. Conor is on the garden patio, then he's on the path heading to his van, when finally she calls, "Wait!" and goes after him.

Standing beside the stone cabin, where a climbing clematis is hanging loosely, she says in a low voice, "I haven't decided about playing. You can't just expect—"

"I was going to suggest another piece if you thought the Whelan piece too tricky. What about 'Over the Rainbow'? If Grappelli and Frankie Gavin can, on violin and fiddle, so can we. Right?"

Conor reaches out to her, but she shoulders him away.

"Sorry. I don't understand what the big deal is."

Rose turns around. There's so much he doesn't understand, she thinks.

"That's all right, though," he says. "You think about it and let me know." He kisses her lightly on the back of her head and says, "Okay, Rose, I had a good time the last couple of days." He waits for a response. "Rose?"

She forces herself to turn and face him. Except for her father's, Conor Flynn has the kindest eyes she's ever seen.

"See you later?" he says.

"Not tonight."

They stand a moment longer in Iris's garden. A strong wind picks up and a petal from a blue clematis floats and lands on his shoulder, then slips off. Rose is motionless. For a second her breath stops. She gives Conor one long look, which leaves him looking confused. Then she turns and heads back to her mother's kitchen.

What Rose hasn't told Conor is that the piece he wants her to play was one of her father's favorites. She hasn't told him of the strange synchronicity and how the moment he'd said it, her heart split. She doesn't know if she can do it. Luke Bowen had collected nearly every single recording ever made of "Over the Rainbow," from instrumentalists like Stéphane Grappelli, Nestor Torres, Jeff Beck, and Keith Jarrett, to singers Frank Sinatra, Ray Charles, Plácido Domingo, Eric Clapton, Eva Cassidy, Willie Nelson, Sarah Vaughan (and, of course, Judy Garland), and his favorite, Israel Kamakawiwo'ole.

As she comes back into the kitchen she hasn't decided if now is the time to tell her mother more about Conor. There is so much to tell now that Iris is back from her crazy trip to Boston. And what the hell? Like, what was her mother thinking? And why Boston?

Then it hits her—her mother is all right! Nothing else matters. Her mum doesn't have cancer. "Mum!" she says when she sees Iris still standing there in the kitchen like a solid piece in the center of a puzzle. That's all Rose can manage. "Mum!" She hugs her mother and cries, gulps for air, and Iris rocks her gently back and forth on her shoulder, smoothing her hair.

"I'm glad you're home, Mum. I have so much to tell you," Rose says. She stands back and sleeves her tears.

Her mother has a look that Rose can't quite interpret. It's happy and sad at the same time.

Iris waits a moment, then she says, "Me, too, honey. Me, too."

Seventeen

Rowan drove westward from Dublin under an iron-gray sky. It was a Friday in the middle of June. The countryside was oddly lit, as if all the forty shades of green Johnny Cash sang about were rolled into one long expanse of vegetation. Asparagus green, Hooker's green, lime green, Dartmouth green. He tried to pick the colors, like crayons from a box, and remembered Burdy withdrawing his hand from his overcoat pocket one Christmas and presenting a pack of Crayolas. "And it's okay to draw *outside* the lines," Burdy whispered.

County Laois brought a sudden release of rain. The weighty sky darkened swiftly and the wipers slashed back and forth in a blind flash. And then, just as suddenly, in the afterrain, sparkling sunlight glimmered on the road. That's how it must be in this country, Rowan thought, light and dark in dramatic play between sunshine and shadow. He drove on, past the city of Limerick and over the Shannon into the west of Ireland. Swans clustered under the bridge. The radio didn't hold stations and so he drove in silence and fell in and out of memory. And hope. And doubt.

Passing a craggy field he heard Burdy's voice in his head, "When you hit a wild shot you know it right away. You swing through and connect with the ball but it flies off, and you know. You know the shot is hooked or sliced and the ball disappears into the rough. You know that you'll never find it. You know it's lost. *But you still look.* You still drag your bag up there into the long grass and you start hacking around with your club at the place you last lost sight of the ball. That's it. That's what you do."

Before Rowan had left Dublin he'd met briefly again with Sonia McGowan and signed the official Register for Adoption Contact. He'd filled in the form, giving his address. He'd ticked the box: *Natural Father,* and farther down: *Willing to Meet.*

"I hope at least you know you've done all you can—to open the door from your side—by stating your preference for contact. Your birth daughter will have the information . . . if she ever comes looking for it."

Rowan took her offered hand and shook it, warmly, and thanked her. "I just want to do the right thing."

She seemed more at ease with herself. Lighter somehow, her dark eyes restful, he thought. "I'm so sorry, Mr. Blake, this has all come as quite a shock to you."

"If she ever comes looking for me, please tell her she has nothing to fear. I will be glad of whatever level of contact she requests."

"And if she never requests it? How will you feel?"

"It's still hard to lose something, or someone, you never had."

Rowan arrived in the town of Ennis, half an hour after crossing the Shannon, and booked into a hotel. The hotel's owner, a man named Allen, bright blue eyes and an easy smile, greeted him, and after remarking on the hotel's garden, Rowan was enthusiastically shown into a room that overlooked it, and beyond which, across the street, stood the town's cathedral.

Tracking down Iris and Luke Bowen on the Internet had been easy, although the manner in which he'd discovered them was still troubling him. Any person with even the skimpiest of profiles could be traced these days. He'd found out that all Irish birth records (adoptions included) were open to the public, and with just a few facts (a name and a date of birth) and a little detective work, he'd been able to apply for Rose's birth certificate, which arrived at the Merrion Hotel through the Irish postal system two days later. If it wasn't in his own interests, he'd have objected. It was too easy. Her adoptive parents were named on Rose's birth certificate. Iris and Luke. (Not as adoptive parents.) Rowan searched for a "Luke Bowen," and from a link to the *Irish Times* archives learned that Luke Bowen, solicitor, beloved father of Rose and husband of Iris, had died after a short illness two years previously. Sad. Uncomfortable and all as it was, Rowan forced himself to take it in: *beloved father.* Poor Rose.

He had Googled "Iris Bowen" and within seconds her garden blog came up. The few photos showed a cottage-style garden and some quirky entries that had made him smile. (He'd posted a message telling her so.) The fact that she was a gardener somehow comforted him.

That night at the hotel in Ennis, he spoke with his brother on the phone.

252

"I've got to tell you, buddy," Pierce said, "I'm afraid you've got no rights."

"I know, I know. The lady in Dublin told me that."

"So what are you doing, then?"

"I don't know. I'm . . . I'm . . . I'm just following the line of the ball."

"Huh?"

"Listen, Pierce, I'm not going to do anything stupid. I'm not going to butt in where I don't belong."

"That would be a wise choice. This isn't some Hollywood movie, Ro. This is real."

"I *know* that. I just . . . shit. I don't know." There was a long pause. Rowan stood at the window of his room. Through ancient birch trees in the garden, he saw a sculpture of a pair of giant hands holding nothing but free air in the soft, gray limestone of its open palms. He thought of the statue of Robert Emmet. Although not a religious man, Rowan thought he'd stop into the church on his way out and say a prayer. There was always a first time for everything.

"I just want to see she's all right. Nothing more." He paused. "Trust me. I'll do the right thing."

"For whom?"

"Pierce . . . I said I'll do the right thing."

Rowan hadn't presumed to have any rights as a birth father, not this many years after the fact, but that didn't stop him from wanting—something. It was as if a hungering had slowly been growing in him for years and only now had he recognized it. He longed for some part of him to be . . . what? Unspoiled? To know he'd done something good in his life? Something he could be proud of? That whatever goodness was in him, passed down from Burdy, survived? Natural fathers have rights only within the marital family in Ireland, so Pierce said. As far as Irish law was concerned, if the parents aren't married the child has *no* father. *Beloved father*—it stuck into Rowan's heart like a thorn. But he needed to know. Something. He wouldn't just show up and say, "I'm your birth father. I'm your *natural* father." No. That wasn't how it was going to go. He would do the right thing.

From Ennis the road led west to the Atlantic Ocean about thirty kilometers away. Allen at the hotel had explained that West Clare was rather isolated, but suggested he go to Doonbeg where a golf course, built alongside the sand dunes, had one of the finest views in the west and its hotel was a nice spot to have lunch. (Rowan had Burdy's ashes and planned to drop them casually on one of the greens. He and Burdy would make the golf trip, after all.) He drove westward from the old market town, with its narrow streets and pubs and coffee shops, into an uneven landscape of whitethorn and fuchsia and black-and-white cattle. Twenty minutes later, just shy of Kilrush, there was a turn to the right. According to the directions, it would take him across the western part of the county to the sea.

If he'd had an address for the Bowens he still wouldn't have knocked on their door. He had checked the phone book. There was no listing. As he drove he noticed there were no street names, no road signs.

Point was, he'd lectured himself that he had no real intention of finding where Iris Bowen and Rose actually lived. He just wanted to see that somewhere place in the world, the *whereabouts,* of their home. Where Iris made her garden. Where Rose grew up. That was all.

He wanted a moment of nearness.

As he passed along a stone bridge over a small river, the road forked. A red van was awkwardly parked in a gap where a lone cow was rubbing her head through a farm gate. Beside it a young man was thumbing a lift. Rowan slowed. The guy looked okay to him so he stopped and leaned over to open the door.

"Hey, thanks." The man held the open door. "Where you going?"

"West, I think. Hop in. I can take you somewhere."

The young man got in and laid what looked to Rowan like a violin case across his lap. "My van died back there." He didn't look at Rowan as he spoke. He had some urgency or upset in him and took off his hat and worked his hair roughly with both hands, as if trying to free his head of some unpleasant idea. He then tapped the dashboard and continued. "It survives a journey to London and dies in the locality. What's up with that?"

"Huh?"

"Oh, my van, I mean."

"That's too bad. Sorry to hear that."

The passenger turned his head toward Rowan then and said, "You're American?"

"That's right."

"On holiday?"

Rowan nodded. "From New York," he said. He wanted to say more. "I'm hoping to play some golf for a couple of days." Rowan sensed his passenger looking for clubs in the backseat, but it was only his imagination. A delusion he was committing a crime weighed uneasily on his mind.

"Nearest course is Doonbeg. Is that where you're headed now? Doonbeg?"

"I hear it's a good course."

"Yeah, but even better surf."

The road quickly came into a small village, and as they passed a pub at the crossroads, Rowan glanced at his passenger, a tall man, probably late twenties. He noted the checked shirt he was wearing was freshly ironed but the look on his face was one of agitation. Rowan entertained the thought of asking him if he wanted to stop into the place called Morrissey's, a yellow pub with an old wooden door. A pint of Guinness in the west of Ireland had been on his bucket list. But, as he admitted to his brother, he was turning over a new leaf. And as his mother had told him, one day at a time. It'd been six days so far. One day he hoped he would be able to stop counting.

"I'm going to try to persuade my girlfriend, if she still *is* my girlfriend, to play with me tonight. If she says yes, we'll run through our piece . . . not that she needs much practice. Then head over to the festival later. But now, feck it, I have to get a mechanic! And my phone is dead." He moved in his seat and all his limbs made jerky motions as if he was trying to escape the weight of his own burden.

Rowan passed on by the pub and nodded. After a moment he said, "Festival?"

"Yeah."

He gestured toward the case on the man's lap. "You play?"

"Fiddle. But my girlfriend . . . she can play anything. She's the real thing."

Rowan drove slowly through the village because at any moment he expected the fiddler to ask him to pull over and let him out. But he didn't. A flock of birds transformed into a curling wave blown back against the gray sky. The road, barely wide enough for two cars passing, was dotted into the distance with white bungalows clustering as it turned toward the sea. Low houses were strewn like a bunch of colored blocks in otherwise green fields. Beautiful and all as it was, it seemed a lonesome kind of place. There were dunes off to the right. Rowan eased the car to the side of the narrow road at the edge of the village.

"So how can I help?"

"What?"

"Why not? I'm in no hurry."

"What about your tee time?"

"That's not until tomorrow," Rowan said, lying so easily it startled him. "I can't check into the hotel until later, anyway."

The fiddler's face softened and he relaxed back into the seat. He resettled on his head his yellow wooly hat. "Could you ever drive me back to the garage? I don't want to arrive at her house without my van, without my phone. What class of eejit would I look like then? Not too dependable."

Rowan laughed. "Yeah, sure. I'd be happy to." Something about this felt right, but Rowan couldn't put his finger on it. He wasn't old enough to be the age of this guy's father, but the situation had that feel about it. He felt, what? Paternal? Rowan did a three-point turn on the country road and drove back through the one-street village.

At Fitzpatrick's garage, he pulled the car in. As the passenger opened the door to get out, he asked, "Maybe you could drive me? After I speak with a mechanic?"

"Sure."

"That'd be great. Rose actually lives only three miles from here," he said, "when she's at home, that is."

The pit of Rowan's stomach did a somersault and he forced himself a pause and a breath.

"Be right back."

Rowan's heart pounded. Rose? He quickly reasoned—because he had to, because to think this man's Rose was also his was too much—it must be a common enough name. Rowan got out of the car and leaned against it. He bent over, anchoring his hands on his knees, and breathed. Christ almighty, what were the chances? He straightened up. Across the street was a row of small one-story houses. Outside of a blue bungalow an elderly woman was washing and polishing windows. She was using newspaper. Rowan concentrated on her movements until the man returned.

"All set. The guy knows where Rose lives and said he'd drop up the van. He said it sounded like it was maybe just the fan belt." He hesitated. "You all right?"

"Um. Yes. Sorry. Jet lag."

"Listen, I can hang here."

"No. No. It's all right. You said it isn't far."

"The thing is we had a bit of a row yesterday," the man in the wooly hat said as Rowan pulled out of the garage. "Although to be honest, man, I have no idea why. But she mightn't want to see me. It wasn't exactly a row. It wasn't a fight, either. Wasn't any right kind of argument, really. It was . . . I don't know what it was, but she was cross with me," he said. "I'm still trying to figure it out."

Rowan said nothing and drove on, waiting to be directed. His face felt hot, so he lowered the window. A drizzling rain misted in and he concentrated his mind on it and on the narrow country road before him that stretched long and up a hill. Not a house in sight. Not a saint nor a sinner. All the time his heart was beating in a fast, staccato rhythm. *Taa-ta-ta-tut-a-at. Taa-ta-ta-tut-a-ta.*

A little farther on, his companion said, "It's this road, up here on the left. The house is about a half mile down." Rowan turned left onto perhaps the smallest road he'd ever seen. He seemed to be entering into a green kaleidoscope. When he cleared the top of the hill, two horses nosed over the stone wall, facing the sliver of ocean that met the horizon farther to the west. Huge bushes with tiny red flowers whose name escaped him were closing in, and the road had grass growing in the middle of it.

"*Deora Dé.* Tears of God."

Rowan turned his head, not understanding and somewhat alarmed. Had he spoken? Had he voiced his thoughts? Maybe he should let the guy out here.

"The red flowers. Fuchsia. It's Irish."

Rowan nodded outwardly, he even smiled, but inwardly he was dissolving, as if all his strength was becoming liquid and leaking from him, joining the rain, and soon his whole being would slip away into the vast river of tears of other lonesome souls. He couldn't help the groan that seeped from him and when his passenger turned in surprise, Rowan coughed. He forced his mind back then to the small road, and as he considered what he would need to do if a car or tractor came toward him, his companion suddenly offered, "Rose is studying in London to be a classical violinist. We met the first time when her parents contacted me to make a violin for her. It was love at first sight for me, but it's taking her some time to feel the same. Seven sights so far."

Rowan watched the road, his mind rushing through: He'd said "parents," right?" He breathed a mixed sigh of relief and yet disappointment, too. The *Irish Times* said Rose's father was dead. This Rose was *not* his Rose.

"I wanted to be a musician myself, once," Rowan said quietly, regaining his composure. "But I was never going to be good enough."

"Yeah? What do you play?"

"Saxophone. Below par, but available for weddings and funerals," Rowan said, a self-effacing smile reviving his mood.

"That's cool." The guy tapped his fingers against his case. "We musicians are one big happy family, right? It's just around the bend. The next house."

Rowan turned his head slightly toward him. "I'd be happy to wait in case she, I mean Rose, isn't speaking with you."

"Ha. No. Not to worry. I'll win her back. Beg . . . if I have to. And then I'll convince her to play with me tonight. And she will. I think." He smiled. "But thanks."

Rowan pulled the car into a bit of a driveway alongside a stone building with a faded, black-painted door with a hint of crimson showing in peeled places. A blue clematis arched over the top of a low building on the opposite side of the entrance and draped onto an open wooden gate. (He knew that clematis. It was an Alice Fisk.) Names were coming back to him. Several potted agapanthus, lady of the nile, lined the wall. Something about all this seemed impossibly familiar.

As his passenger was getting ready to open the car door, he stopped, then opened his case and, from underneath the bow, took something. "Here's a ticket," he said, handing it to Rowan. "You should come tonight. The concert's in the community center."

Rowan smiled and took the ticket. "Thanks. I'm not sure. But thanks."

The fiddler got out of the car, but as he was about to close the door, Rowan wanted to prolong the moment and said, "Nice place your Rose has here."

The young man looked at it for a moment, then nodded. "Yeah. Her mum's a gardener."

As if a great wind had swept through the car taking all the air, Rowan lost his breath.

Seven hours after Hector sat into row 18, seat C, aisle seat, on the Aer Lingus flight from Boston to Shannon, he arrived in Ireland. It was six in the morning and raining. Talk about shock. He was freezing when he came out onto the concourse. He headed straight for the information desk, where a pretty young lady with a line of tiny earrings adorning her left ear looked like she was expecting him.

"Welcome to Ireland," she said and smiled at his shirt and his general goose bumps. "Not Hawaii out there." The talons of the eagle tattooed on his arm were showing beneath his short sleeve.

"This is summer, right?"

"Be lovely in a little while," she said. "How can I help?"

"I need to rent a car. Get a hotel room. Find a place called Ashwood." He gave her the slip of paper on which Grace had written Iris's address.

"I see." She pointed to the car rental desks. "When you're done there, come back to me and I'll sort you out with a room and a map." She smiled again. The girl was sweet.

When he returned with the rental keys she showed him where Ashwood was on the map. "It's a townland in West Clare," she said. "Here's the route. It's about an hour. But I'm afraid all the B and Bs nearby are booked solid because of the festival this weekend." She looked at Hector from across the counter. "I can book you a room at a really nice hotel, though."

"Festival?"

"There's a jazz festival. It happens every year."

"What do you know." And he rembered then Iris had mentioned it.

"Sorry?"

261

"Jazz . . . it's my thing."

"Oh," she said. "The Lodge so. You'll like it. And they'll take you right away."

"And the rain?"

"Five more minutes."

Rain was gone in ten. He could barely keep his eyes open as he drove, but from what he could see it was farming country with cattle and horses and a medley of small green and yellow fields separated by stone walls and some savagely shaped bushes. He'd gone the extra mile and hired a car with SatNav, thank God, because there was barely a street sign to be seen. The SatNav lady spoke with a kind of motherly affect. "At the next crossroads, turn *left*" and "On the next roundabout, take the *second* exit." She was like the Spirit of Grace commanding him not to screw up and to get there. The landscape got country. Real quick. Talk about rural. It was a strange thing, but the nearer Hector got to the part of the world where Iris lived, the more he wanted her.

The Lodge, as the lovely earringed girl had called it, turned out to be a rather grand five-star hotel perched on the edge of a long stretch of sand dunes. Awesome, but to Hector oddly discomforting. From his room, the Atlantic Ocean stretched endlessly, melting into a leaden sky on the horizon. Rain fell in the distance. He thought about the lovely Julia and how all those years ago he'd first heard the phrase "aggressive Stage 3 breast cancer." Fuck. He hoped to God he would never hear those words again. He hoped to God that wasn't what Iris was facing. Poor, sweet, gentle Iris. He had to know. He remembered her promise to her husband and now guessed that was why she had wanted to find Hilary. For Rose.

A few hours later, after a nap and some lunch, Hector showed the concierge his map, in case Lady SatNav didn't know the way, and was told it was only fifteen minutes inland. So, at four in the afternoon, Hector Sherr left the coast behind and set out for Ashwood. There was no rain, but he took the road slowly because it was narrow and windy. Low houses were strewn like a bunch of colored marbles in otherwise green fields. He turned right at the bottom of a curving hill when directed, but that was the end of the line as far as SatNav was concerned. She spoke no more.

Without directions now, he drove up the hill before him. Huge bushes with tiny red flowers closed in on the thin road. Grass was growing in the middle. Wild, he thought. He hoped Spirit of Grace knew where she had taken him because he seemed to be disappearing into the thickest greenness he'd ever seen. Even the air he breathed seemed green, and smelled of hay. When he cleared the top of the hill, two horses, a speckled gray and a chestnut mare, nosed over the stone wall. They faced toward the sliver of ocean that crossed the horizon about ten miles back to the west. He stopped the car and got out. The road evened out ahead but there was no house in sight. The horses came toward him. He saw his reflection in the eye of the mare and he thought she spoke to him. He shrugged and got back in the car, feeling giddy.

Another quarter of a mile farther, at a bend in the road, a driveway appeared, huddled between two stone buildings, one with a black door. A blue flowering vinelike plant spilled over a lower building on the other side of the entrance and fell onto an open wooden gate. Several potted plants were lined up against the wall.

This had to be the place. It said Iris all over.

He parked the car at the gate. His heart felt five sizes too big for his chest. It was thumping a big drum rhythm full of ache and regret and hope, *ba-bam ba-bam ba-bam*, drying up his throat. *She's in here.*

"Come on now, Hector, keep going, man." He hopped in over the stone stile and followed the line of potted flowers that led through a gap in a high hedge. A jaw-dropping, mind-blowing, breathtaking garden materialized. He stood a few moments as if in a trance. *I've arrived in Emerald City where the blue Iris lives,* he thought.

"Um . . . hello? Can I help you?"

It was a young woman with long brown hair who came out from the house.

"I'm looking for Iris. Iris Bowen?"

The young woman considered the stranger a moment and got up. "She's not here."

"Is she all right?" He spoke with a little too much urgency and a little too quickly and he knew he'd surprised her.

"Yeeesss. She's fine," she said cautiously. "Um . . . does she know you?"

"You must be Rose . . ." he said then, and walked a little nearer. "I met your mom when she was in Boston last week."

"O . . . kay . . ." Rose paused. "She didn't mention meeting anyone except the lady at the guesthouse."

"That'd be Grace Hale. Another nice lady . . . like Iris . . . I mean, your mother." He took another step closer and held out his hand. "I'm Hector Sherr." They shook hands. "It's a real pleasure to meet you, Rose."

Neither of them spoke for a moment. Hector shifted his weight, but Rose stood still. "Your mom talked a lot about you. You're a musician, right?"

"Yes."

"Me, too."

"Oh. Nice . . . um . . . was Mum expecting you?"

"Actually, no. It was a sort of a spur of the moment thing. I just wanted to see how she was. I mean—"

"I don't know when she'll be back, but I'll tell her you stopped by."

"Yes. Please . . . I'd really like to—"

"Where are you staying?"

She was a tough marker, Hector thought. How could he blame her? A stranger walks into your mother's garden, out of the blue, and starts nosing around. "In a place called Done Beg."

"Doonbeg." She smiled. "I'll tell her so."

"I hear there's a music festival on this weekend?" Still, she didn't say anything. Hector wanted her to say, Yes, there's a festival and we'll be there and I'll bring my mother and we'll all have a nice time. But this girl didn't give anything away. And she wasn't going to. She wasn't going to tell him what he wanted to know: Is Iris all right? Hector, man, he thought, be cool. What if the news wasn't good? She wasn't going to tell him. It was none of his damn business.

"I'll get going then." But he didn't move. He waited, still hoping Rose would give him some encouragement. "Nice to meet you, Rose," he said at last, then he turned and walked back along the line of potted plants, through the gap in the high hedge, and out. He got in the car and headed west.

He would return there the next day.

And the day after that.

And all the days after until he saw Iris Bowen again.

The small village of Doonbeg was an unlikely setting for an international music festival and, except for its position so near the sea, it might have gone unnoticed in the calendar of Irish summer festivals. It was a thing the Irish did to counter the often-compromising weather, organize and attend festivals. Every year since the turn of the millennium a group of local people orchestrated the event that brought semiprofessional musicians from all over the world to play. One of their tenets was to make the festival free to all, so volunteers came from all walks of life from the West Clare community to lend support. Tess's husband, Sean, was on the development committee and Tess took tickets for the raffle at the door on Saturday night. For her part, Iris contributed a floral arrangement. The festival was a boon for local hotels and guesthouses that helped sponsor it. Before Luke died he, too, had volunteered, ferrying musicians from the airport and coordinating their accommodations.

The day of the opening concert Iris met Tess for lunch in the garden of the hotel in Ennis. They were lucky to find a bright spell in an otherwise gray day and sat in the sunshine filtering through an old copper beech. Gardeners were trimming the boxwood hedge. She would have preferred to be in her own garden as gardening had a way of helping her work things out—and she did have some things to work out, like the surprising appearance of a young man in her daughter's life, and what was she going to do with herself now that she wasn't going to die—but she was anxious to confide in someone about Hector. Her garden could wait. The more she thought about Hector, the more she believed perhaps she'd been too hasty in her judgment to leave without saying good-bye. He'd been a breath of fresh air and, to be quite honest, she missed the attention. Keeping him a secret made her feel as if she'd done something wrong.

But still. She wanted someone to know there had been sparks. That there was some life left in her. Just when she was about to tell her friend, Tess's phoned buzzed. She read the text: Boys to be collected from football training, then I have to get to the community center. She sighed and, as she stood, she asked, "What were you going to say?"

"Oh, nothing. Tell you later." Iris waved a hand and smiled and Tess dashed away. Iris sat a while longer in the garden.

Now, shortly after four, Iris arrived back home with groceries. She could hear music playing when she stepped from the car. She paused, listening, stilled by the rising melody that leapt up above the trills of the fiddle. It was "Over the Rainbow." So Rose *is* going to play at the concert, she thought. With Conor. She was glad because her daughter's account of the stroppy Mr. Ballantyne made her wonder if she should suggest Rose take a break from her studies in London. Maybe she would be better off back home in Ireland. Take one of those gap years and travel. Or something. Rose had never had a job, maybe she'd like that. They'd put down two very demanding years and now that Iris had been given the all clear, now that her architectural distortion was just some calcification, maybe the two of them should travel. But it was all conjecture. There was someone new in Rose's life now. And for a moment Iris was happy-sad thinking about it, the way only mothers know.

More petals dropped from the clematis, leaving behind feathery heads with silver threads. The summer was already transitioning toward autumn. She stood listening a few moments longer before entering the house.

"Hey, Mum!" Rose laid down her violin. "Nice lunch?"

"Yes. Lovely. I stayed until the rain threatened." Iris put her shopping on the counter. "The piece sounds really great. I can't wait to hear your duet."

"Rose Bowen is an actual star," Conor said. "Festival crowd won't know what hit them when this classy violinist starts playing jazz—with the fiddler from Kinvara, Conor Flynn."

Rose smiled and Iris began to unpack. "So . . . Mum?" Rose glanced to Conor and then back at her mother. "Do you know someone named Hector?"

Iris froze. She turned to Rose and stared but said nothing.

"Wasn't that the name I told you, Conor?" said Rose, keeping her eyes on her mother.

"Tall guy, you said, and friendly, American. Hawaiian shirt."

"Hector?" was all Iris could manage.

"He said he met you in Boston," Rose said.

Iris looked away and continued unpacking. She couldn't believe it. Hector? Here? It made no sense. Hector? She lined up the sugar and raisins and buttermilk and tomato sauce. Incongruous and mad, and yet . . . she turned away her blushing face.

"Mum?"

"What?"

"Tell me."

"I can't. Not . . . I can't. No. I'm too busy now. I have to . . . I have to post on my blog. And I promised Tess I'd make an arrangement for tonight." She opened the refrigerator and stood, shielded behind the door.

"He seemed pretty nice," Rose finally said. "Maybe a bit loopy, but in a nice way."

"Shouldn't you be practicing?"

"Details, Mum."

"No. Go. Not now, Rose."

Rose shrugged and led Conor to the sunroom, but she threw her mother one over-the-shoulder glance. Rose had caught her smiling.

"I'll tell you later," Iris said. "Okay?"

"Sure. Can't wait."

Soon Rose and Conor were playing and Iris was left to think. What? Hector? How had he got here? How had he found her? Hector? It was as if a Californian poppy had unexpectedly appeared in her flower border. What did he want? It was mad, just mad.

She escaped outside to finish making the centerpiece. Tons of lady's mantle bloomed along the path. Somewhat wildly, Iris clipped a large bunch and dropped it in her basket. She gathered a few love-in-a-mist seed heads and two fat hosta leaves, then began to arrange them with cosmos in a black watering can she had chosen as a container. She needed more color and hesitantly snipped her two last red poppies from the border in front of the sunroom.

Inside the shed her hands were shaking as she made final adjustments. What the . . . Hector? Here in Ashwood? Had he seen her garden? Talked with Rose? She tried to concentrate on the arrangement, but the flowers kept falling sideways. She placed a long red rose in the center and the arrangement held.

"Mum?" Rose was on the path. "Mum? Conor's van is back. All fixed. We're going to get a bite to eat in Doonbeg. Is it okay if we see you there? Conor needs to meet someone."

"Of course."

"You're okay?" Rose waited.

"Sure . . . you're home. That's all I need. And . . . I get to hear you play tonight."

Rose only half smiled. She turned and followed Conor, but

had only taken a few steps when she came back to her mother. "Do you think he'd mind?"

Iris was holding the centerpiece in both hands. The large faces of the poppies obscured her own face. "Who? Mind what?"

"You know! Dadda?"

Iris's face flushed.

"Would he mind me . . . ?"

"Oh!" Iris said, realizing Rose wasn't asking if Luke would mind about Hector.

"Would he mind me playing 'Over the Rainbow'?"

Iris lowered the centerpiece. "I think he'd be happy."

"And you?"

"Me? It's wonderful." She put the centerpiece on the wooden table under the porch and then her arm around Rose and led her out to where Conor was looking at his repaired van, like it was a temperamental friend he'd now forgiven.

"All right, then, ready for road?" he said. " 'Bye, Mrs. Bowen."

"I think you can call me Iris."

Rose kissed her mother and whispered, "You're not off the hook yet. I want to hear all about Mr. Hector Sherr."

Iris waved her hand at her daughter. "Go!"

Along the path back to the house she picked up Cicero and brought him inside. She decided against making a supper just for herself and instead got some crackers and some cheese from the refrigerator. She cut a few slices for the cat.

"Is he a nice man?" she asked Cicero. "Hmmm? Isn't he?" Waiting for the kettle to boil, she ran her hands over the cat's back. She hadn't gardened in two weeks and noticed her fingers were beginning to look, well, normal. The chapped edges of her forefingers were softening. Even her nails were growing. Her wedding ring clinked against the cat's collar and, all of a sudden, she remembered the dream of Luke smiling and walking out of the sea toward her. He was carrying a box. It was an open box.

She had just enough time to wash her hair, so she grabbed some shampoo from the cupboard and washed in the sink. The lather released a scent of apples and cinnamon. Then with toweled-up hair, she sat and finished the blog post that had been gathering in her mind.

Sea change. Rainy summer is in full swing, but nothing can dampen the turning of the world. It goes on with or without you—the seasons and the garden and the very music of life itself. You'd think the rain might have a slowing-down effect. Even hope it will. But nothing can deter the steady passage of summer into autumn. The cuckoo flies south. The baby swallows leave the roof beams. The purple moor grass turns orange.

Neither wind nor rain nor sun nor gray skies can hold back the changing seasons. So perhaps they change in us, too. The thing your slow, redheaded gardener realized in her garden today was not to resist. The garden teaches trust. Accept the change.

Cry out: Onward, hail and olé.

And celebrate.

At seven o'clock Iris drove westward toward the sea. She was running late and so drove fast, constantly glancing sideways to mind the old black watering can doddering in the backseat. She should never have filled it with water. The rain had shifted east and the sky showed blue between parting clouds. Sunlight shone out beyond Spanish Point. In midsummer dusk didn't fall until eleven. This was her country at its best.

Iris had decided not to tell Rose about Hilary, at least not yet. There was no need now. Iris wasn't going to die. Not yet, anyway, thank God. She had reacted out of fear. Fear that Rose would be alone, and unable to manage without her. Tess was right. You can't prepare for every eventuality. Rose had her own life to live and, judging by recent events, she was doing pretty damn well on her own. Hadn't she managed her master class? Hadn't she landed herself into a promising-looking relationship with Conor? In fact, she was blooming before Iris's eyes. Blooming in a way that proved, beyond the shadow of a doubt, that all the nurturing, nourishing, wiping away tears, encouraging, consoling, challenging, and battling at times, all the guiding, supporting, parenting, and mothering—yes, real mothering—had given Rose the best possible circumstances in which to flourish.

In time, life was going to take her daughter away from Ashwood, probably before Iris was ready. That was one eventuality she could prepare for—and she would, and somehow it would be fine. Sonia McGowan, too, had been right. It was up to Rose to ask questions if she wanted to know about her birth mother. That's the way it works. And even though there was no indication of a birth father, it would still be Rose's decision to initiate the process of tracing information about her birth parents. Her *natural* parents.

It was ironic, but in discovering that Hilary was dead, Iris felt anchored to Rose in a way she hadn't before. *That* was natural.

The fact was, hard as it was to take, Iris had lost her mate. And the truth was, she was learning, albeit slowly, that she had to get on without him. As for her promise to Luke, she *had* tried to find Hilary. The journey had taken her though a season of melancholia.

A new season was emerging. It wasn't exactly an epiphany, but Iris acknowledged, today, she hadn't been able to see grief as a process that takes its own time. Waves come and go. And wash over you. Allow grief to be a badge of courage, an inspiration, a transformative sea change—Luke was saying in the dream. Honor what is best. See it in me. In yourself. In Rose. That is my gift to you.

Fifteen minutes later she arrived at the Doonbeg Community Center. Cars were arriving and parking every which way as was the custom in that part of the world. She pulled over as near to the front door as she could and got out and eased the centerpiece from the backseat. Inside the foyer, a small crowd had gathered and stood admiring a children's art competition on the walls, the theme being jazz. There were drawings of wild-haired drummers, and yellow saxophones, and crazy crooked pianos. One blue guitar had won first prize.

"There you are!"

"A bit late, sorry, Tess."

"No bother, pet." She stood back. "You look nice."

"Have you seen Rose?"

"Inside. Bring the flowers and we'll put them on stage." Tess started through the double doors in the hall, then stopped and said, "You really do look nice."

Iris blushed. She knew she had made an effort. And that was something new. But was it so noticeable? She followed Tess, snaking through the rows of chairs and up the stairs to the somewhat-bare stage. A drum set was arranged against a black curtain in the corner. Tess looked around for a place to put the flowers. "The piano will have to do. There's nothing else. I'll find something to put under it. Sean will have my head if I scratch the new piano.

I'll be right back." Tess was wearing a sleeveless summer dress with a crazy patchwork pattern of flamboyant colors, some Spanish label she was fond of. Iris hated it. Tess knew that and knew, too, Iris preferred her flamboyant colors to be *in* the garden.

Iris stood on the empty stage holding the flowers, feeling somewhat conspicuous. She'd missed last year's concert and the one before that because of Luke. And now she realized there were a dozen people she hadn't seen in two years. Marjorie O'Neill was waving to her. Una Brew and Mary O'Dea, school friends of Rose's, were signaling: *Is Rose here?* Was Iris obliged to approach them all and redeem herself? Apologize for her absence? Maybe later. Musicians nodded as they ambled up onstage and passed by on the way to the dressing rooms. A young man with a black baseball cap unpacked a bass in the corner.

Iris spotted Conor in the now crowded auditorium. He was talking with a tall man she could only half see, his back was to her. Hector? *Was he here?* Her heart skipped. Conor saw her and nodded. The stranger in a white shirt and jean jacket turned.

It wasn't Hector.

Iris swiftly scanned the crowded room. No Hector. Why hadn't she asked Rose what he'd said? Had she told him about the concert? She couldn't spot Rose, either. Where was she? Practicing? Was she anxious about the piece? Did I not put her at ease about playing?

"Here we go." Tess hurried back onstage and laid a gold cloth on the piano. "It's the best I could find." It had the name of the local drama group and their mascot, a greyhound, emblazoned in green. Tess laughed and stood back while Iris lifted the flowers and centered them on the piano.

"Looks rather fab," Tess said. "You did a good job. Don't you think?" She checked her wristwatch.

Iris didn't answer.

"Iris?"

Movement down at the door had caught Iris's eye. She let out a gasp and abruptly turned to face the back curtain of the stage.

"Iris? What's wrong?"

"I have to get out of here," she whispered.

"What? Why?"

Iris ducked past the piano, slipped through the curtain, and was gone.

Tess quickly followed her into the women's dressing room.

"Something's happened," Iris said, "I tried to tell you earlier . . . at lunch. But . . . oh . . . I met someone in Boston. He's here. Rose met him. He came to the house when you and I were at lunch. He's been to my house, Tess. . . . And now . . . he's here!"

"Okay. Okay. Calm down."

"Tess! I don't . . . he's here . . . and I don't—"

"It's all right. Slow down." Tess's hands were waving up and down like she was softly combing the air. "Breathe."

Iris blew air at the ceiling.

"Did you know he was coming?"

"No!"

"So he just—"

"Followed me."

"Wow. I mean—"

"What should I do?"

"What do you want to do?"

Iris brought her hands to her face and felt the heat there. She shook her head and said, "I don't know."

Tess laughed. "You poor thing."

"It's not funny."

"Okay. Sorry. But listen. You can't leave. You have to hear Rose and Conor. Wait until most of the seats are taken. Before the music is about to start, which is in a few minutes! Slip out and take your seat. Easy peasy. I've put a reserved sign on our chairs anyway. At the front." She squeezed Iris's hand. "I'll mind you."

Somebody had bumped into the drum set onstage and set the cymbals clanging. It made Iris jump. "*Where* is Rose?"

"She's probably tuning up."

"I don't think so."

Tess checked her watch again. "I've got to get back to the front and help with the raffle tickets. You'll be all right, pet." At the door, Tess turned around. "What's he look like?"

Iris gave her a helpless look.

"Gorgeous? Tall?"

"Tess!"

When Tess had gone, Iris caught herself in the dressing room mirror and sighed. She paced the room, casting her eyes about and listening for sounds of someone approaching. She hoped any moment Rose would come. The door opened and closed, but it was only the musicians gathering in the next dressing room. She heard Italian spoken and laughter rising from children running in front of the stage. It was time for the concert to start.

She stayed in the curtained wings, determined not to look out, but she couldn't help herself. The community center was packed, every seat taken. Long benches had been carried in from the local school and placed up along the side walls. Rows of twenty seats now took twenty-five. The buzz of chat and shuffling noises of chairs and shoes and coughs and children's squeals built around the auditorium.

She looked out into the faces, but she couldn't see Hector's. What was she feeling? She wasn't sure. She couldn't pinpoint it but it felt something like a mortified schoolgirl might feel. If he wasn't so . . . so Hawaiian shirt!

For a moment her eyes locked on the man with whom Conor had been speaking. He was walking toward a seat at the back but looking directly at her. She lowered her eyes and went down the stairs and slid into one of the empty chairs at the front marked "reserved." She held her hands in her lap and tried to be still and silent and invisible and studied the program notes.

A few moments later she felt someone standing in front of her.

"Mrs. Bowen. Hey. Exciting, isn't it? Can't wait to play with Rose."

"Yes. Yes, I'm sure, Conor. Where is she, though, I wanted to speak with her."

"She said she needed to clear her head. She drove down the road to the beach. Took Gerty. I mean, my van. She should be back soon." Conor paused, eyeing the auditorium. "No worries. We're not playing till after the intermission."

"She used to go there with her father," Iris said quietly. "To the White Strand. Just the two of them."

"Ohhhh. Right. I didn't know . . . okay. I'll wait for her by the door so." As he walked away he pulled out his phone.

Tess was hurrying up the aisle. She had the metal cash box with her. "Great crowd! Isn't it just mad?" She sat down, leaned in to Iris, and whispered, "Did you see him yet?"

Iris shook her head. "I'm not looking!"

"Right." Tess turned her head around but Iris grabbed her arm.

"Don't. Please."

Something onstage caught their attention. A group of young men in tuxedos in various states of wear came on carrying a bass, guitar, and violin. The man with the electric guitar introduced them as Tuxedo Jazz.

"Oh, they're cute," Tess said. Iris nodded, but she was only half listening. They started playing. Tess rocked to the beat of the bass. Iris closed her eyes and tried to concentrate on the violin part. And before she knew it, the piece was over.

Tess nudged her and whispered, "You okay, pet?"

"Not really. And where's Rose?"

Tess's eyes swept the audience and she gave a little wave and turned back.

"She's at the back. Look over your shoulder to the left of the door."

There was Rose standing with Conor. She seemed all right. In her brief scan of the audience she hadn't seen Hector. It gave her time to think. For an encore the Tuxedo Jazz group played "Sweet Georgia Brown" and behind Iris someone was singing. It seemed as if half the audience was singing or humming and tapping their feet. Iris relaxed a moment and felt lifted, slightly. Rose was there. Okay.

Maybe Hector had left.

Maybe she had only imagined him. And in that moment, when she felt somewhere deep inside a swelling warmth, she realized she *did* want to see him.

When Tuxedo Jazz finished, they bowed and the crowd clapped wildly. It was as if their jazz was an exotic thing that landed in West Clare only once in a blue moon. It lifted the audience and with it came a greater freedom in their lives, if only for that evening. At the intermission the back doors were opened and evening sunshine spilled in. Some of the audience stood and chatted and some went out for cigarettes and some over to Tubridy's for a pint before the second half. Three women started through the audience selling Tess's raffle tickets. First prize was a dinner for two at the Doonbeg Lodge. Second prize was a family ticket for Bunratty Castle Folk Park and third prize was a wash, cut, and blow-dry at Peter Marks in Ennis.

"You want first prize," Tess whispered. "I need third." And she stuck two tickets into Iris's hand.

The two women stood and stayed where they were facing the stage. Rose and Conor came toward them. Rose had changed into a black dress and her hair was pulled back. She wasn't wearing any makeup and she looked tired, her mother thought.

Tess said, "Rose, you look wonderful."

"Yeah, super," said Conor.

"Are you okay, honey?"

"Um. Yeah, I guess. I'm fine." She looked down. "A little nervous maybe." Conor put his arm on her bare shoulder and she faced him, but in moving, his arm slipped off as she seemed to intend. "Who was that man you were speaking to when I came back?"

"The white shirt guy?"

"Yeah."

"He's the guy I told you about. He picked me up when my van broke and brought me to your house. I gave him a ticket. You should have come over. I wanted to introduce you. Nice guy. American. Golfer, he said."

"Oh, that was him? Nice," Rose said distractedly.

"Seems it's the day for meeting the Yanks, hey?" said Conor.

Only Tess laughed and when she did Iris darted her a look.

"Okay, then. I'll leave you all for a bit," Tess said to Iris. "Better check on what trouble my boys are into," and to Rose and Conor added, "I'm so looking forward to hearing you play." As she darted off she crossed two fingers on both hands and held them up. "Best of luck!"

"Rose?" said Conor. "White shirt guy? I sort of told him all about you. He was superimpressed. He said he'd love to meet you one day. He gave me this." Conor reached into his pocket. "He said to give it to you . . . some sort of good luck charm." He dropped a little silver coin into Rose's hand.

She turned it over. "What is it?"

"Old money. It's got a hare and harp on it."

Rose handed it to Iris.

"It's an old Irish threepenny piece," her mother said after a few seconds and handed it back.

"He said he hoped it would bring you luck."

"That's kind of random," Rose said. "Nice, but random."

"Luck sometimes is. Isn't it, Mrs. Bowen? I mean, Iris."

Iris smiled.

"He told me he wanted to be a musician himself. Hadn't worked out for some reason. He said he was hopeful *you'd* have a wonderful career, though."

Rose looked at both sides of the coin, at the hare and the harp, and then slipped it into the pocket of her dress. She looked around at the crowd as if to see him, to even thank him perhaps, Iris thought, as recognition crossed her daughter's face.

"Hey, Mum, isn't that your new friend, Hector? Over there?" She pointed.

Without thinking Iris turned to look, diagonally to the far side of the room.

There.

"Oh. He's seen us," Rose whispered.

Hector came gingerly toward them, excusing himself as he weaved though the audience, his head nearly a foot above most of them.

There was no way out unless Iris made a show of herself. Rose sensed her mother's disturbance, as if somehow the very air in the room was changed and she could feel her steadying against it. She stepped forward as Hector approached.

"Hello, Mr. Sherr."

"Hello. Hello, Rose." He carried a bouquet of flowers. He'd acknowledged Conor with a nod but he looked directly at Iris. "Hello, Iris." He laughed self-consciously. "I had to see you again." He spoke as if they were the only two there. "I'm sorry, I just had to."

Iris felt she had fallen off the world, or into it. She couldn't tell. She had too many feelings scrambling for her attention and no thoughts for any of them. Except one, the understanding that she couldn't deny she was happy to see him. Hector. Hector Sherr. Mr. Jazz Piano Man was standing in the Doonbeg Community Center in the middle of the west of Ireland.

"Rosie?" Conor said, nudging her. "We'd better get—"

"Mum?"

Iris found herself looking from one to the other. Then to Hector: "You've met Rose . . . she's playing . . . with . . . with . . ."

"Conor," Hector said. Iris looked surprised. "I saw it on the program." He turned to Rose. "Yeah, you're performing one of my favorite pieces." He handed her the flowers. "Good luck."

"Two good luck tokens in one evening. You must be on to a winner," Conor said.

"Thanks. Thanks, Mr. Sherr." Rose's expression showed she was somewhere between bewildered and bemused. She took a deep breath and let it out with a long, slow whoosh. She gave her mother the flowers and hurried up the stage steps with Conor and disappeared behind the curtains, leaving Iris somewhat thunderstruck and standing alone beside the tall, tanned man in the colorful shirt with his fair, midlength hair behind his ears, like wings, and his eyes sympathetic and glad.

"May I sit with you?" he asked.

Iris nodded and sat down with the flowers on her lap. Hector took the seat to her left.

Tess suddenly reappeared and, without batting an eye, seeing her seat was taken, sat down on the floor alongside some children seated in front of them. They giggled and Tess shushed them.

Tess's husband, Sean, introduced the second half of the evening as being devoted to duets, and then acknowledged the great work of the volunteer committee. He announced the winners of the raffle and thanked the sponsors, saying it couldn't be done without them.

"And if anyone has a free seat, would they be so kind as to give it over to my wife, the tireless Countessa, who's sitting down there on the floor!" The audience laughed and a few shouts went up and Sean said, "There, Tess, at the back. Thank the good man and let the music begin." They all watched as Tess got up and spiritedly jogged her way to the seat vacated by the man in a white shirt and jean jacket who moved to the back wall of the auditorium.

First up was a jazz version of "As Time Goes By"—on violin accompanied by harmonica. Hector turned briefly but Iris refused to look at him or anyone and kept her eyes straight ahead. The duet of two young musicians, a teenage boy on harmonica and a young woman in her early twenties on a blue electric fiddle, began. By the end of the first verse Hector was humming. *Dear God, he's humming.* And then he started singing, softly, though.

Iris knew the words, too. The facts of life . . .

Hector then put his hand on top of hers. He stopped singing.

She closed her eyes but faced slightly toward him, and she let her hand be covered until the end of the piece. Then she slipped it away to clap with the rest of the audience.

For Rose to perform in front of the local community was not in and of itself a challenge. She was used to playing in front of audiences. Iris watched the first duo leave the stage, then Conor and Rose appeared. They stood side by side. A cold sweat broke out on Iris's forehead. The audience stopped clapping. An expectant hush hung in the air.

Conor bowed, lifted his fiddle up under his neck, and brought his bow to the strings. He began with the musical introduction, playing the way into the piece for Rose. She stood with her violin and bow hanging. She caught her mother's eye and in a single flowing movement took a step back and lifted her violin. She rested it on her shoulder and settled her chin into the rest. Her bow arm still hung at her side but it was already moving in time. Then she lifted her bow and joined Conor.

There are some people in the world whose presence is such that when they stand before you, whether in conversation, or performance, or whatever, they are met with awe. Rose's presence onstage commanded this attention. And she was beautiful. It wasn't just Iris's imagination that the audience hushed as she played. It was like there was always this secret part of her daughter that only achieved perfect expression through her playing. Her bow arm was flawlessly positioned. Her violin was held high and her elbow was angled exactly the way Andreas had taught her.

Iris felt her heart expand beneath her breast as if something was let go and there was more room in her, wide and free, and she felt like encompassing everything and everyone. The pink light coming through the windows. The raffle sellers paused in counting money. The children with their noisy snack wrappers. The blue guitar that won first prize (and the one that didn't). The rapt countrymen. The coughers. The man in the white shirt. Her best friend, Tess. Conor. And the man beside her. Hector Sherr.

Sensing this easing in her, Hector started the quietest humming. *Bluebirds fly . . .* She turned to him, wanting to both smile and shush him.

Then the music weakened.

Onstage, Rose had lowered her bow. It was like she was frozen or dumbstruck, or had she lost the notes? The audience paused with her. Iris caught her breath. She knew that pose of Rose's: At any moment she would burst. Tears streaming. Body shaking.

Hector turned to Iris. "What's wrong?"

Iris kept her eyes on her daughter and opened them wider as if to say, *It's all right. Everything is all right.* Conor continued playing but he, too, looked at Rose, his eyebrows raised questioningly and turned slightly away from the audience to face her. Rose was starting to shake.

"May I?" Hector asked.

"What?"

"I know this version."

Iris didn't know what to say. But now Hector Sherr was standing and in his long-legged stride was hopping up the steps two at a time. Within seconds he was seated at the piano with the watering can full of flowers on top. Conor had slowed the tune, pulled the melody into melancholy, but he had kept it going. He was waiting for her but Rose was riveted to her spot, looking down to her mother. Iris was nodding her head and mouthing the words all mothers know, and all have said, after every fall down and disappointment and heartbreak: *It's okay, honey. It's okay. Everything is going to be okay. Go on . . .*

And then Hector played. Joined right in with Conor.

At first Rose didn't react. So Hector played a jazzy solo. Conor moved toward her and exaggerated his own playing, encouraging her to join in. And finally Rose shifted gears and came back to the moment, to herself. She returned to the melody. Even Iris's centerpiece came alive, the lime flowers of lady's mantle pulsing as Hector's fingers beat the piano keys.

And by God, he could play. Conor grinned and Rose's face relaxed. *Troubles melt . . .*

Tess didn't miss a beat in reclaiming her seat. She put her arm around Iris. "It's all good, you know. Luke would be happy. Happy for Rose. And for you, Iris."

The sad, sweet, beautiful longing of "Over the Rainbow" continued to fill the hall. In it every single person in that audience found their own yearning, and for a time dared their dreams to come true.

And because Rose and Hector were real musicians, they knew when to accompany and when to solo. They had fun with the piece and the audience loved them. When Hector nodded, Conor stepped back, Rose stepped up, and like one of those bluebirds flying, her bow took flight and she was in the music.

When it was over, the audience rose in ovation with one long roar. It was the kind of big-game roar Iris was sure Hector had never quite heard before at a jazz concert. He stayed seated at the piano until Conor bowed and beckoned him. Then he came to stand, with that particular awkward shyness of his, beside Rose. He bowed to her and the audience applauded louder. Then he exited the stage, disappearing through the curtain and leaving Conor and Rose to bow once more.

A moment later all the musicians appeared onstage, but Hector wasn't among them. They bowed and, after accepting more exuberant applause, returned to the dressing rooms behind the curtain.

"Oh my God, Iris. That was fab. Just fab! And what about that knight in the Hawaiian shirt riding in to save the day? I want to be introduced!"

Iris was too dazed to speak. She nodded and looked to Tess, her eyes wet.

"Ah, pet." She gave Iris a quick hug. "It's all okay. Hey, the doctor was right when she said there's a lot going on in there! Ha! If she only knew! I've got to get going. I've got some bits and bobs to tidy up but I'll see you in a moment. You'll be okay. Oh, and the gang in the back are going to have a bit of a celebration. Sean bought some champagne, so don't expect them to hurry straight out."

Iris stayed where she had been sitting. The audience had emptied out to the still light evening. She closed her eyes, singing the words silently to herself.

Then she felt a hand touch her shoulder.

"Mrs. Bowen?"

"Yes. What?" Iris, startled, opened her eyes and looked up.

"I'm sorry to disturb you." It was the man in the white shirt.

"That's all right." She stood, still holding the flowers Hector had given Rose.

"I just wanted to say . . . um . . . she . . . your daughter, Rose, is really terrific. And so . . . so . . . beautiful."

"Yes. She really is," Iris said, the after-music still echoing in her.

"She plays brilliantly. You must be very proud."

"Yes, I am. Thank you. Very proud. But she's done it all herself." It wasn't the first time a stranger had come to share their appreciation of Rose's talent. But there was something about him. Was it his eyes? Had she met him before? "You gave her the coin?"

"Yes . . . for luck."

"That was so nice. But are you sure? I mean, it's—"

"It belonged to someone very special. It was my grandfather's. He died recently and I—"

"Oh . . . I'm sorry for your loss." For one moment, Iris thought the man was going to cry.

"His name was Burdy." He looked down at the program he was holding. "He always wanted me to come to Ireland. I think he hoped one day I'd—"

His eyes glanced up quickly at the empty stage, and came back again to Iris's. Suddenly all his features broadened, as if caught by surprise. Iris waited, expecting he was going to say more.

"I was just remembering something someone said to me a long time ago, which I had forgotten until now. 'You will go to Ireland and find a girl and it will change your life.' " He stood quite still as if he needed to so the meaning of the words he'd just voiced could sink in.

"And?" Iris said, watching his face slowly relax as if it was a bud, untightening. A poppy shedding its shell ready to unfurl.

"Yes. Well. Here I am."

"I mean . . . have you found her?"

"I have. Yes." He paused. "I *have* found her."

Iris waited for him to continue, to finish the trebled prediction, but he didn't. She wondered if she should perhaps ask him, but something in the way he spoke, and looked, made her feel the answer was, *Yes, his life would change.*

"Won't you stay and meet Rose? She'll be out in a minute."

"No, no." He glanced at the stage once more, and made to move, but didn't. "But maybe some other time." It took him another long moment. Then he looked directly at her. The smile he smiled was bittersweet and his eyes seemed ready to tear again. He offered his hand and Iris took it. "Will you tell Rose I wish her all the luck in the world. And . . . even though she never met him, I know h . . . I mean . . . I know my grandfather, Burdy, is looking out for her. And—"

Iris looked at him searchingly. She could see there was a whole story in him, but before he could continue, and before she could find out what it was, his phone rang. He let go of her hand and looked at the number. Then he looked at her and said, "It's been my great pleasure to meet you, Mrs. Bowen. I *hope* our paths cross again." His phone was still ringing. "Good-bye."

Rowan Blake walked down the aisle of the auditorium, out through the open double doors of the hall, and into the beginnings of evening twilight.

Then he answered his phone.

"Pierce. Hello . . . yes . . . it's all good. . . . Yes. I did. She's all right. . . . No. No, I didn't. . . . But I'm fine. It was the right thing. . . . I'm happy. Really, it's okay. I'm okay. And Pierce, she's soooo beautiful." Rowan told Pierce to tell his mother he'd be home the day after tomorrow. Or, maybe the day after that.

He walked along the street of parked cars and a few tractors. It seemed as if the whole audience from the concert had decamped en masse to the village pubs. The festival hadn't ended with the concert, Rowan thought. People were out on the street, leaning against the walls, sitting on chairs taken from inside, drinking pints and half glasses, lingering and chatting, enjoying themselves. He delighted in their celebration. It had a kind of pureness. A kind of organic, grassroots simplicity. And although he felt as far away from his life in Manhattan as he'd ever felt before, their optimistic voices filled him with the nearness he'd hoped for.

This is where Rose is from. This is her home, he thought. And she's fine. She's better than fine, she's great.

That was all he needed.

Soon he was back at the hotel. He went to his room. Got the package Pierce had given him and tipped the contents into a small plastic glass. And as the last light of the sun sunk off the western Irish Coast, Rowan Blake walked onto the green of the 18th hole of the hotel's golf course. The whole of the Atlantic seemed to be stretched in front of him, with rows of waves breaking far out. He stood for a few moments, filling his lungs with the sea air blowing in across the water. Then, with the cup in his hand, his arm stretched its full length, he angled it just so, and like a boy with a kite, he ran the circle of the green, scattering the ashes to the wind.

"Now, Burdy," Rowan said, letting his head fall back and looking up into the sky, "keep an eye on her."

The ashes lifted on the air like they were floating feathers.

Rose bounded across the stage and down the stairs. She was laughing and pulling Conor's wooly hat down his face.

"Well?" she asked her mother.

"Wonderful," Iris said, and hugged her. "Stunning. Fab, as Tess would say. Really, honey . . . it was pure magic. I wish I had recorded it."

"Not to worry, Iris, we'll give you a private performance. And now that we have a trio—" Rose elbowed him.

"Just saying," Conor said, glancing at Iris, who smiled ever so slightly. "So . . . Tubridy's?"

"Morrisey's," Rose said. "Mum?"

"Be there in a minute," Iris said. "You two go." Rose gave a look that meant she understood her mother was waiting for Hector. "And tell Tess I'll see her there."

Iris sat down again in the front row and looked up at the stage, at the piano and the centerpiece and the flowers. Her flowers, the white cosmos shone and the petals of the poppies held even though she hadn't singed them.

The audience had all gone, the auditorium was as quiet as it had been loud. She waited. He would be out in a moment. Iris was left with the sense of completion and a satisfying feeling of the resolution of a cycle. Life moves on. With all she was already experiencing, she thought of the word, the feeling, the miracle of *grace*. And, she felt that feeling that can't be explained in words, that feeling that makes you take a breath but lets you know that in its long, slow, easy exhale somehow something has been healed.

Then, out of the wings, eyes down and stepping quietly, Hector Sherr appeared on the stage. He stood a moment and looked down at Iris. Then he bowed to her. He pulled back the stool. He sat again at the piano, and once more, for Iris Bowen, he began to play.

CPSIA information can be obtained
at www.ICGtesting.com
Printed in the USA
LVHW08s1322030818
585867LV00001B/65/P

9 781250 092311